SISTER MARGUERITE

AND THE

A NOVEL BY
MARK BARIE

Best wishes

Barringer Publishing, Naples, Florida
www.barringerpublishing.com
Cover, graphics, layout design by Linda S. Duider

ISBN: 978-1-7352525-0-6

Library of Congress Cataloging-in-Publication Data *Sister Marguerite and the Captain/Mark Barie*
Printed in U.S.A.

Names:	Barie, Mark, author.
Title:	Sister Marguerite and the Captain : a novel / by Mark Barie.
Description:	Naples, Florida : Barringer Publishing, [2020]
Identifiers:	ISBN: 978-1-7352525-0-6
Subjects:	LCSH: United States–History–Revolution, 1775-1783–Fiction.	United States–History–French and Indian War, 1754–1763–Fiction.	Women and war–America–History–18th century–Fiction.	Female spies–United States–History–Revolution, 1775-1783–Fiction.	Plains of Abraham, Battle of the, Québec, 1759–Fiction.	Ticonderoga, Battle of, N.Y., 1758–Fiction.	Bunker Hill, Battle of, Boston, Mass., 1775–Fiction.	LCGFT: Historical fiction.
Classification:	LCC: PS3602.A77539 S57 2020	DDC: 813/.6--dc23

SISTER MARGUERITE

AND THE

Captain

by Mark Barie
Barringer Publishing
book review by Kate Robinson

The author relays an interesting, slightly more distant, male-oriented viewpoint of the romantic connections while still fully exploring Antoine's and Marguerite's foibles and complexities. Although reminiscent of Diana Gabaldon's *Outlander* series—one also set amidst two eighteenth-century wars and across two continents at this explosive juncture in history—Barie's star-crossed protagonists are more at odds with one another and their worlds, grappling with a gritty reality without the fantasy of time travel and the homely comforts of true love. Still, the more intense and tragedy-driven conflicts surrounding Antoine and Marguerite will keep readers up all night turning pages, so compelling is the need to discover if love will ultimately triumph over adversity.

RECOMMENDED by the US Review

Other Books by the Author

Other novels by Mark Barie include:
"War Calls, Love Cries," available at Amazon.com.

Barie has also authored or co-authored several local (upstate New York) history books, all available at Amazon.com. They include:

"Crossing the Line"

"The President of Plattsburg"

"The Boat People of Champlain"

**The author can be reached at:
authormarkbarie@gmail.com.**

DEDICATION

To my grandchildren: Josie, Jocelyn, and Noah.

Never has a grandfather been so blessed.

ACKNOWLEDGMENTS

Writing a book is never accomplished in isolation.

An honest author will readily admit that friends, family, and colleagues all contribute.

In this instance, I must acknowledge and thank my family; Christine, my wife, and my children; Eric, Oliver, Alexandra, and Sebastian. They never once complained about my incessant babbling regarding "the book." Even their significant others were polite!

But I especially want to thank my son-in-law, Eric Ashline, whose fifth great grandfather prompted this book and whose interest and encouragement were a true inspiration.

And then there are hundreds of friends on Facebook, Linkedin, and subscribers to my newsletter, (see: markbarie. com), many of whom took the time to express their support and enthusiasm, for my second novel.

Thank you all for your kind words and sincere encouragement.

TABLE OF CONTENTS

HISTORICAL NOTES

This novel was inspired by the life of Antoine Poulin, a well-known historical figure in New France and, later, in the American Revolutionary war. The book is neither an accurate description of his life nor a review of his service to the patriot cause—hence the name change to Antoine Dauphin

The Royal Roussillon Regiment came to New France on several ships. For purposes of simplicity I assigned Captain Dauphin to the *Leopard.*

The arrival of Montcalm's ship in New France is depicted as occurring shortly after the arrival of the *Leopard*. In fact, the two ships were weeks apart.

While the vast majority of historical references are correct, the reader may discover occasional minor discrepancies. All of these are deliberate and intended to simplify the narrative.

A NOVEL BY MARK BARIE

CHAPTER ONE

On Board the *Leopard*

"In Paris, you wore a red dress," he said.

The soldier leered. Sister Marguerite bowed her head.

"You speak of the past. I have taken the vows of the Ursuline."

She recognized her unwanted visitor from the meals they shared at the ship Captain's table. Adolphe Lezard served as a Captain in the Royal Roussillon, a regiment of the French Army. The Regiment, like Sister Marguerite and her colleague, Sister Helene, journeyed to Quebec City. They sailed on the *Leopard*, a French man-of-war traveling to New France, in April, of 1756. The intruder, several inches shorter than Sister Marguerite, wore his jet-black hair tied, in a greasy ponytail. The officer's black, pencil-thin moustache squirmed like a snake whenever he flashed his crooked, yellow teeth. And the man seemed to sweat, profusely, regardless of the cold or heat.

The soldier accosted Sister Marguerite below deck, in the tiny area where she slept. Stained walls of old sail canvas and flimsy hammocks, three-high, separated men from women, soldiers from passengers, and strangers from friends.

Sister Marguerite, frantic to understand why this man would harm her, raced through the chapters of her life. As the daughter of a wealthy financier in Paris, Marguerite Valtesse enjoyed the life of a princess, without the responsibilities of a throne. She appeared at every party, social gathering, and formal ball, in the city. Her long, flaming red hair, brilliant green eyes, and stunning beauty mesmerized all who saw her. She regularly teased and taunted the men in her life with innocent but evocative looks. And for good measure, the girl recklessly splashed her father's money and credit, wherever she went.

Lezard inched a step forward. Sister Marguerite, barely able to breath, could not stop trembling.

"You don't remember me, but I remember you," said Lezard.

"We are not alone, Captain Lezard. My friend, Sister Helene, will return shortly."

"No, she will not. A soldier in my regiment requires her immediate assistance," said Lezard, a calculating smile covering his face.

He took another step forward, removing his black tricorne hat and tossing it on a nearby cot. With her back to the chamber wall and hammocks on either side, the Ursuline nun could not escape. He reached for the snow-white coif that covered her head and yanked it to the floor. Lezard cringed when he first glimpsed her shorn locks. The beautiful woman's shoulder length hair disappeared several years ago when she entered the convent.

"You have changed your appearance, my friend. But it is not your red hair that interests me, he whispered.

His black eyes drilled into her innocent face. She focused on his boots, tears rolling down each cheek, now flush with fear.

"Please, Captain. I am begging you."

He pulled at the waist-level cincture that wrapped her body in layers of cotton and wool, leaving her tunic to hang loosely from the nun's tiny frame. Marguerite did not resist, as if his lustful cravings were required penance for her sins. Lezard lunged. He used both hands to slam her head against unyielding wood. Her knees buckled. He pressed his lips against hers and bit the soft flesh until the woman's blood oozed onto his darting tongue. He released her head and in a single motion, ripped the tunic from her shoulders. Her tattered undergarment and a single, milky white breast lay exposed. Instinctively, she reached to cover her bosom.

He shoved her arm to the side and yanked at the fabric once more. The sight of her bare chest drove Lezard into a ravenous frenzy. He smothered a breast with his wide-open mouth. The innocent Ursuline nun suddenly resisted with all her might. She yanked on his hair with both hands and screamed when Lezard's teeth lacerated her flesh. Marguerite's closed fists pummeled the monster's head and shoulders. He pulled away and used the back of his hand against her face to stop the woman's onslaught. Marguerite's eyes rolled to the back of her head when an unknown force jerked her assailant backwards. Lezard crashed into several of the empty hammocks. When he tried to stand, a crushing blow from a large fist rendered the man unconscious. Sister Marguerite smothered a sob and choked her response.

"Captain Dauphin."

Antoine Dauphin draped his spotless blue coat over her bare shoulders.

"You are bleeding, Sister Marguerite," he said.

Dauphin reached into his pocket and retrieved a fine silk handkerchief.

"Are you hurt?" he asked.

Marguerite could not respond. She took a series of rapid breaths but continued to gasp for air. Her head convulsed in tremors and her hands shook like delicate flowers in a windstorm. Overcome, she leaned forward and embraced her savior.

Antoine held the nun close but snarled in Lezard's direction when the assailant stirred. When Marguerite noticed Lezard's movements, she broke the Captain's embrace and backed into the far corner of the tiny chamber. Antoine pulled Lezard to his feet and, with a mighty shove, propelled the intruder from Sister Marguerite's enclosure. She whispered her gratitude.

"Thank you," she said.

Their brief moment together ended when Sister Helene appeared at the entrance.

"Sister Marguerite, have you no shame?"

Antoine interceded.

"I am Captain Antoine Dauphin, an officer in His Majesty's army. Sister Marguerite has been attacked and needs your immediate assistance."

He tossed Lezard's headwear through the opening, bowed low, and exited the chamber.

Sister Marguerite lay still, while Sister Helene attended to the lacerated lip and a large bump on the back of her head.

Marguerite closed her eyes and traveled back to Paris and her riotous past. Her wealthy father, in regular contact with the princes and nobles of 1753 France, indulged his only daughter. She knew him as the man who occasionally visited the nursery, her mother visited slightly more often, but neither of them on a regular basis. One of the servants, Annette, acted as Marguerite's nurse maid and later, as a chaperone. But an aging woman is no match for a rambunctious and flirtatious teenager.

It began with the dances at court, fancy floor length dresses, elaborate hairdos, sparkling jewelry, and evenings that seemed to last forever. Men of all ages, attracted by her stunning beauty and conspicuous wealth, flocked to her side. She grew bored with her admirers and left in her wake, dozens of frustrated suitors. The fifteen-year-old girl remained blind to the effects of her provocative behavior and, while most of her victims recovered and moved on, Adolphe Lezard did not.

She suddenly recalled one night in particular.

The painfully short man followed her everywhere. He pestered her for a dance, brought her unwanted glasses of champagne, and looked ridiculous, in his ill-fitting, sequined, evening coat. Marguerite thought him overly flamboyant and much too old. She eluded him by slipping, unseen, into the cool and dimly lit courtyard.

That was the first time she laid eyes on Jean-Claude, the young and handsome gardener who worked for the master of the house. To Marguerite, Jean-Claude, the gardener, might well have been a handsome knight, in shining armor. His bare chest and rippling muscles were an erotic invitation to the girl's raging hormones. More importantly, the two of them were of the same generation. For a moment, she watched in silence as the boy-man struggled with the limbs, of a recently pruned fruit tree. She approached.

"Why must you work even as the sun goes down," she asked.

"I apologize if I have disturbed you, my Lady."

"It is I who have interrupted you," she said.

He blushed.

"Please forgive me, my Lady. I must go now."

"Wait!" she said.

He stopped and swiveled his head in her direction.

She scurried to his side and kissed him on the cheek.

His smooth, bronzed face reddened. She giggled. He ran into the darkness.

The young couple did not know that a witness to their innocent encounter lurked in the perfectly manicured shrubs. Infuriated, Lezard threw the glass of champagne, he intended for the girl, on to the stone walk. He stormed back into the ballroom and made no effort to hide his angry exit. Marguerite laughed at his back, as

Lezard disappeared behind a set of glass paneled, French doors.

Inside the ballroom, Marguerite, once again surrounded by admirers, alternately demurred, blushed, and batted her eyelids, while each man did his best to attract her interest.

"If you remove your shirt, she will kiss you," said a voice from the back of the scrum.

Marguerite's spurned suitor, Adolphe Lezard, pushed his way to the center of her circle.

An enraged onlooker came to the girl's rescue.

"You, sir, are no gentleman," he barked.

"And she is no lady," said Lezard.

When the admirer stepped forward, fists clenched and wearing a snarl, Marguerite intervened.

"Ignore this little man. Like my poodle, he is all bark but no bite," said Marguerite, gently patting the top of Lezard's head as she floated by.

The witnesses, all men, could not hide their laughter. Lezard's face blushed a deep pink and he stomped out of the ball room.

In the weeks that followed, Marguerite returned to the mansion on an almost daily basis. She enjoyed the visits, with her new-found friend. Lezard, who regularly stalked the girl, reported the couple's innocent encounters to the master of the house. Lezard implied that the young couple engaged in illicit behavior. The gardener was fired. Marguerite's parents, mortified by the possibility of a social disaster and fearful that Lezard would be less than discreet, deposited the girl at an Ursuline Convent, in the French countryside.

The angry young lady struggled mightily against the iron hand of the Ursuline's Mother Superior. Marguerite refused to believe that all men are evil and that a person's sexuality needed to be repressed. The nuns, with few exceptions, knew little or nothing about the real world, thought Marguerite. She, on the other hand, understood the opposite sex and the clever ways of rich, beautiful women. But her parents, old fashioned and set in their ways, conspired with the nuns and the wayward ward of the Catholic Church eventually surrendered.

The teenager could not escape the Ursuline prison and, despite her stubborn protestations, eventually acceded to the demands of her captors. The daily ritual of her new environment forced a slow but inexorable transformation. In time, she resisted the demands of her community less and less. Strict discipline forced the young lady into a new life.

Marguerite traded her reckless independence, for a humble life of prayer and penance. She constantly repented for her "sins" and gradually retreated into a quiet, guilt ridden, and genuinely humble existence. She became a woman of grace and devotion, convinced that her eternal salvation depended upon her willingness to change. She accepted her penance and prayed only for His eternal mercy. Before the end of her first year at the convent, she became a Postulant. After an additional year, Marguerite decided in favor of the religious life and "took the veil." Sister Marguerite, now seventeen years of age, would wear the white veil, until she swore her permanent vows, two to three years hence. At that time, she would be presented with the black veil, a sign of her life-long commitment to Christ. When ordered to New France for teaching and missionary work, she went willingly. She took note of Mother Superior's dire warning. There would be great hardships, tremendous temptations of the flesh, and danger. But her faith in God and her sacred vows would save her.

Nevertheless, her vivid recollection of Lezard made Sister Marguerite tremble in fear.

"The Captain will be with you, shortly. Wait here" said the Ensign.

Antoine Dauphin stood outside the captain's cabin, ordinarily reserved for the ship's commander. Today, it served as the temporary office of the regimental commander. While he waited, Antoine focused on the ship's top deck, studying the crew members as they scurried across the surface like ants in the dirt. The *Leopard*, a triple-decked ship designed for the high seas, carried sixty-four guns and two hundred seventy crew members.

On this journey, in April of 1756, it also transported the second battalion of the Royal Roussillon, a Regiment of more than four hundred men. The French soldiers represented a fraction of the forces now in route to New France, as reinforcements for its war with England. The ship's other passengers included merchants, a number of missionaries, and a handful of prisoners, all destined for Quebec City. Antoine did not envy the hardworking crew members. Most of them received no more than a soldier's wages and constantly worked in four-hour shifts to keep the *Leopard* afloat and on course. Soldiers, such as Antoine, were neither expected nor permitted to help with onboard chores, unless the crew lost too many of its men as a result of sickness or an attack at sea.

Antoine recalled his boyhood decision to join the military. His father, a retired engineer from the Bearn regiment, encouraged and expected it. The boy's mother, a victim of her husband's military career, constantly alone and worried sick about the fate of her soldier-husband, openly expressed opposition to Antoine's desire to imitate his father. An older brother, already an ensign in the French Navy, also cautioned the boy against it. But Antoine ignored his mother's resistance and his brother's admonition. At one point, Antoine's mother unilaterally enrolled the boy in a seminary near Avignon, to begin formation for the priesthood. When the confused seminarian and his disobedient mother were discovered, she received a beating and the boy received an appointment to the Royal Roussillon.

In short order, the freshman soldier demonstrated a physical prowess that quickly catapulted him to the head of his class. Antoine received excellent grades, in horsemanship, marksmanship, and skill with a sword. Military tactics, world history, the languages, and even philosophy came easily to the new recruit. His teachers and fellow students convinced Antoine that the genteel ways of his ultra-Christian mother were the things of women, not men. He was destined to lead soldiers into battle, they said. Others would do the praying. Antoine, flattered by his colleagues and encouraged by his superiors, fell in love with the military life, as if it were a beautiful woman.

But more so.

"The Lieutenant-Colonel will see you now."

Antoine, at six foot-two, stooped as he entered the small cabin and respectfully saluted his commanding officer, Leopold Charles, the Marquis de Hautoy. Traditionally, a regimental leader enjoyed the rank of full Colonel. But the Royal Roussillon, also known as the King's Regiment, had as its Commander, the King himself, Louis XV. Lieutenant-Colonel Charles served as the King's representative.

"Sir."

"I have been informed of your complaint against Captain Lezard.

"His victim is an Ursuline nun." said Antoine.

"You expect me to flog a member of his Majesty's army, in full view of the ship's crew and all of its passengers?"

"Captain Lezard may be a member of the Royal Roussillon regiment, but he is the undeserving beneficiary of his friends in government. He commands no men, performs no meaningful function, and is a captain, in name only."

Antoine's piercing blue eyes flashed in anger as he repeatedly squeezed both hands into fists. But he refrained from challenging his superior officer, in a more direct manner.

"It is my decision that the accused will apologize to the woman, at table, tonight. If I am so inclined, I will pursue the matter further when we make landfall. Until then, Captain Lezard will receive a warning only," said the Lieutenant-Colonel.

"Marguerite, excuse me, Sister Marguerite, is injured," replied Antoine.

Antoine's slip of the tongue did not go unnoticed.

"I note that you and Sister Marguerite are often seated together at the captain's table," said the Lieutenant-Colonel, stepping forward to closely observe Antoine's reaction.

Antoine's face reddened. He took a deep breath and opened his mouth to speak. He thought better of it and chose to study the floor instead. The Lieutenant-Colonel arched his eyebrows and waited for Antoine to explain. Antoine bit his lower lip, mentally scolding himself for the foolish error. The wooden ship creaked in protest as the waves slammed into the ship's hull. The Regimental Commander waited no longer.

"Is there anything else, Captain?" he asked.

"No sir," said Antoine.

Antoine retreated to the storeroom rather than his bed chamber, surrounding himself with onboard supplies and foodstuffs.

He preferred the smell of rancid meat and rotting food to the constant chatter and noisy games of bored soldiers and fellow officers. His self-imposed isolation allowed him to recall the first time he saw her. Sister Marguerite's stunning beauty, easily visible from behind the dull, gray habit she wore, captivated the captain, in ways he did not expect. Her green eyes, full lips, high cheekbones, long eyelashes, and cream-colored skin mesmerized Antoine. The woman could not be ignored. With her soft voice and graceful demeanor, she appeared as a delicate rose, in an ugly world of thorns and weeds.

On their first night at dinner, yards of table and other diners, separated them. Antoine, reduced to furtive glances, watched closely as she prayed before eating, nibbled at her food, and smiled constantly. On the second night, he sat opposite the woman, now obsessed by her beauty but irritated by Sister Helene, who continually dominated their conversation. After thirty days at sea, he grew accustomed to occupying the chair nearest Sister Marguerite. Their banter quickly became the ardent exchange of soulmates. She expounded regularly on the nature of love, beauty, God, sin, and forgiveness, but grew quiet whenever he inquired about her past. He regaled her with his knowledge of military history, world affairs, and battle tactics. He opined on the glory of battle and the nobility of military service. She listened with rapt attention and his reaction to her soft voice and quiet countenance went far beyond polite conversation. He lost himself in her eyes, wrapped himself in her charms, and regularly abandoned much of his meal for fear that a single word from her lips might escape his notice.

With only barrels of salted pork and kegs of rum as his confessors, Antoine wrestled with confusion. He contemplated his feelings for Sister Marguerite and struggled with his inappropriate passion. She served God. He served the King. She turned the other cheek. He lived by the sword. She preached to lost souls. He led soldiers to their death. His thoughts concluded with a bitter grimace.

Any type of relationship with Sister Marguerite stood no chance of success.

Lezard, summoned by Lieutenant-Colonel Charles, defended himself with disparaging remarks about his victim.

"She is a whore masquerading as a nun," said Lezard.

"You will not use that word in my presence. Is that understood, Captain?"

Lezard remained at attention.

"Yes sir."

"You are here because Bougainville made the request. Were it not for your relationship with the general, I would flog you myself."

The lieutenant-colonel's reference to Bougainville, prompted Lezard to shove his nose into the air. Louis Antoine de Bougainville, Lezard's well-placed friend, currently served as an *aide-de-camp* to the Marquis de Montcalm, leader of French forces in Quebec. Montcalm and Bougainville, traveling well behind the *Leopard* on the *Licorne*, did not expect to arrive in Quebec City for weeks.

"You will apologize to Sister Marguerite at dinner this evening or I will make a full report to the Marquis," said the Commander.

Lezard scowled and glared at the senior officer.

"Sir, I do not wish to apologize to this woman," he said.

"You have been given an order, Captain Lezard. Dismissed!"

The angry captain saluted, spun on one heel, and left.

Lezard fumed as he climbed below deck to the canvass-walled room which housed his hammock. He thought back to the days when his living conditions were much worse. Until he reached the age of twelve, Adolphe shared a room with his mother, who shared it with strange men. Lezard's father, rarely home and rarely sober, beat the two of them, until his mother paid the drunk to go away. She earned decent money as a prostitute, in the slums of Paris, but did not part with it willingly, a fact to which the bruised, battered, and usually hungry boy could testify. On one occasion, when the alcohol and the money flowed freely, little Adolphe waited, until his mother and her two guests passed out. He then absconded with all three purses.

The boy lived well on the streets as a pick pocket and a petty thief. But for an accident with a horse and carriage, Adolphe Lezard might never have left Paris. One day, a speeding carriage sent the urchin boy flying. Lezard sustained only minor injuries. But the distinguished passenger riding in the carriage, scolded his reckless driver, and decided to protect the waif from further mishaps. He enrolled Lezard into a local boarding school and ensured the boy's entrance into a military academy. Lezard, with a natural penchant for lying and flattery, did well. His adept use of the carriage owner's name, Louis Antoine de Bougainville, guaranteed the young man's rapid rise through the ranks.

And while Adolphe grew accustomed to his new life as a member of the military class, the baggage from his horrid childhood, remained. He distrusted everyone, held most of his subordinates in contempt, and viewed all women as ignorant or whores or both. Adolphe slammed his fist against a low-hanging wooden beam.

"I will not apologize to that whore," he yelled.

But no one heard him.

Antoine Dauphin's timely arrival at Sister Marguerite's enclosure, after the dinner hour, occurred for a reason.

On that evening, Sister Helene, feeling dizzy, asked to be excused. Sister Marguerite accompanied her, but the two nuns separated when a soldier requested the older nun's assistance. The captain thought it wise to check on them, shortly after dinner ended. Lezard decided to do the same, but for a less honorable reason.

At dinner, the next day, Antoine stared at the two empty chairs opposite him, wondering if his religious friends remained ill. He refused the tureen of soup and fidgeted instead with his bowl. At the far end of the table, Adolphe Lezard stood and used a spoon to bang on his metal plate. He waited until the diners stared in his direction.

"Although Sister Marguerite has chosen not to grace us with her presence this evening, I wish to offer my sincerest apologies for our misunderstanding of the evening last," he said.

Antoine scowled when Lezard flashed his crooked grin, sat down, and reached for the wine. No one at the table, except Antoine, knew what prompted Lezard's feigned apology.

Captain Dauphin rose, tossed his spoon into an empty bowl, and left the table without excusing himself.

A canvas sheet, which afforded the Ursuline nuns a small measure of privacy, covered the opening to their enclosure.

Antoine, hearing no voices, cleared his throat.

"Sister Marguerite, please forgive me for intruding, I am concerned that you and Sister Helene did not dine with us this evening.

The canvas curtain moved to one side and Sister Marguerite appeared.

"Sister Helene has a fever. I know not what to do."

"May I see her?" he asked.

"Yes, of course."

Antoine studied the old woman's gaunt face, covered in beads of sweat. The sickly nun stared at the captain through glassy eyes. Her lips were so dry and swollen, they cracked and bled. Sister Helene took rapid, shallow breaths and wore the gray look of death on her face. Despite several blankets, the old woman trembled violently.

"And there is this," said Sister Marguerite, carefully pushing the ailing nun onto her side. She exposed the nape of her patient's neck and lower back.

Antoine stepped back, as if the circular, rose-colored patch on the old woman's wrinkled skin posed a physical threat. He stared at Marguerite and motioned toward the opening.

"Please," he said.

Outside of the bed chamber, he spoke in a whisper.

"She suffers from the purple fever."

"What must I do?"

"The surgeon-major sails with us. I will speak with the lieutenant-colonel, first."

Sister Marguerite reached for the Captain's hand and squeezed.

"I pray to God that you will help us once again."

Antoine swallowed hard and drew a short breath, the touch of her soft, cool hands—unexpected but pleasing.

"I take my leave, but first you must tell me why Captain Lezard chose an Ursuline nun as his victim," said Antoine.

Marguerite blushed and averted her gaze.

"Sister Helene requires my attention," she said, disappearing behind the canvas curtain.

"Two of our men suffer from the fever as we speak and several dozen of the crew are similarly plagued. No one on the ship is safe," said the surgeon-major.

Antoine turned to the lieutenant-colonel, questioning the officer with his eyes.

"I am sorry, Captain Dauphin," said the lieutenant-colonel.

Antoine inquired of the surgeon-major.

"What are your instructions?" asked Antoine.

"Large quantities of our fresh water and, if she is able, bring her top side. The salt air seems to have a positive effect," said the surgeon-major.

"And what medicine should we give her?" asked Antoine.

"Captain, there is no medicine for such a fever. Your friend is going to die."

Antoine returned at once to Sister Marguerite's enclosure.

"Will she recover?' she asked.

Antoine studied the canvass wall that separated one enclosure from the next. The stained piece of sail prevented prying eyes, but it did not stop purple fever. Antoine could do nothing. Sister Marguerite's red, swollen eyes, framed by dark circles and tear-stained cheeks, melted the man's heart.

"I am truly sorry, my friend. I am truly sorry."

"It is God's punishment." she said, her eyes fixed on the ashen face of her fellow Ursuline. "It is penance for my sins."

"Marguerite, you must not think that way," he whispered.

She did not remark on the inappropriate use of her first name, consumed only with Sister Helene's worsening condition. The fluids which pooled in the sick woman's lungs rattled and her shallow breathing slowed. The symptoms signaled to Antoine and Sister Marguerite that their vigil would soon be over.

"You must leave now, Captain Dauphin," she ordered.

She turned her back to him. He stood in place.

"Sister Marguerite," he pleaded.

"Go. I wish to be alone with my friend," she announced.

The most dangerous portion of the ship's cross-Atlantic voyage to Quebec City occurred at the end of the journey.

Navigating the Saint Lawrence River, its rocks, reefs, and treacherous northwest winds, frightened even the most experienced of ship captains. Daily stops, required for soundings which measured the water's depth, extended the journey by ten days. From the French settlement in Rimouski, the *Leopard* hugged the south shore of the St. Lawrence to St. Anne de Beaupre, a tiny community twenty miles east of the city. The crew fired several of its cannon in gratitude to the patron saint of sailors, for the ship's safe arrival.

The *Leopard's* journey to New France came to an end shortly after Sister Helene's journey on earth came to an end. Except for Sister Marguerite's whispered prayers, the disposal at sea of the nun's body occurred without pomp and circumstance. The ship, now totally infested with disease, lost more than one hundred crewmembers and soldiers. More would die in hospital at Quebec City.

Antoine and Adolphe Lezard received their orders when the *Leopard* dropped anchor.

Antoine reported to headquarters, to assist with preparations for the imminent arrival of his new commander, the Marquis de Montcalm. Lezard reported to François Bigot, intendant for all of Quebec. Sister Marguerite, alone and caring for other patients, walked alongside wagons filled with litters, to the Ursuline monastery where young girls went to be educated and sick people went to die.

"You were accompanied by Sister Helene, were you not?"

The distressed novitiate, on her knees before her Mother Superior, reached for the elderly woman's outstretched hand, kissed the sacred ring, and murmured her response.

"Yes, my Blessed Mother, but I failed in my duties. Sister Helene contracted the fever and is now with our Lord in paradise. I beg your forgiveness my beloved Mother Superior."

Mother Mary of the Nativity, a crusty old woman with decades of experience as an Ursuline nun, showed no emotion. The Mother Superior naturally questioned the motives of her novitiates and instinctively challenged their devotion.

"Sister Angelique will show you to your cell. You are to remain in prayer, until you are summoned. Do you understand, Sister Marguerite?"

"Yes, my beloved Mother Superior."

Sister Marguerite ignored sharp pangs of hunger and fell to her knees even before the cell door slammed shut. A crucifix, on the wall above her cot, decorated the otherwise barren room. A few pegs in the wall served as her armoire. A small, bedside table, with a bowl and pitcher, served as her bath, and an old wooden bucket, as her toilette. She thanked her Savior for such luxurious accommodations, begged His forgiveness for her sins, and asked Him for the strength and courage to sin no more.

CHAPTER TWO

Hungry and Alone

In Quebec City, Adolphe Lezard watched as Intendant François Bigot paced the floor in his elaborate offices, barking orders, waving papers, and tugging on his custom-made wig.

The Intendant received word that Pierre Francois de Rigaud, the Marquis de Vaudreuil, would arrive that day. As the newly installed Governor, appointed by King Louis XV, Vaudreuil served as the supreme civil authority for New France and as the technical commander-in-chief of all military forces in the area. Bigot reported to Governor Vaudreuil.

Lezard, the Intendant's aide-de-camp, could not resist a wry observation, as Quebec's most powerful civil servant walked back and forth, while mopping his brow.

"Governor Vaudreuil causes great concern for the intendant, yes?"

"My only duty is to assist the governor in any way he desires," said Bigot.

Lezard smirked and rolled his eyes. Bigot returned the grin. Bigot enjoyed an ownership interest in almost every import company, shipping concern, fur trading outfit, contractor, and supplier that did business in New France. Over the years, Bigot amassed a small fortune. He expected the Marquis de Vaudreuil to cooperate with the Intendant's crooked ways or look the other way. Bigot could not assure himself of Vaudreuil's "cooperation," until the outcome of their first meeting.

Antoine, told by his superiors that the Marquis de Montcalm would not arrive in Quebec City for at least a week, searched for something to do.

He thought of Sister Marguerite but resisted the urge to visit the Ursuline monastery. The landmark convent occupied a city block and lay within walking distance from Montcalm's headquarters where Antoine worked. After a week of mind-numbing boredom and constant preoccupation with the nun, Antoine ignored his best instincts and visited the convent.

He stood at the entrance of the walled structure, pulled on the rope several times, and heard the ring of a distant bell. One of the two large wooden doors, in the main building, opened. A diminutive nun, wearing the habit of a novitiate, approached the large, black, wrought iron fence. She did not attempt to open the locked gates, which towered above the captain and effectively prevented unwanted guests.

"May I help you?" she asked.

"My name is Captain Antoine Dauphin, with His Majesty's Royal Roussillon regiment. I am here on government business. I must speak with Sister Marguerite Valtesse," he announced.

Antoine suspected that a simple inquiry would not permit him access to the cloistered community and decided on a slight deception. The young woman frowned and quickly retraced her steps across the stone-paved courtyard, disappearing behind the large, wooden doors. Antoine waited at the gate, until the novitiate reappeared, this time with a nun, in full Ursuline regalia. The much older woman brandished an ornate ring and a long string of beads around her neck, ordained with a gold crucifix. Antoine licked his dry lips and fidgeted with the buttons on his colorful jacket, bracing himself for the repercussions of lying to a nun.

"I am the Mother Superior. What is your business with the monastery?"

Antoine bit his lower lip and removed his hat, struggling to compose his response. Mother Superior turned to the novitiate.

"You may return to your work," she said to her young charge.

The novitiate scampered across the courtyard and disappeared into the large stone building.

Mother Mary of the Nativity leaned forward, looked for ear witnesses, and whispered.

"Sister Marguerite speaks of you often, Captain Dauphin."

Antoine exhaled deeply and beamed his relief.

"I wish only to speak with her, Mother Superior," he said.

Mother Mary stepped back and spoke in a loud voice.

"Captain Dauphin. We are a cloistered community and leave the monastery only when it is necessary. We receive those who are seriously ill and the little girls who come for instruction. That is all."

"But, surely . . ."

"Your gallantry and your compassion are known to our Lord. You should be concerned with nothing else. May God bless you."

"Please, I must see her," said Antoine.

The woman closed her eyes, bowed, and walked away.

"The ship is sturdier than the crew."

Captain Pellegrin and his distinguished passenger, the Marquis de Montcalm, watched the deckhands on the *Licorne*, secured by no more than a rope around their waist, struggle to maintain their footing. The ship's surface, now awash in foam, exposed the men to volley after volley of wind driven bullets of saltwater. The *Licorne*, constructed two years ago, carried a crew of two hundred thirty men plus six hundred French soldiers and thirty-two guns. For General Montcalm, the French frigate, still days from Quebec City, could not slice through the waves quickly enough. British forces threatened French territory, on most of the continent. The French general intended to eliminate the English threat.

Montcalm, now forty-six years old, entered the French Army at the age of fifteen. Twice wounded in battle, he repeatedly distinguished himself as a military man and became the clear choice to lead French forces, in North America. With the exception of Canadian born Governor Vaudreuil, who was disinclined to accept any general officer that hailed from France, Montcalm was loved and respected by those who knew and served him.

"You are as skilled on the St. Lawrence as you are on the high seas," said Montcalm, a flattering reference to the ship captain's impressive skill while traversing the treacherous waterway that led to Quebec City.

Pellegrin grinned as he skillfully steered his ship at an angle to the vicious storm.

"A fully loaded vessel is safer when we are at sea. But that is not the case here, in the St. Lawrence," he observed.

The general nodded in agreement. In time, conditions on the water improved. The ship's sails soon billowed gently in the breeze. Mother Nature's powerful temper tantrum ended. Quebec City lay over the horizon.

"Burn it."

Antoine swallowed hard to stifle an inappropriate cheer. He watched as several of his colleagues, in the Royal Roussillon regiment, reacted to his order and climbed onto the deck of the

Leopard. They touched their torches to small mounds of dry wood sprinkled with gunpowder and sprinted to the side of the infested vessel, to board their waiting *bateaux.* The decrepit heap of pestilence received its death sentence from the military brass, as retaliation for a failing hull and because the ship's diseased interior lay waste to half the ship's crew and dozens of passengers.

The French man-of-war threw its flames high into the air, as if to protest its fate. It would share the same watery grave that swallowed Sister Helene and so many others. Antoine, partially avenged by the intentional arson, said a silent prayer for Sister Helene and his fellow soldiers. Again, his thoughts shifted to Sister Marguerite. Her voice and image burned in his mind with the same intensity of the conflagration which now consumed the *Leopard.* He could neither explain nor did he justify his interest in a member of the religious community. His attraction to the woman, like his obsession with the military, would not be denied. He furrowed his brow and muttered to himself.

"I will not surrender to that crusty, old nun," he said, referring to Mother Superior.

Montcalm could wait no longer for the slow moving *Licorne,* to drop anchor in Quebec.

The impatient veteran abandoned the *Licorne* and rode a *caleche* into the city. The two wheeled, horse drawn vehicle, did not perform as expected, however, and much to General Montcalm's chagrin, he arrived several hours after the *Licorne.*

Antoine, increasingly anxious as he waited for Montcalm's arrival by carriage, stood on the docks, with a number of soldiers. Several carriages would deliver them to Intendant Bigot's residence, where Montcalm would be formally greeted. The Intendant acted in Governor Vaudreuil's absence, the governor currently in

Montreal and expected to formally greet Montcalm, at a later date.

The general and his entourage arrived at Bigot's luxurious quarters, graciously acknowledging their host's bubbly and overly gratuitous welcome. Antoine, a mere captain, remained at the entrance to Bigot's offices while the dignitaries exchanged pleasantries. He could discern portions of their conversations, including Bigot's announcement that a grand reception and banquet in honor of Montcalm, would take place the next evening.

"You may wait outside with the horses."

Antoine recognized the slithery voice of Adolphe Lezard. He chose not to respond.

"Did you hear me, Captain Dauphin?"

Antoine's face grew red as he glared at the man's crooked teeth.

"We are of the same rank, Captain Lezard."

"Intendant Bigot is my superior."

"And the Marquis de Montcalm is my commanding officer. Now leave me to my post or you will suffer the same fate which you experienced on the *Leopard*.

Lezard, emboldened by the presence of his employer, took a step forward. Antoine did the same. Neither man blinked, and both of them scowled their refusal to retreat. The approaching voices of Bigot and Montcalm prompted the adversaries to step back. Each of them held one of the double doors through which their respective superiors walked.

Antoine followed Montcalm. Lezard retreated to Bigot's inner office.

"This is not possible."

Mother Mary of the Nativity gesticulated wildly and spoke in a loud voice. The Superior pointed an arthritic finger at Sister Marguerite and demanded to know more.

"What, precisely, did the man at the dock say?" she asked.

Sister Marguerite and Alemos, the Abenaki Indian boy who pulled the two-wheel cart used to transport supplies, looked at each other and at Mother Superior.

"Please forgive me, Blessed Mother, the man at the dock had nothing for us to purchase."

"No flour, no salt pork, no rice?" asked Mother Superior.

Sister Marguerite lowered her eyes. Alemos, with his limited skills in French and English, managed a single word.

"Warehouse."

"Ah, yes. Monsieur Bigot, our unscrupulous intendant, has gathered everything into his warehouses where we shall pay and pay and pay."

"Is it your wish that we go to the warehouse?" asked Sister Marguerite.

"We shall go together and at once," said Mother Superior.

Two soldiers stood at the entrance to Bigot's building, one of several large structures, all of them heavily guarded.

"You may not enter." barked one of the soldiers.

"I am Mother Superior at the Ursuline Monastery. If I refuse to do as you ask, is it your intention to shoot me in the back or will you simply run me through," asked Mother Mary of the Nativity.

The soldier stepped back and looked to his fellow guard. He studied the Indian boy and proposed a face-saving compromise.

"The savage stays here."

"May God have mercy on your soul," said Mother Mary, brushing past the stunned guards, with Alemos and Sister Marguerite in tow.

A series of stairs brought the threesome to a set of double doors, made of hand-carved wood. Brass fittings, and the king's seal inscribed on a brass plaque, adorned the entrance. Mother Superior did not knock, opening both doors and taking several strides into the ornately furnished office.

"You will leave, immediately."

The man who barked at Mother Superior fixed his gaze on Sister Marguerite.

The younger nun used her hand to stifle a scream. Mother Superior took several steps forward, now inches from the French officer.

"And you are?" she asked.

"I am Captain Adolphe Lezard, assistant to the Intendant, Francois Bigot.

"Yes, of course. I know exactly who you are—and what you are. I wish to speak with the intendant. You will summon him, now," she ordered.

"I refuse. And now, you will leave, immediately, or I will summon the guard," Lezard announced.

"I will not leave, and you will summon the intendant," she repeated, as she wagged a finger at Lezard.

While the Mother Superior and Lezard remained locked in an unspoken battle of the eyes, Sister Marguerite stood frozen in the doorway, trembling and standing behind the much smaller Indian boy. The impasse between nun and soldier ended when the sound of rustling silk distracted each of the warring parties.

"Mother Superior, I am extremely honored by your visit," said the woman.

The voice belonged to a beautifully dressed lady, in her mid-thirties, with perfectly coiffed blonde hair, large hazel eyes, and a floor length, pink dress. She entered the office from a rear door. The woman reached for the nun's hand and fell to one knee. After kissing Mother Superior's ring, she rose to her feet and hugged the nun.

"You can't possibly know me, Blessed Mother. I received my education at the monastery many years ago. But you bring with you so many beautiful and cherished memories." said the woman, motioning Mother Superior to a large overstuffed chair. The old nun required a moment to recover from her initial confusion.

"Bless you my child. Your continued faith in our Lord God makes you beautiful, in His eyes.

"Permit me to introduce myself, Blessed Mother Superior. I am Mademoiselle Pean, a grateful student of the Ursulines."

"I thank God in heaven for sending to our school, students such as yourself, imbued with the grace of God. And your great beauty is proof of his divine creation," said Mother Superior.

"You are too kind," replied the Mademoiselle, smiling her appreciation for the compliment.

"I must confess. We are here to see the intendant, but our visit is unannounced," said Mother Superior, her hands clasped in supplication.

"Blessed Mother do not worry yourself. François will see you immediately. I will insist. Captain Lezard, have you no manners? Please invite all of our guests to be seated. And tea. We must have tea," she smiled.

As the beautiful woman waltzed from the room, Lezard, unsmiling, moved two, large overstuffed chairs. Mother Superior motioned to Sister Marguerite, but the frightened nun remained at the door. Alemos, clearly enjoying himself, fell into one of the large chairs and smirked at his reluctant host. When the beautiful woman returned, minutes later, she walked hand in hand with Bigot.

"An unexpected surprise, Mother Superior, but a delightful one indeed," Bigot said, as he bowed from the waist.

Francois Bigot, a short and stocky man, in his early fifties, did not impress Mother Mary of the Nativity. She betrayed no emotion and did not rise from her chair. She knew of the intendant. He acted no better than a tyrant, exercising complete control of all goods and services which flowed in and out of the province of Quebec. Bigot, a glutton, loved to drink and gambled to excess. But, most of all, he loved his spectacularly beautiful mistress, Mademoiselle Paen.

The Mother Superior, knowing all of this, extending her ringed hand, closed her eyes, and looked away. Bigot kissed her ring and noticed the beautiful nun standing in the doorway.

"You are accompanied by an angel," said Bigot.

Mother Superior glared her disapproval. Mademoiselle Paen blushed.

"We are in desperate need of foodstuffs for the monastery," said Mother Superior."

"Francois, my love, will you help these poor sisters?" asked Paen, stepping to within inches of Bigot's face and caressing his cheek.

The Mademoiselle purred her request and Bigot, drowning in the beautiful woman's eyes, beamed his approval. He snapped at Lezard.

"Captain, you will assist the friends of Mademoiselle Paen and you will receive from them only what they desire to pay, nothing more. Do you understand what I have told you?"

"Yes, Intendant, I will do as you say."

Sister Superior stood and acknowledged her benefactor and his paramour.

"You have been most kind. Thank you very much," she said.

After leaving the warehouse, Alemos struggled with his wooden cart, overflowing with foodstuffs. Sister Marguerite joined the Indian boy and pushed the contraption up the hilly terrain.

Mother Superior chuckled to herself—all the way to the convent.

Antoine, included in Montcalm's entourage to Montreal, did not expect that his superior officer would be treated as a homecoming hero.

Governor Vaudreuil arranged for his new general to be welcomed with cannon fire and great ceremonial splendor. Their meeting went well, despite the fact that the two leaders, intent on pleasing the other, did not wish to deal with the other. Antoine overheard a number of Bigot's aides, as they echoed Vaudreuil's complaint that a general officer from France could not be as effective as a Canadian-borne soldier. The whispered murmurs, from Montcalm's inner circle, were equally unsettling. Many of them quietly complained, as did General Montcalm, that the poorly trained, backwoodsmen of Canada and their redskin friends, could never be an effective military force against the English. That job belonged, more properly, to the professionally trained French Army.

At least for a while, the native, Canadian governor and the thoroughbred French general worked together. After his trip to Montreal, Montcalm visited Ticonderoga (Carillon) and installed his best number two general, the Chevalier de Levis, to defend the garrison. Montcalm also ordered an additional 3000 men to the fort; a move designed to distract the English army and obscure the French general's true objective—Oswego.

Antoine, refusing to give up, made another visit to the convent.

"They have a recreation period?" he asked.

Antoine, quizzing the novitiate behind the iron gate at the monastery, could not believe what she told him.

"Yes, Captain, once, each week on Sunday afternoon. Your

entrance at that time would be permitted."

Antoine reached through the bars, retrieved one of the young lady's hands, and pressed his lips on the unblemished, white skin.

The young nun, red-faced, at once withdrew and ran to the stone cloister.

"Why are you here?" asked Sister Marguerite.

The nun's head swiveled, as she looked about the courtyard. In her mind, everyone stared at the novitiate and her male visitor. A captain in the French Army, no less. It was too scandalous for her to even contemplate. In fact, when she first learned about Antoine's arrival, Sister Marguerite refused to leave her cell. Antoine too, refused to leave and Mother Superior intervened, once again.

"Go, and tell the captain, goodbye," she ordered.

Antoine announced the purpose of his visit.

"I leave in three days. We are off to war," he said.

Sister Marguerite studied his solemn face. Her anxious look disappeared, replaced with genuine concern that her gallant friend might never return.

"You will not be alone, Captain Dauphin. The Lord is with you, always." she said.

He motioned to a nearby bench, hewn from rock, and further away from the other visitors. She hesitated.

"Please?" he begged.

They sat on opposite ends, eyes straight ahead. He spoke in a soft tone of voice.

"The Lord may be with me, but it is you that I think of, day and night, without relief."

She jerked her head in his direction and jumped to her feet.

"Captain Dauphin. You must not speak to me in this manner. I am married to our Lord and Savior," she said, retreating several steps away, from the still seated Captain.

He rose to his feet and reached for her hands. Her entire body spasmed and she stepped further away.

"Can a man deny his own heart?" he asked.

"I pray that you will be safe, Captain Dauphin. But I do not pray for your return."

As she walked away, Antoine watched the gray habit float across the stone-covered courtyard and disappear behind the two, large, wooden doors.

Chapter Three

The Enemy

Antoine contemplated the fruitless meeting with Sister Marguerite for most of his voyage to Fort Oswego on Lake Ontario.

For a brief time, he wrestled with feelings of infatuation, personal attraction, and yes, lust. In the end, he dismissed the entire episode as a foolish waste of time and quickly returned to his one, true mistress, the military.

Although Governor Vaudreuil and General Montcalm agreed on the strategic importance of Fort Oswego, Montcalm took on the logistical nightmare of delivering more than three thousand men, two armed ships, tons of ammunition, and foodstuffs, to a remote British outpost. And all of this needed to be accomplished while maintaining the element of surprise. Montcalm succeeded and, upon his arrival at Fort Oswego, wasted no time in the final preparations.

"We begin the first parallel, tonight," he announced to his officers, Captain Dauphin among them.

Parallels, hand dug trenches parallel but close to the walls of a fort, protected the attacking soldiers and their artillery. The trenches also had the effect of isolating the enemy. The deep ditches prevented supplies and men from entering the fort and made it impossible for the defenders to escape.

Antoine supervised his assigned duties in the massive undertaking, under almost constant fire. And while the men around him feared for their lives and cowered as musket balls exploded in the dirt, Antoine relished the danger. He embraced the thrill of battle with a fervor that exceeded his passion for Sister Marguerite. A victory would be his mistress.

At sunrise, their digging came to an end and the firing commenced. It required less than forty-eight hours for the British to conclude that, unless they surrendered, they would be annihilated. Antoine and his men spied the white flag of truce flying over the enemy's fortifications. A series of loud cheers erupted.

"The English have surrendered," one of the men shouted, jumping up and down.

Antoine's eyes closed as he murmured to himself.

"Victory is ours," he said, falling in love, once again, with the lure of battle.

Antoine and his colleagues left Oswego ten days after they arrived.

The French attack left all British fortifications in the area, leveled to the ground. Montcalm and his men, victorious in battle, enjoyed a hero's reception when they reached Montreal. Word spread throughout the province that French forces defeated the English Army, until now acknowledged as the greatest army in the world.

The tally of Montcalm's victory impressed the masses. In less than a month, the General and his men, travelled more than 650 miles, destroyed all three British forts, in the Oswego area, captured a British war flotilla, and seized an immense store of

British provisions for use by the French Army. Governor Vaudreuil received and posted the captured British flags in Montreal churches. The Bishop of Quebec declared a public thanksgiving and the locals expressed their amazement that French forces accomplished all of this, with minimal loss of life. Ironically, General Montcalm expressed his frustration.

"The General is angry, even in victory," said Antoine to a fellow officer.

"Yes. It is now public knowledge that the Governor assigns most of the credit for our victory to his local militia and their redskin friends," said the officer. "The King's regiment means nothing to this Canadian Governor," he added.

"And this fighting between Montcalm and Vaudreuil will lead to our defeat," Antoine predicted.

Sister Marguerite's chosen life as an Ursuline nun, plummeted her into a daily routine of strict sacrifice, suffering, and self-imposed, solitary confinement.

Marguerite refused to participate in the weekly recreation periods, ostensibly because she wanted to pray. She performed all of her required tasks and volunteered for additional chores—scrubbing stone floors on her hands and knees, cleaning the latrines, and working in the kitchen. She rarely ate a full meal, satisfying pangs of hunger with an occasional cup of hot broth. Marguerite also labored in the hospital ward, an unpleasant assignment where doctors regularly mistreated their religious volunteers and where dying patients lashed out at their Ursuline caregivers. Marguerite withstood it all.

Late one morning, Mother Superior noticed Sister Marguerite, asleep on her knees leaning against a bench, scrub rag still in hand.

"Sister Marguerite."

The novitiate jerked to attention and immediately bowed her head.

"Forgive me, Blessed Mother, for my failings. I am guilty of the cardinal sin of sloth and deserve your just punishment."

"Come with me, Sister Marguerite."

The pair marched to the Superior's office chamber. Mother Mary sat behind a large, oak desk. The young Ursuline fell to her knees, head bowed, and hands clasped, expecting a harsh penance.

"You may be seated."

Sister Marguerite hesitated. Her Superior insisted.

"You may be seated, Sister Marguerite."

Mother Superior rested her hands, palms down, in front of her, and leaned forward.

"I have observed you closely, since the day of your arrival and, most especially, since your visit with Captain Dauphin."

"Please forgive me, Blessed Mother."

The old nun shook her head and slapped at the desk, with both hands.

"Sacrifice, self-denial, and prayer. We do these things because we seek the love and mercy of our Lord and Savior."

"Yes, Blessed Mother."

"Do you seek the Lord, Sister Marguerite or do you hide from the captain?"

Sister Marguerite stared at the floor, in an effort to hide the pink heat which now covered her face.

"I do not understand." she said.

"Yes, I believe you do. You are avoiding the captain and doing penance for your sins. What sins have you committed with this man?"

Sister Marguerite looked up, her eyes wide with fear and denial.

"My sins are of the mind and heart, not of the flesh."

"Is there a difference?" asked Mother Superior.

A long period of silence enveloped the inquisitor and her captive. Sister Marguerite spoke first, her voice trembling, her lips quivering.

"I have prayed for His guidance but His will remains a mystery to me. What am I to do?"

The aged woman rose to her feet and thrust an accusing finger at the young nun.

"You will soon take the permanent vows of the Ursuline. Your sacrifice, your suffering, your very life, is for the glory of God and no one else. You are married to Christ. Put this soldier out of your mind and live your life with no thought for anyone or anything, except the Lord your God." she ordered.

"Do you understand me, Sister Marguerite?"

"Yes, my Blessed Mother."

Antoine's heart grew colder as winter enveloped the city of Quebec.

He stayed that way even as the river's ice melted and the trees blossomed green, with the buds of spring. The captain made no further attempt to visit the monastery, devoting himself instead to the daily chores of an officer in the Royal Roussillon regiment. He prepared for yet another attack on a British outpost, this one built on the shores of Lac Sacrament. (Lake George) Fort William Henry lay immediately north of Albany, New York. The need for supplies forced Captain Dauphin to visit Intendant Bigot's warehouse, on a number of occasions. Antoine and his counterpart, Adolphe Lezard, managed the bare amenities when they encountered each other. With time, their meetings became easier for Antoine, as his feelings for the woman he once rescued from the clutches of Lezard, faded from memory.

On one morning, while leaving the building and simultaneously inspecting Lezard's, more often than not, inaccurate paperwork, Antoine walked headlong into a small, two-wheeled cart. While the officer and the young Abenaki Indian exchanged apologies, a familiar voice addressed the captain.

"Captain Dauphin, please forgive us."

Antoine instantly recognized Mother Superior, but his face grew red when he noticed the Superior's assistant, Sister Marguerite. Antoine pursed his lips, in a failed attempt at a smile. He removed his hat, executed a perfect bow, and stepped to one side.

The older nun did not continue on her way, pursuing a conversation with the captain.

"We are thankful to the Lord and to General Montcalm, for your great victory and for your safe return," said the Mother Superior.

Antoine adjusted his hat and stared at his boots. After what seemed a long period of silence, he faced the older woman, studiously avoiding eye contact with Sister Marguerite.

"Thank you, Mother Superior. And I apologize to Sister Marguerite."

"And why do you apologize, Captain Dauphin?" she asked.

Antoine's eyes darted to the novitiate, flashing their anger.

"Sister Marguerite prayed for my safety, but not my return," he replied.

He bowed once more and crossed the street.

Sister Marguerite, alone in her cell at the monastery, hurled her prayer book across the room.

She reached for the wooden crucifix on the wall and slammed it on the stone floor, splintering the sacred icon into pieces. The pitcher and its basin did not escape the woman's wrath. She watched as ceramic shards flew in every direction and clenched her teeth as she yanked the veil from her head and threw it at the door. Marguerite fell onto the cot and sobbed into her woolen blanket.

Her recent encounter with Captain Dauphin left the novitiate confused, angry, and frustrated. The vows she made, to love the Lord and no one else, weighed heavily on her mind and heart. And yet, the distinct possibility that she might never see Antoine Dauphin again, left her unsettled and filled with regret. And while the admonitions of Mother Superior rang loud and true in her head, a tiny voice in her heart, questioned Marguerite's willingness to spend the rest of her life as a celibate Ursuline.

In between sighs and sniffles, Marguerite thought back to her days, in Paris. She cursed her parents for abandoning her at the convent. She resented the Ursulines for her life of misery. And she regretted those times when she allowed others to make decisions for her.

A knock on the cell door forced Marguerite to jump from the cot. The debris on the floor prohibited her from opening the door any more than a few inches. The inquiring novitiate spoke to a sliver of darkness.

"Mother Superior wishes to see you."

"Yes, of course," said Marguerite.

"You will go to Bigot's warehouse, deliver this letter, and remain there until you are given the money that he owes us," said Mother Superior, clearly irritated that the intendant cheated the monastery once again.

"I will do as you have instructed, my Blessed Mother, but Captain Lezard is certain to be present," said Marguerite.

"You will be safe, my child. If he is by himself, leave immediately. He will not attempt anything in the presence of others," said

Mother Superior.

Sister Marguerite walked to Bigot's offices, her mind a jumbled tangle of thoughts about the two captains in her life, Dauphin and Lezard.

Lezard came to the door. Marguerite took a deep breath.

"I wish to speak with the intendant," she said, remaining in the doorway.

Adolphe Lezard sneered as he looked up at his visitor.

"Of course, you do. I will announce your presence. This way please," he said.

He pointed to a chair in Bigot's massive office and left the chamber through a side door. Marguerite stood close to the entrance, her intended escape route. She jumped when Lezard reappeared behind her and slammed the large doors shut. He locked them, twisted in her direction, and laughed.

Sister Marguerite, eyes wide with fear, ran to the side door, but it too could not be opened. She stole a quick glance over her shoulder. Lezard held the key aloft, grinned, and slowly nodded his head to confirm the woman's worst nightmare. Marguerite's mind, driven by panic and fear, raced through the lessons of her past.

"Turn the other cheek." "You must forgive the trespasses of others." "The Lord will protect you from all evil."

The loud sound of her beating heart overpowered the admonitions of her Ursuline instructors. She could not catch her breath and struggled to speak.

"Captain Lezard, I harbor no ill feelings against you. And I beg you to forgive me, if I have offended you in any way," she pleaded.

"You are a whore. You do not deserve my forgiveness," said Lezard, removing his jacket and loosening his collar.

Marguerite stood trapped between Lezard and Bigot's oversized desk. A similar scene from years ago, flashed in her mind.

While attending a raucous party at a Paris mansion, an aggressive, young suitor pulled Marguerite into a private office, belonging to the host. When the young man's lurid intentions became clear, Marguerite panicked. She intended to scream for help, but the young man suddenly changed his mind and left the room of his own accord. Only after she looked around, did Marguerite understand the man's unexpected retreat. They were not alone. Another young couple, their amorous intentions obvious, occupied a far corner of the room. Marguerite, too curious to leave, remained for a brief moment, unable to avert her gaze. She watched unseen, and listened as a voluptuous blond, her back to a large, mahogany desk, spoke to her male friend, in a husky voice.

"Finally, Gaston, we are alone," said the woman.

As the man rushed to the woman's side, Marguerite, embarrassed by her voyeurism, slipped quietly from the room.

When she looked up from her daydream, the glint of Lezard's evil grin, appeared yards away. In that instant the innocent nun became the voluptuous woman in the mansion. With great effort and trembling limbs, Marguerite fixed her eyes on Lezard and calmly removed her veil.

"Finally, Captain Lezard, we are alone," she whispered.

Lezard's eyes watered and for a moment, he stood motionless.

Marguerite cast her eyes downward, after a quick glance to the right side of Bigot's large desk.

"Today, you will be mine," he said, his voice choked with lust.

As he approached the woman in gray, licking his lips and using a sleeve to wipe the sweat from his brow, she reached for the long, brass, candlestick holder which adorned Bigot's desk. Lezard's carnal cravings, now out of control, blinded him to the threat of Marguerite's cunning plan.

The brass implement landed squarely on the side of the smiling

Captain's face, opening a long gash, which spurted blood onto his uniform and the oriental floor rug. Her next blow, backhanded, sent the man to his knees, the opposite side of his face similarly lacerated and the bottom half of his right ear, now hanging from a small strip of bloody red flesh. He collapsed to his knees and for a brief moment, the red uniform kneeled before the gray habit, as if in silent adoration. He fell forward and lay motionless at her feet. When she saw his hand twitch, she reached for the large oil lamp and threw it at the body. The fragile globe struck Lezard squarely on the head, forcing shards of hand-painted pink and green glass deep into his face, forehead, and scalp. For a moment, she stood there, shocked by the violence of her resistance.

She stepped over the crumpled heap and grabbed her blood-speckled head dress. After retrieving the key, she scrambled to a side door and used a snowbank to launder her red-stained veil. Marguerite walked the alley ways and side streets, so as not to be discovered.

After an hour of walking, the exhausted woman stumbled into the cold confines of her cell at the monastery and collapsed into the cot.

CHAPTER FOUR

No Memory

Captain Dauphin, like most of his military brethren, wintered in Quebec City.

The fall of 1757, a constant celebration of Montcalm's victories on Lake Ontario, gave no warning of the harsh winter which lay ahead. The troops and the locals suffered an extremely cold winter and the frigid spring brought no signs of a thaw. A famine spread through the land. Bread, when it became available, was rationed. Foodstuffs and fresh meat grew prohibitively expensive, if available at all. Vegetables disappeared altogether.

A brief respite from the struggles which plagued the soldiers and the inhabitants of Quebec, occurred when a French merchant ship unexpectedly appeared in the river. The locals climbed up to roof tops to witness their floating dream of food and badly needed supplies. A large crowd assembled dockside to greet the ship's captain and to negotiate if and when the precious cargo could be accessed. Intendant Bigot boarded the ship first, Lezard, noticeably absent. And although Antoine Dauphin repeatedly scanned the crowd, he could see no gray habits. A scuffle near the ramp, where cargo from the hold of the ship made its appearance, caught Dauphin's attention. He pushed and shoved his way into the center of the crowd and discovered Bigot, bloodied and disheveled, despite a dozen soldiers using bayonets to keep Bigot's attackers at bay.

"Ignorant pesants! Do they not understand? Were it not for me, they would all perish," Bigot growled.

"The people are without food, sir. Surely you understand their desperation," Dauphin replied.

"I do indeed, Captain Dauphin. The evidence of their wrath lay bleeding and unconscious in my office, days ago," Bigot said.

The intendant recounted for Antoine the attack on Adolphe Lezard.

"No one has come forward to identify an assailant and the only witness, a nun, seems to have disappeared," Bigot grumbled.

Captain Dauphin pretended to survey the growing mob but in fact, struggled to hide his thoughts.

"You are not safe here, Monsieur Bigot," said Antoine.

Bigot shook his head, frowned, and stormed off, the troops scurrying to stay by his side.

When Sister Marguerite failed to appear at morning vespers, Mother Superior, red in the face and clenching her teeth, decided to confront the young nun.

She didn't bother to knock, and Marguerite did not rise from her cot, much less fall to her knees, when Mother Superior entered the cell.

"Sister Marguerite, you dare to disrespect me in this manner?"

Marguerite did not respond, her eyes fixed on the ceiling, a broken crucifix in her hands, and tears rolling down her cheeks. Mother Superior noticed the blood-stained coif that lay on the floor.

"You must tell me everything," she said, kneeling at the novitiate's bedside.

"I think I killed him," said Marguerite, her whispered words becoming an uncontrollable series of sobs.

Mother Superior jumped to her feet. She reached for the black rosary beads that hung from her neck and repeatedly crossed herself, with the crucified image of Christ. She painted the Sign of the Cross in the air above the crying woman, not once but thrice, each time imploring "Our Lord and Savior" to forgive the novitiate for her sin.

"You must confess your crime and go to the authorities," said Mother Superior.

"He fooled me into thinking that Bigot was there. Instead, he trapped me. I had no choice but to defend myself," said Marguerite.

"Did you invite his lust, Sister Marguerite?"

"No Blessed Mother. You must believe me," said Marguerite, choosing to withhold the details of her clever deception.

"Surely you are guilty of provoking this man's desire. This is Captain Lezard's second attack. Who will believe you? They will hang you for murder. Of that you may be certain," said Mother Superior.

"I will not go to the authorities," Marguerite announced, daring to disobey an Ursuline nun for the first time, since entering the convent.

Mother Superior, shocked at the young woman's refusal, surveyed the debris strewn about the room.

"First you will get cleaned up and then you will leave the monastery," she ordered.

"But where will I go?" asked Marguerite.

"You cannot stay here. This is a religious community and we do not give sanctuary to criminals," she said.

After hearing Bigot's flustered remarks at the docks, Antoine suspected that Sister Marguerite either knew what happened or attacked Adolphe Lezard, herself.

He wrestled with the thought of going to the convent. Afterall, the sordid scandal did not involve him. And what could he possibly do to help this woman? Lezard, however, deserved to be punished. He disgraced the uniform of His Majesty's Regiment, not once, but twice. Antoine struggled with his thoughts, for most of a sleepless night. In the end, his concern and his curiosity forced him to the convent's main gate, once again. He arrived shortly after sunrise and wasted no time with the novitiate, who scrambled to answer the captain's persistent ringing of the cloister bell.

"I must speak with the Mother Superior, immediately. I insist," he ordered.

The young woman responded, almost too quickly, thought Antoine.

"I am sorry. Mother Mary of the Nativity is unavailable," she announced, her words spoken in a monotone, as if memorized.

Antoine changed his request and demanded to see Sister Marguerite. Again, the novitiate seemed prepared and rehearsed.

"Sister Marguerite is no longer with us. She has left the Order," said the young nun, clasping her hands and stepping back from the gate, as if expecting a violent reaction.

"That is not possible," said the captain, raising his voice. "I don't believe you," he added.

The young woman bowed her head. Antoine slammed his hands into the wrought iron barrier. The nun covered her face and shrieked. He shook the gate in anger and screamed Marguerite's name, as if she might suddenly appear. But she didn't. The novitiate, unable to move, fixated on the captain, wide-eyed and trembling. After a few moments, Antoine's angry breathing slowed. He took a deep breath. When he composed himself, Antoine closed his eyes and bowed his head.

"Please forgive me."

Mother Superior announced her decision with respect to Sister Marguerite.

"You will go to the Ursuline convent in Three Rivers. Alemos will be your guide," said Mother Superior.

"Blessed Mother, I thank you for your kindness," said Marguerite.

"The Community at Three Rivers has been informed only that you are a young woman in trouble. If you share your story with anyone, they will ask you to leave, at once," said Mother Superior, closing her eyes, stunned that she had become a co-conspirator in the murder of a French officer.

"Now please. Leave me."

"Surely you remember who attacked you?"

Francois Bigot stood at the foot of Adolphe Lezard's hospital bed. The patient required days to regain consciousness, after suffering serious wounds about the face, scalp, and skull. A bandage wrapped around the man's head, hid Lezard's right ear, half of which was severed in the attack. He received dozens of stiches to repair deep gashes on both cheeks. Additional stiches and weeks of healing would repair, but not hide, dozens of smaller cuts on his face, forehead, and scalp.

The intendant threw his hands into the air. Bigot worried that he, and not Lezard, was the intended victim of the attack.

"This man tried to kill you and you can remember nothing?" Bigot shouted.

"I regret that I have no memory of the attack," said Lezard.

"This is most unfortunate," Bigot complained.

Lezard's eyes fluttered and closed. Bigot cursed under his breath and stormed from the room. Lezard watched, with one eye open, and grinned when the door slammed shut. He examined his wounds with both hands, gingerly touching the bandages, stitches, and superficial cuts. He grimaced in pain and snarled at the crucifix, which hung in his room as well as every other room of the Catholic hospital.

"That whore will pay for this, with her life," he vowed.

Captain Lezard, released from the hospital several weeks ago, stood in front of the polished, metal mirror, with the ornate, gold colored frame.

The expensive wall hanging, brought to Bigot's office from France, allowed Lezard to examine the scars which covered his face and scalp. The remaining portion of his right ear could also be seen. Lezard winced and looked away. He never enjoyed the self-confidence of taller, more handsome men, but the image in the mirror looked more like a monster than it did a man.

A knock on the door prompted Lezard to clear his throat. He used a red, silk handkerchief to dry his tear-filled eyes. A pause, before he opened the door, allowed the horribly injured man to compose himself.

Mother Superior waited on the other side. The old nun covered her open mouth and gasped. She swallowed hard and spoke in a measured tone.

"You have been injured," she said.

Lezard's eyes narrowed to slits and he glared at the old woman.

"I was viciously attacked, without warning or provocation," he said.

"And your assailant, has he been apprehended?" she asked.

"He," and then Lezard paused, "or she, has not yet been

apprehended," Lezard said.

Mother Mary studied her list of needed supplies.

"This is most unfortunate," she answered.

Lezard, stepped forward.

"You are not accompanied by Sister Marguerite. Why is that?" he asked, arching his eyebrows and searching over Mother Superior's shoulders in both directions.

Mother Superior pretended to read the scribbles on her list.

"Oh, didn't you hear? Sister Marguerite is no longer a member of the Ursuline community," said the nun.

Lezard spun in the direction of his desk.

"How very convenient. What is it you require?" he asked, standing with his back to the woman but near a large, red stain on the carpet.

"We have no food. Surely you can spare some flour for bread and perhaps some corn." she pleaded.

"You are no doubt aware, Mother Superior, of the famine which has plagued our entire region?"

"And yet, your superior, the intendant, continues to entertain lavishly and his guests never leave hungry," she replied

Lezard pointed a finger in her direction and snarled.

"The intendant's affairs are none of your concern. Now unless you have something on your list which I wish to grant, I have more important business to conduct," he said, dismissing her with a wave of his hand.

Mother Superior folded her list and jammed the paper into her bag.

"I pray that you recover from your injuries," she said.

"You should pray for the person who did this to me. I will not rest until justice has been served."

Lezard waited for the gray habit to disappear. He kicked over a wooden, office chair and cleared the desk of its contents, sending the lone candlestick, along with stacks of documents, and writing paraphernalia, flying to the floor.

"The mother hen lies to protect her chick," he snarled.

Captain Dauphin gave no thought to searching for Marguerite.

Now in route to Fort Carillon, (Ticonderoga, New York), he focused on the battle which lay ahead. English forces outnumbered the French Army, by a margin of more than four to one. Despite the overwhelming chance of defeat, Antoine did not shrink from the danger. This is what he trained for. This is what he lived for. He relished the prospect of battle and functioned with little or no sleep for most of the week which preceded it.

When the two armies finally clashed, French preparations, in advance of the battle, paid handsome dividends. Despite repeated attempts to storm the bastion, British troops could not overcome the network of abatis, felled trees, and trenches, installed by the French Army. The British lost a popular general in the attack and suffered both killed and wounded far in excess of the French.

Despite overwhelming odds, French troops defeated the English army, once again.

CHAPTER FIVE

The Siege

Marguerite Valtesse, although grateful to her Ursuline hosts in Three Rivers, decided to return to Quebec City.

A letter from Mother Superior triggered her decision. The Ursuline Superior reported that Captain Lazard did not recall the circumstances of the assault in Bigot's office and could not identify his attacker. The old nun also reported that she and her colleagues had no food and faced the real possibility of starvation. The second bad harvest, in as many years, left the inhabitants of the city in a life-threatening situation. Some of the settlers now ate horse flesh, which Bigot's men sold at great profit. Grass became a regular staple in the French family diet, along with potatoes which, previous to the famine, most of the population detested.

Worse yet, the English captured the small French fort at Frontenac, (Kingston, Ontario). While no one mourned the imprisonment of its 110 occupants, the garrison also housed 800,000 pounds of food stuffs and supplies, all of it destined for Quebec. When word of the defeat reached Quebec City, panic spread like typhoid. Mother Superior inquired if Marguerite could assist the community in any way.

Marguerite also learned from the letter that Captain Dauphin remained in Quebec City. She wondered why the Mother Superior, who previously enjoined the novitiate to forget about Dauphin, now mentioned him by name. The answer to Marguerite's question came at the end of Mother Superior's missive:

"You may no longer wear the habit of the novitiate, as I have released you from all your obligations as a member of the Ursuline community. I believe it is God's will that I do this, and I pray that you will continue to serve Him, in other ways."

Marguerite's expulsion from the Ursuline Community, now official, prompted sadness but also, relief. She quickly plotted her return to Quebec City. A recent, hoped-for gift of funds, from her parents in France, allowed Marguerite to make the necessary arrangements. She secured a horse-drawn wagon, filled it with supplies, and retained the services of a driver.

And while she thought mostly of her Ursuline friends, the possibility that she might, once again, see Captain Dauphin, made her look forward to the journey.

Marguerite arrived at Quebec City in January, dressed as a peasant woman.

The new year (1759) did not bring food or comfort to *"les inhabitants"* but the former nun brought all of that and more to the Ursuline monastery.

"You have risked your life to help us and even now you remain in danger, said the Mother Superior.

Marguerite furrowed her eyebrows and tilted her head.

"Captain Lezard may be lying about his knowledge of the attack," Mother Superior whispered.

Marguerite took a deep breath and continued to unload the wagon.

"I will not leave my friends in their time of need," she said.

"You will stay here at the monastery," said Mother Superior. "And you must remain within the walls of our cloister," she ordered.

"Thank you, my Blessed Mother."

Spring approached and still, Antoine did not appear at the Ursuline's gate. On visitors' days, Marguerite appeared in the walled garden, disguised as a chamber maid. She prayed that Captain Dauphin might show himself. He did not. Marguerite struggled with her feelings. In the past, she rejected the man's advances and used her Ursuline vows as an excuse. And now, her excuse was gone. But so was the captain.

As summer approached, word reached the city that British ships might soon arrive. By the end of May, signal fires informed "*les inhabitants*" that the enemy now occupied the river. Many of the residents climbed to the roof tops to watch the silent invasion. By the end of June, a total of twenty-two British ships dropped anchor, at the south end of Isle d'Orleans. Behind them followed forty frigates plus transports for more than 8,000 soldiers and seamen.

Most of the locals considered Quebec City unassailable by water because the Saint Lawrence river could only be traversed by experienced, local, boat pilots. Nevertheless, the British prevailed. They pressed a local ship captain into service and used a number of flat bottom boats to mark the channel with colorful signs. Within days, the English assumed positions north of Montmorency Falls, a few miles from the city itself.

Fear and panic spread throughout the city

"Prepare to fire the boats."

Antoine's stomach churned when he heard the order. Earlier that week, his troops assembled a number of old, merchant vessels, along with a series of smaller boats and loaded them with incendiary materials. Now, they would set them on fire and push them in the direction of the English fleet. With luck, the floating conflagrations would collide with English ships and do great damage to the enemy's vessels. The attempt failed miserably, and Antoine watched in horror, as English forces easily deflected the burning boats and escaped unharmed.

As French troops moved in every direction and barricades magically appeared, a large number of residents abandoned the city. In days, the British bombardment began. English cannon, ensconced on Point Levis, across the water from Quebec City, pelted parts of the city with red-hot balls of steel. Buildings not destroyed by the shelling burnt to the ground, as a result of dozens of fires, most of them out of control. The lower portions of the city stood well within range of the enemy artillery and suffered the most. Nearly every home was destroyed, burnt to the ground, or still burning.

Able to observe much of the shelling and many of the troop's movements from the monastery, Marguerite and her colleagues moved into the chapel. As shells fell around them, they prayed in front of the Blessed Sacrament.

Marguerite focused on the broken stained-glass windows and watched as the Cloister's outhouses burned to the ground.

"What is it?" asked Marguerite, as she entered the convent's kitchen area.

"A tarte made of eel meat," said the novitiate, smiling despite the grueling and gory task of slicing eel into edible bits.

Sister Josephine, the youngest member of the Order, spent many hours in the kitchen, her skills greatly tested by the food shortage that continued to plague the Quebec region. Marguerite frowned and reached for a slice of the freshly baked crust, instead.

"Delicious. Why would you ruin it with an eel?" she asked, prompting the usual grin from the ever-cheerful Sister Josephine.

Marguerite went searching for Mother Superior. The Superioress, surrounded by novitiates busy with their needlework, smiled her welcome to Marguerite.

"From my bench in the garden, I could see entire families with children. They are leaving the city," Marguerite reported.

"And we too shall leave, said Mother Superior. "I have, today, received permission from his Excellency, the Bishop, to evacuate."

"Where shall we go?" asked Marguerite.

"To the Hotel Dieux."

The large hospital across town, already cramped with sick and wounded from previous battles, stood beyond the range of British artillery.

"We should not abandon the cloister. I wish to remain," said Marguerite, no longer bound by the Ursuline vow of strict obedience.

After a series of searching looks, several of the nuns nodded their agreement. Mother Superior did not argue, instead choosing a combination of ten nuns and novitiates to stand guard, as the British onslaught continued. Their Chaplain, the Reverend Resche, also volunteered to remain behind. As the elderly nun rose from her seat, the community rose with her and dutifully made the Sign of the Cross as she blessed them.

"May God be with you."

Captain Dauphin watched as a long line of local men and boys marched past his building. A directive, issued by Montcalm, ordered every male citizen between the age of sixteen and sixty into action. But anyone younger than sixteen or older than sixty did not get turned away.

"General Levis wants you."

The messenger's desperate voice told Antoine that the invasion had begun. Francois-Gaston de Levis served as Montcalm's second-in-command. He addressed the officers in charge of the Royal Roussillon regiment.

"The British are advancing from the Montmorency. I've sent 500 French fighters and 500 Indians to reinforce the Repentigny Regiment. I want the Royal Roussillon to reinforce our troops at Beauport in case the enemy lands there."

"The high tide will not last forever," said Dauphin.

"Precisely. If we can keep them at bay, for a short while, their attack will fail."

By 5:30 that evening, the tide went out and several of the British boats ran aground. The English troops still managed to form in large numbers, at the foot of the hill. A sudden and violent downpour made their steep ascent almost impossible. The Royal Roussillon, waiting patiently behind their breastworks, took advantage of Mother Nature's intervention and rained down a volley of musketry. Large numbers of dead and wounded English troops rolled helplessly down the wet, grassy slope. Antoine cheered loudly and urged his men to continue their assault.

The heavy rain continued but eventually made the soldiers' weapons useless. The British used the pause in bloodshed, to affect an orderly retreat. They set fire to several of their own vessels, now stranded in the muck and mud of the St. Lawrence, so as to deprive the French Army of their reuse.

Antoine estimated at least 400 of the enemy lay dead. And while he took solace from the fact that only a few dozen French soldiers lost their lives, the captain and his fellow officers knew that a much larger battle lay ahead.

English General James Wolfe chose the tiny cove at Anse au Foulon from which to launch his attack on the Quebec fortress.

He ordered transports to travel past the point of embarkation and use the river's current to drift back in silence. Although guided by starlight only and twice fooling French sentries, with the perfectly spoken French of one of their own, Wolfe and more than 4800 English soldiers scaled the Heights, using trees, roots, and bushes to aid their ascent. English General Robert Moncton led the invasion force. He made quick work of the tiny picket of French regulars, charged with protecting that especially unlikely invasion route. British forces quickly took up their positions on the Heights. (Plains of Abraham)

Marguerite studied the landscape through the broken window in the church loft, noting destruction, flames, smoke, and rubble in every direction.

The sudden screams of her colleagues interrupted her depressing solitude. She scrambled down the winding staircase to discover the cause. The Ursuline's loyal, Abenaki friend, Alemos, stood in the kitchen, surrounded by gray habits.

"I tell you true. British Army on Heights. They are here," he said, the boy's broken English good enough to deliver the bad news. Marguerite did not linger. She ran to the chapel and prayed for the nuns' safety.

She also prayed for the safety of the man she loved.

General Montcalm finished his second cup of tea, as the morning of September 13, 1759, dawned on his camp at Montmorency.

His moment of peace ended when several aides, including Captain Dauphin, breathlessly rushed into the General's chamber. Earwitnesses reported musketry fire at Anse au Foulon. There could be no doubt.

"The English have scaled the Heights," said Dauphin.

Montcalm stood motionless. His unblinking eyes focused on Antoine.

"They have got to the weak side of us, at last," he muttered.

Montcalm demanded that his horse be saddled and simultaneously ordered all French troops to assemble on the Heights.

"We must crush them with our numbers," said the General.

When Montcalm finally crossed the Charles, his horse at a full gallop, he fixed his gaze on the path ahead and said nothing to the waiting troops. During a hurried council of war, with his top aides, Montcalm did not hide his concerns.

"The enemy is digging in and already has two pieces of cannon. If we give him time to establish himself, we shall never be able to attack, with the few troops we have," said the General.

As Montcalm surveyed the battlefield, the events of his immediate past, stung in his mind like the wind driven surf of the Atlantic. The corrupt government in Quebec hampered his every move. Vaudreuil and Bigot resisted the General's decisions at every turn. Together they inflicted more damage than the English army. Everything Montcalm required for an effective fighting force, be it men, supplies, weapons, or food, came too little and too late. For months, General Montcalm and his troops watched helplessly, as their strength and morale dwindled to nothing. And now, with only weeks to spare before winter took hold, the English accomplished the impossible.

They stood, in large numbers, on the Plains of Abraham, with a dagger at the throat of Montcalm's army.

After an initial volley of French artillery, British soldiers, told to lay flat so as to avoid grape shot and sniper fire, remained in place and were largely unaffected.

The French Army did the same. Eventually, both sides cautiously moved to within a quarter mile of each other. Neither side pressed their advantage in a decisive way. Captain Dauphin, yards from his commander-in-chief, studied the landscape which lay before him. The blue facings of the Royal Roussillon, the Languedoc, and the La Sarre regiments, stood in sharp contrast to the red facings of the Guienne and Bearn regiments. Each battalion of the French Army carried their own colors and proudly waited for their General's orders. Montcalm himself, wearing a bright red coat and a brilliant white shirt with lace cuffs, brandished his sword, as he rode back and forth on a black horse, exhorting his troops to fight for king and country. He instructed the men to wait for his order to attack.

Across the field, General Wolfe wore no sword, and quietly urged his men to wait patiently, until ordered to fire. The General, uniformed almost entirely in red, presented an easy target for French snipers. And moments later, a marksman's bullet shattered the General's wrist. Wolfe wrapped it in a handkerchief and proceeded as if nothing happened. A second shot, struck the English General in the groin, causing great pain, but still, Wolfe refused to leave the field of battle.

Montcalm ordered his troops forward in three divisions. As soon as they marched within range, the French troops fired at the English line, causing a number of Redcoats to fall. But a dead or wounded English soldier did not diminish the British line. An immediate replacement stepped forward to take the missing warrior's place. As a result, the English line did not move or falter. Not until Antoine and his comrades-in-arms marched to within forty yards of the British line, did the English troops fire their first volley. French soldiers dropped by the dozens. Moments later, another thunderous volley inflicted even more damage. Panicked French troops scrambled for cover, in full retreat.

Montcalm struggled in vain to rally his men but took a musket ball to the lower abdomen. The shock sent him flying off his mount. Across the Plains, General Wolfe realized that French troops were in retreat and immediately ordered his men to charge. Wolfe moved only yards forward when another bullet struck him in the chest. As the English troops broke into a run, chasing after the retreating French, Wolfe limped to the rear with two officers supporting him on their shoulders. On seeing the incapacitated general, an aide-de-camp scurried to inform Wolfe's second-in-charge, General Robert Moncton, that Wolfe could no longer command the army. Unfortunately, Moncton too, suffered a serious wound and the final charge fell to Wolfe's third-in-command, General George Townshend. Wolf, appearing unconscious, woke from his stupor when an aide informed him that the enemy had left the field of battle, in complete retreat.

"God be praised. I die in peace," said the Englishman.

Captain Dauphin, at Montcalm's side, gathered a number of men to load the wounded General onto a litter.

As the red stain on Montcalm's abdomen grew larger, the men struggled to deliver their leader to the apothecary. The medical building housed the king's surgeon, but Doctor Arnoux could not be located and his younger brother stood in.

"The wound is mortal," he announced.

The news of his imminent death did not unnerve General Montcalm. Still in full possession of his faculties, he spoke in a calm and deliberate manner.

"I die content, since I leave the affairs of my king in good hands."

Antoine guessed that Montcalm referred to his number two, the Chevalier de Levis. But de Levis, currently miles away and nearer to Montreal, could do nothing to reverse the French defeat.

Antoine watched as Montcalm breathed his last. He pressed a servant from the monastery, to construct a crude coffin. Several of the men wept. The convent itself served as Montcalm's tomb. A large crater, created by a British shell, became the general's burial site.

Captain Dauphin walked behind the coffin as a slow possession of officers escorted their deceased leader to the monastery chapel. The chaplain, bathed in the glow of a dozen torches, recited committal prayers. As several of the men shoveled dirt into the crater, Dauphin, his own eyes moist, decided to leave. When he exited the chapel and crossed the courtyard, a movement in the far corner, caught his eye. The captain instinctively reached for his blade, but the weapon proved unnecessary.

"Captain Dauphin."

He recognized Marguerite's voice, but her face and head remained hidden behind a knit shawl. She stepped forward, the couple now yards apart. He said nothing. She dropped the wrap to her shoulders revealing her unforgettable bright, red hair. In the faint light of a waning moon, Antoine could see that Marguerite no longer wore the habit of the Ursuline.

"You are in the Lord's Army no longer?" he asked.

She shook her head slowly, refusing to lose her grip on his eyes and searching for a reaction.

"I have been asked to leave the Community," she said.

"They told me you left and would not return."

"I hid at the convent in Three Rivers, but my friends here at the monastery were starving. I brought them food and supplies," she said.

"You went into hiding because it was you who attacked Captain Lezard," said Antoine.

"I was forced to defend myself," she said.

"And Captain Lezard, does he know you have returned?"

"This, I do not know," she said.

Antoine exhaled deeply and slowly shook his head.

"Captain Lezard will seek his revenge. Besides, we have lost the city and we shall soon lose all of New France," said Antoine.

"Where will you go? What will you do?" she asked.

"The governor and his crooked intendant have traveled to Montreal. Ramezay is our new leader. He is a fool and we will soon fly the white flag."

Marguerite stepped forward and embraced the Captain. He stiffened and pushed the woman away, his hands still grasping her shoulders.

"The British will not harm you. Lezard will. You must remain in hiding," he ordered.

She leaned forward and touched her lips to his cheek.

"*Mon Capitan,*" she whispered.

He bowed and disappeared into the darkness.

Many of the French troops that scrambled from the Heights of Abraham, ran into the city, some as far as the countryside.

Most of the defeated soldiers made their way to Beauport where the remnants of the French Army huddled in fear and confusion. Ramezay, calling a Council of War, announced that Governor Vaudreuil agreed to terms of surrender. After discussion of a counterattack, the group reached agreement. A white flag of surrender remained as their only sensible option.

Dauphin, quiet until now, spoke up.

"The men have no food and "*les inhabitants*" are starving to death," he said.

"We will ask the British for food," Ramezay responded.

I don't trust Bigot to pay me," said British General Murray, now serving as the acting Governor of Quebec.

The victorious general referred to the French request for foodstuffs. Although reluctant at first, Murray eventually agreed to provision the hospital, which the British now occupied. He also agreed to provide 1000 pounds of biscuits and an equal weight of flour to the French people. The magnanimous general refused to visit the cruelty of starvation on a vanquished enemy.

"I want a guarantee," said Murray to his aide.

He instructed the lieutenant to inform Ramezay that the food would be delivered, on one condition. As a guarantee that Bigot paid the amount owed, Murray insisted that a French officer serve as hostage, until the debt was repaid. The officer in question would be hanged if Bigot waivered.

Within hours, Ramezay agreed to Murray's demand.

The French regulars at Beauport, unorganized and without provisions, soon left for Montreal.

The troops, Antoine among them, all cheered loudly when they encountered an advance party from de Levis' army, at St Augustine, thirteen miles from Quebec City. The Chevalier, still traveling from Montreal, dispatched his reconnaissance party to learn more about the situation in Quebec City. When de Levis' representative learned that a white flag of surrender had already been posted, he ordered the remaining French troops to Montreal. After the announcement, the aide-de-camp requested a private word with Antoine.

"You will not return to Montreal. You are to surrender yourself to the new English governor, General Murray."

"I will die before I surrender," said Antoine.

"Intendant Bigot himself requested that you do so. You are to be held hostage until payment for supplies, given to the French people by the British, are paid in full. Our fellow countrymen are starving. You surrender for '*les inhabitants*'," said the aide.

Antoine frowned, a puzzled look covering his face.

"Bigot? And why would he request me as their hostage?" asked Antoine.

"I was not present. I do not know. But these are your orders."

Dauphin recalled his occasional visits with Bigot, but the two men rarely spoke. Lezard's obnoxious presence prevented that. Antoine clenched his teeth and his face flushed with anger. He reached for the aide-de-camp, yanking on the man's uniform and pulling the soldier close. Antoine's eyes drilled into the aide's frightened face.

"Lezard," he shouted. This is the work of Adolphe Lezard,"

"I am truly sorry, Captain Dauphin. I do not know this man, Lezard," said the aide.

Chapter Six

Missing

Marguerite welcomed the return of those Ursuline nuns who left the monastery during the siege.

Mother Superior praised the small but stalwart, religious band, who, despite the torrential down pour of English bombs, managed to rescue a number of sacred artifacts. Several Tabernacles, a series of statues and paintings, plus altar furniture, and a long list of valuables, survived the onslaught.

"I thank the Lord that all of you are safe," she said, blessing each one of the them as they knelt to kiss her ring.

Marguerite did not step forward, focusing instead on the scene of desolation and destruction which she viewed, through the broken stained-glass window. Mother Superior approached and spoke in a barely audible voice.

"That which you desire most, continues to elude you," she observed.

Marguerite's blank stare acknowledged Mother Mary's conclusion. Her eyes glistened with tears.

"He came to the chapel when they buried the general. We spoke, but only for a moment. I am to remain here," said Marguerite.

"And remain here, you shall. For as long as necessary," said Mother Superior.

"Come now, we have work, to do," she added.

Marguerite, grateful for the diversion, labored hard and long to restore a semblance of order to the convent. She cleaned and rearranged rooms and removed the dirt and debris of war which covered the cloister. By months end, word reached the convent that Bigot's warehouse lay empty, soldiers and "*les habitants*" pillaging all that could be carried from the intendant's properties. The winter of 1759-1760 marked the fourth consecutive year of famine for New France. Even the Ursulines' most loyal and ardent supporters brought to the convent only handfuls of food stuffs and supplies.

Ironically, the small army of Ursuline nuns would be rescued by the English army.

General Murray's appearance, at the front gate of the cloister, startled its occupants.

But the Englishman's first meeting with Mother Mary of the Nativity occurred without incident.

"We serve the Lord first and most, but if I am able to, we will serve the general as well," said Mother Superior.

Murray bowed and informed the Superioress that her monastery would henceforth be protected by English troops.

"You will also receive a large supply of foodstuffs, before dark, today," said Murray.

Murray announced that a number of his wounded and sick required housing at the cloister.

"This, we can do, but I must ask if we will be allowed to continue our religious practices and traditions," asked Mother Superior.

"Yes, but if it is possible, we should like to utilize your chapel for Anglican services," said the General.

Mother Superior inhaled deeply and closed her eyes. She recalled the specific instructions of Bishop Pontbriand, to avoid anything that might irritate the new government, even unto their use of Catholic churches.

"We will accommodate the British Army in any way we are able," she said.

By mid-October, the monastery housed dozens of wounded soldiers and on Sundays, dozens more of England's faithful. The English congregation included a number of Highlanders, whose kilts prompted a furious flurry of knitting. For reasons of modesty or charity or both, the nuns decided that the warriors' exposed legs required hosiery.

Captain Dauphin stood before the English Governor, Murray.

"Mr. Bigot is not trusted by his own people and yet, your life is in his hands," said the governor.

Murray stopped short of offering to release his prisoner.

"I am prepared to die for my king," said Dauphin, acknowledging the distinct possibility that he would swing by the rope, if Bigot failed to pay his debt to the English.

"Your people are without food. How much longer will your king wage this horrible war?" asked Murray.

Dauphin's head drooped as he studied the stone floor in Murray's temporary headquarters.

"I am a soldier, not a king," said Antoine.

"Very well, then. You will return to France on the next transport and you will refrain from rendering services to the French King, for a period of two years. Do I have your word as an officer in the French Army, that you will respect my wishes?" Murray asked.

Antoine looked up. The general's question forced Dauphin to

choose life in France, as a civilian or life in Quebec, on the run from the English.

Antoine's eyes closed as he winced.

"Yes sir. I will honor your request."

Antoine remained under arrest for several weeks more.

During that time, he befriended a guard and traded his sidearm for writing materials. He stared at the blank paper for hours, struggling with the words that would accurately and properly express his true feelings.

My dearest Marguerite,

It is my great misfortune to have become a prisoner of the English army. I have been ordered to return to France and to refrain from any and all activities against the English King. Of this, I have given my word.

I am therefore unable to assist you, during these dangerous times.

The English transport sets sail tomorrow, and I am forced to bid you a fond farewell, from my cell.

I shall think of you always.
AD, Cpt

One of the jailers agreed to deliver Antoine's letter, for the few remaining livres in the captain's pocket.

Marguerite accepted the letter from Mother Superior, in silence.

"I pray it is good news," said the older nun.

Marguerite ran to the privacy of her cell, ripped the letter open, and prayed for the words to disappear.

"Taken prisoner . . . ordered to France . . . a fond farewell."

Tears burned in Marguerite's eyes as she walked through the courtyard and onto the streets of the upper town. With no shawl or wrap to protect her from the cold, September winds, she shivered uncontrollably. The woman gave it no thought, attracting stares from passersby as she made her way to the Heights of Abraham. She focused on the water as she approached the edge of the cliff, challenging the jagged rocks below. Another step brought her perilously close to the edge as she leaned forward against the wind.

A cold hand on her bare arm stopped Marguerite's final step. She gazed into the tear-stained face of Alemos, the Abenaki Indian boy who regularly helped at the convent.

"I see you as I cross the Heights," said Alemos.

Alemos, fifteen years old, lost his father at the age of ten. The Ursulines effectively adopted the boy. Mostly, they supplied Alemos and his remaining family, with foodstuffs in exchange for his labor. Although not yet full grown, the boy-man grew up fast— surrounded by war, famine, and discrimination.

Marguerite, her face covered in pain, moved her lips but no words could be heard.

Alemos, struggling with his own loss, did not press the woman for an explanation.

"I go to convent. Rangers destroy my village."

The boy's words disrupted Marguerite's suicidal thoughts. She reached for the boy, a hand on each shoulder.

"Your family?" she asked.

"My mother, my two sisters, and my grandfather—they are dead. Some of them, burn alive; rest are scalped," he announced, his voice a sad monotone and his eyes, dry.

"English soldiers?" asked Marguerite.

"Rangers," Alemos replied.

Marguerite reached for the boy and held him close.

"I am so sorry, my friend. I am so sorry," she cried.

Alemos looked to the rocks below. He stiffened and stepped between the woman and the cliff's edge. He pushed her back a step but gripped both of her arms.

"You wish to die?"

Her lips did not move but her face and eyes could not hide the truth.

"Enough have died. Yes?" he asked.

She nodded, her overflowing eyes making conversation impossible.

He removed his wrap and placed it on her shoulders.

"We walk now. You and me. Together," he announced.

They said nothing as they navigated the narrow and hilly streets of the city. When their destination appeared in the distance, a gravelly voice interrupted their silence.

"I have been searching for you, Marguerite."

The shock to Marguerite's system made her weak at the knees. She made a wobbly turn and faced her tormentor.

"Did you think I would forget?" asked Captain Lezard.

Alemos stepped between them. Lezard shoved the boy to one side. Alemos retaliated and pushed Lezard to the snow covered walk. The boy reached under his shirt and flashed a small, hunting knife.

"You wish to hurt my friend. I will hurt you," said Alemos, pointing the blade in Lezard's direction.

Lezard rose and brushed the wet and dead leaves from his clothes. He kept a respectful distance from Alemos and wagged an index finger in Marguerite's direction.

"We shall meet again, Sister Marguerite. Soon."

Marguerite held the boy's arm and trembled with fear.

The unexpected encounter with Lezard sent Marguerite to the edge of another cliff.

She rushed into Mother Superior's office, barely able to describe her chance meeting with the evil man. She paced the floor and pulled at her hair with both hands, babbling hysterically.

"He's going to kill me. What shall I do? I should never have returned to Quebec City. But you were starving, what was I to do? Please, Mother Mary, you must help me," she cried.

"There is the community in Three Rivers, but I must first write to them. I believe the last ship to France is about to sail and we have no mission in the English colonies. There is nothing I can do at this time," said Mother Superior.

Marguerite fell into a chair and bawled.

"God continues to punish me," she choked.

Mother Superior rose, went around the desk, and pulled Marguerite to her feet.

"You have not been punished by the Lord. You have been saved by Him. Repeatedly. On the ship, at the intendant's palace, and today, on the street, with Alemos at your side."

Marguerite focused on the older woman through watery eyes. The nun continued.

"You almost murdered this evil man. What did you expect?"

I will write to the cloister in Three Rivers," she announced.

Marguerite nodded her acquiescence.

When Antoine waited to board the English ship, destined for France under the white flag of truce, he discovered several other exiles.

From them, he learned that officers and members of the regular French Army must return to France. But members of the French militia, Quebec natives, received permission to return to their farms, so long as they swore an oath of allegiance to the English King. Antoine groused about the irony. The Militia men often refused to fight, citing the planting season or requirements of the harvest. Antoine concluded that part-time warriors received better treatment than professional soldiers. The bitterness in his heart overpowered the captain's promise to Governor Murray.

As he surveyed the confusion around the dock, he noticed a large man wearing French Army-issue leggings. Although members of the Canadian militia did not receive uniforms, they wore a single item of the regular French Army uniform, so as to distinguish them during battle. Antoine waited for an opportune moment and hailed the rotund Frenchman, in his native tongue. A quick conversation revealed that the man wanted to go to France. He lost his parents and a young wife to the fever and no longer considered New France as his home. He also lacked the necessary funds.

"If you wear the uniform of a captain, the transportation is free," said Antoine, with a wry smile.

The soldier cocked his head and frowned. Antoine pointed to the man's clothes and explained the British rules for members of the French Army.

"Were I wearing your clothes, I could remain in Quebec," said Antoine.

He flashed his best conspiratorial grin. The native understood the captain's meaning and both men began a series of furtive glances, in every direction. There seemed to be a hidden enclave behind a large stack of dockside barrels. The two of them walked to the makeshift changing room, taking pains to attract no attention. In moments, Antoine emerged as a member of the militia. The lowly army grunt, now promoted to the rank of Captain, walked triumphantly onto the ship, proudly wearing his tight-fitting jacket.

Antoine disappeared into the crowded streets of Quebec, struggling with a pair of loose-fitting trousers.

Captain Lezard watched helplessly from the street, as "*les habitants*" and a small collection of militiamen, wondered in and out of the intendant's palace and warehouses.

They searched for anything of value but left empty-handed. Earlier raids by English troops left nothing worth stealing. Lezard still enjoyed access to a modest apartment near Bigot's palace and remained grateful to the intendant, for a last-minute allocation of 1000 livres, more than a year's salary for most of Quebec's civil servants. Lezard recalled his last conversation with Bigot. Lezard's offer to secure a "volunteer" when Bigot required a hostage for English Governor Murray, was pure genius he thought—a perfect way to ensnare Captain Dauphin.

But the grin on Lezard's face disappeared when he contemplated his current circumstances. The governor and intendant left the city, along with the remaining French troops. The government in France would soon suspend all financial aid to its former North American colony. Lezard, more than anyone, knew the significance of that decision. With the opportunity for profiteering at his government's expense now ending, Lezard might be forced to work for a living. He also anticipated a series of investigations, too many prying questions, and arrests. In fact, Lezard feared the retribution of the French government more than he feared the conquering English. On the other hand, the newly installed English government might appreciate his assistance, thought Lezard. He would remain in Quebec City and pursue that option.

Not coincidentally, the object of his lust for revenge also remained in Quebec City.

Marguerite's thoughts switched back and forth from her encounters with Lezard to her numerous engagements with the magnificent Captain Antoine Dauphin.

She imagined the worst as she considered the conditions on board an English ship, tasked with the return of exiled enemy soldiers. The man whom she most wanted to see might never be seen again. And the nightmare of another winter, in Quebec City, left the woman discouraged and overwhelmed. In the midst of her depression, she recalled the words of Mother Superior.

"The last ship to France leaves today, if it hasn't left already."

Marguerite's heart skipped a beat. Ships never leave on schedule. Perhaps it remained at the dock, she thought.

As she flew across the courtyard, Sister Josephine shouted after the fleeing woman.

"Marguerite, where are you going?"

"If the ship is delayed, he might still be here," she yelled over her shoulder.

"We have eel tartes for dinner," said the novitiate.

But Marguerite did not hear the menu. Her mad flight to the water's edge left her breathless. As she approached the docks, she saw the ship's English colors whipping in the wind. When the English flag grew smaller, her hopes diminished. The ship which carried her dreams became a meaningless speck on the water.

Her beloved Antoine was gone.

CHAPTER SEVEN

Reunited

Marguerite wandered aimlessly on the streets of Quebec City, not caring that Lezard might be waiting for her in the next alleyway.

She concluded that Antoine, now in route to France, would never return to Quebec City. It would be too dangerous. The English would hang him. She wrestled with the thought of another winter in the frozen wilds of Quebec and decided to write her father as soon as possible. He would provide her with the funds, for a return trip to France.

Marguerite's mind stopped racing when she heard the sound of footsteps, approaching from behind. She increased her pace calculating that only a soldier's thick, leather, footwear could make such a distinctive sound when they hit the cobblestones. She focused on the street ahead, where a small line of mourners escorted several coffins, to their final resting place. Marguerite did not know the deceased, but she decided to join the procession and hide among the grief-stricken family. When the footsteps accelerated, Marguerite began to run. So did the footsteps. She ran faster.

"Stop." said the voice in pursuit.

She could hear his heavy breathing. A large hand pulled on her shoulder. Marguerite stumbled but her fall was prevented by two muscular arms. She pivoted to attack her attacker, raising fingers in both hands to scratch at the man's face.

"I did not mean to frighten you," said the man, his face and head, masked by a woolen sash.

Marguerite's hand flew to her mouth, smothering a scream. She recognized his voice but refused to believe it was him. The masked man unwound his head wrap.

"Marguerite," he said.

"Antoine!" she gasped.

"How did you escape?" she asked.

"I will explain later. We must return to the safety of the monastery."

They walked, arm in arm, saying nothing. As they approached the iron fence which surrounded the monastery, the relief in their faces shown like a small sun. They waited impatiently as a novitiate bid them enter. When the couple followed the nun across the courtyard, a pair of unseen eyes glared at the duo like a lion about to pounce.

When the large set of heavy, wooden doors slammed shut, Captain Adolphe Lezard flashed his trademark, toothy smile.

Mother Superior, not given to public displays of emotion, beamed at the young couple.

"Our Lord and Savior has brought joy to this city of ruins," she said.

Antoine explained the details of his capture and escape.

"I am abandoned by one army and an escaped prisoner in the other," he said

The Superioress grew somber.

"Captain Dauphin, you are within sight of English wounded and their many friends, she whispered.

"Can you help us?" he asked.

Mother Superior returned to the chair behind her desk.

"Yes. I believe I can," she said.

"It is dangerous for either of us to remain in Quebec City," said Marguerite.

"And so, the two of you will travel to the convent at Three Rivers. It is scandalous of course, but Alemos will be your chaperone. You will carry my letter to their Superior and you will wear the clothes of a novitiate and her confessor," announced the Mother Superior.

"You are most kind," said Antoine.

"May the Good Lord, guard and bless you both," said Mother Superior.

"I wish to speak with Governor Murray," said Lezard.

The governor's aide-de-camp openly studied the man's facial scars and grimaced when Lezard's half-severed ear came into full view.

"Who are you and what do you want?" asked the junior officer, hypnotized by Lezard's monstrous appearance.

"I am Captain Adolphe Lezard, former assistant to the Intendant, Francois Bigot."

The aide studied Lezard's otherwise polished appearance and glanced at the closed door which separated the guard from the governor.

"Wait here," he ordered.

Lezard smiled and bowed his head.

Murray remained seated at his desk when Lezard stepped into the office chamber. The French traitor spoke quickly, beads of sweat traveling in different directions as they traversed scarred trenches on the man's face.

Lezard promised the English Governor valuable intelligence on the French troops that wintered in Saint Foy. He also predicted that his former comrades-in-arms would counterattack, rather than capitulate. And finally, he informed the governor that a dangerous prisoner, a French officer, recently escaped.

"I have heard rumors of a possible counterattack by the French, but this escaped prisoner is of no consequence to me." said Murray, looking away as if disinterested but simultaneously avoiding Lezard's ghastly appearance.

"Oh, but it is of great consequence," said Lezard, correcting the governor.

The governor leaned forward and scowled.

"Who are you to correct His Majesty's representative?" asked Murray.

An avalanche of words fell from Lezard's tongue. He explained, in heavily accented English, his personal role in the designation of Antoine Dauphin as collateral for Murray's delivery of foodstuffs to French locals. Pausing for effect, he squinted his eyes and lowered his voice to a whisper.

"And I am, at this very moment, prepared to disclose the precise location of this traitor," said Lezard.

Murray rose to his feet and stepped to the window with its view of the St. Lawrence.

"Captain Dauphin impressed me as an honorable man. He gave me his word as an officer in the French Army," Murray groused.

"He is no gentleman," said Lezard. "And he makes the governor look like a fool."

"If this is a trap, you will hang," said Murray, turning from the window and confronting Lezard, with a pointed finger.

"I will lead your men to the lair of the fox," said Lezard.

"In that case, it is Captain Dauphin who will hang," said Murray.

Marguerite, once again, wore the uniform of an Ursuline novitiate.

Antoine dressed as a monk. They traveled by bateaux to the Ursuline monastery in Three Rivers, the next day. As agreed, Alemos served as their guide and chaperone. The journey required an overnight stay near the banks of the St. Lawrence. The young Indian set up their camp and, after a meal of freshly caught walleye, the threesome settled into their beds of pine boughs and blankets.

Marguerite waited until she heard the regular breathing of her Abenaki friend. She pushed her blankets to one side and tiptoed to the captain, kneeling at his side. For minutes, she studied the man's face, gently lit by a half moon and strikingly peaceful for a soldier in such turmoil. Abandoning her strict upbringing and the admonitions of her Ursuline superiors, Marguerite eased under the captain's blankets and reached to caress the man's face.

When her fingers made contact, Antoine reacted, as if ambushed by the enemy. He rolled onto the woman and used both hands to strangle his unknown assailant. Marguerite, unable to scream, grabbed at his face and pushed on his chest. She pulled on Antoine's muscular arms and kicked her legs, in a fruitless attempt to throw him off. Alemos heard the sounds of their struggle and tackled Antoine, as the soldier straddled his victim. Antoine did not release his grip. Marguerite's eyes bulged in their sockets. Her red face became a light shade of blue. Alemos, hanging onto Dauphin's neck with both arms, screamed in the captain's ear. When the sleep cleared from the soldier's brain, he loosened his grip on Marguerite's neck and rolled to one side as the woman wheezed loudly, desperate for a deep breath. Still gasping, Marguerite scrambled to her feet and with hands on her hips, yelled at Antoine.

"You almost killed me," she complained.

Antoine bolted upright, threw his arms into the air and gesticulated wildly.

"Are you mad, woman? It is your reckless conduct that places you in danger," he screamed.

Alemos intervened.

"Tomorrow is long day. We must rest," he said.

Marguerite stormed off. Antoine snorted his disgust, as he yanked the blankets over his body and flipped on his side.

Alemos scratched his head and whispered to the captain.

"I sleep here," he said, pointing to a spot on the ground in between the Captain and Marguerite.

Upon their arrival in Three Rivers, the trio did their best to keep busy.

Antoine and Alemos worked as handymen and gardeners, Marguerite as a helper in the kitchen. But the couple's movements, unlike those of Alemos, remained severely restricted. Neither Antoine nor Marguerite could risk discovery, by members of the public. French and English wounded, cared for by the Ursulines, posed an additional risk. Although Antoine currently served in no army, he remained the sworn enemy of one and the disobedient orphan of the other. Marguerite's stunning beauty and her shoulder-length flaming red hair, made the woman far too memorable. This too could prove dangerous to both of them.

Their predicament, made worse by the duo's simmering anger, showed no sign of ending.

"She lies. The Mother Superior lies to protect them," Lezard shouted, as the governor walked away.

Governor Murray, intending to confront Dauphin in person,

stormed across the courtyard, at the Ursuline convent in Quebec City. He stopped and spun around, triggering a near collision with Lezard. The governor pushed Lezard away, as if the man's scars might be contagious.

"Will you return the funds that I have remitted, or must I continue to pay you for worthless gossip?" Murray demanded, as he resumed his angry pace.

Lezard scrambled along-side the governor.

"Your Excellency, I will locate the traitor, Dauphin. This I promise you but there is a matter of much greater urgency. The French have decided to counterattack," said Lezard.

Murray halted, staring directly at Lezard.

"I have received a number of reports about French troop movements. What do you know?" asked Murray.

"Walk with me, Governor, and I shall tell you," said Lezard, purring like a well-fed cat.

With the spring thaw, weeks away, wisps of new grass and green, tree buds made their first appearance, in the Quebec countryside.

So also did thousands of French troops, as they marched through, sailed past, or bivouacked at Three Rivers. Antoine, listening surreptitiously, learned from a series of conversations that the soldiers traveled to Saint Foy. They planned to conduct a large-scale counterattack on Quebec City.

"But they abandoned you," she said, throwing her hands into the air.

Marguerite could not hide her anger, pacing the kitchen floor and shaking her head, as if that would change Antoine's mind or ameliorate her concerns.

"I must return to my regiment," said Antoine.

"And you will be killed," she screamed.

"And I intend to pay my respects to Captain Lezard," said Antoine, shoving his meager belongings into a leather pouch.

The reference to Lezard did not impress Marguerite.

"Why must you go, why?" she demanded.

"It is not your place to question my decisions," he replied.

Marguerite hesitated, the obvious truth of his statement giving her unexpected pause.

"This battle will decide if New France is ruled by the French or the English. I cannot abandon His Majesty's Army even if his army has abandoned me. I am a Captain in the Royal Roussillon. His Majesty himself, is our Commander-in-Chief. My oath of allegiance is to the King and to the King alone."

Marguerite inhaled deeply and shoved Antoine into the wall. She cried in anguish, as she beat on his chest, until her arms tired from the effort. She stepped back.

"I hate your King. I hate your Army. And I hate you."

Antoine glared as he watched the door slam shut.

"I go with you."

Alemos confronted Antoine as the captain closed the gate to the iron fence which surrounded the Ursuline cloister, in Three Rivers.

"No. That is not possible," said Antoine.

"Why?" asked Alemos.

"You seek revenge for your family. I go to serve my country, said Antoine.

"My people have no country. The white man steal it. They take our meat and our fish and our women. They kill my family. And now, you say to me, 'you are not Abenaki warrior.' I am warrior and I will fight these Rogers Rangers that butchered my family," said Alemos, arms folded, his feet apart, and deliberately blocking the captain's exit.

Antoine exhaled loudly and looked behind him, as if Marguerite might intervene.

"You must promise to remain at my side. Understood?"

Alemos nodded his agreement.

"Go and tell her goodbye," said Antoine, jerking his head in the direction of the cloister.

Antoine caught up to the French Army at St. Augustine, a short distance from Quebec City.

At a Council of War, de Levis presented the details of his planned attack. When Antoine walked into the gathering, de Levis recognized General Montcalm's trusted aide-de-camp and interrupted his meeting to greet the Captain.

"The intendant sent our best captain to the English as a hostage. I do not understand his decision, but I am grateful for your safe return," said de Levis, embracing Dauphin and ceremoniously kissing the captain on both cheeks.

Antoine bowed as General de Levis motioned and a captain's jacket, along with weapons and accoutrements, magically appeared for Antoine's use.

"The English are nearby," said de Levis. "We must form up as quickly as possible," he added.

As the officers scurried to their respective units and 7000 men prepared for battle, Antoine learned from his colleagues that Governor Vaudreuil and Intendent, Francois Bigot, remained in Montreal. Antoine assumed that Bigot's aide, the crooked Captain Lezard, accompanied his superiors and vowed to himself that he would return to Montreal.

But first, he would fight the English.

The English army, although mostly confined to the fortress during the winter months, now numbered only 3000.

They suffered from widespread illness and, like the locals, worked feverishly to secure foodstuffs and supplies. When word arrived, that French troops might soon attack, a number of the English soldiers, sick or even hospitalized, reported for duty anyway. Governor Murray's forces would engage the enemy with an outnumbered and considerably weakened army.

Deserters passed this information onto the French. General de Levis, Captain Dauphin, and the troops, openly contemplated the likelihood of their success. Alemos relished the prospect of revenge.

"The soldiers talk of Rangers. They are here. I wish to fight them," said the boy soldier.

Antoine shook his head.

"That's not the way we fight," he said.

"They destroy my village, butcher my family. I will fight the Rangers. I must," Alemos insisted.

"Follow me. You will meet the Rangers, soon enough," said Antoine.

Marguerite, angered that Antoine Dauphin cared more for his military career than for her, struggled to remain busy.

She devoted more time in the cloister's hospital ward, tending to mostly French soldiers, all of them, sick or wounded. One of them, originally assigned to Montreal but unable to take part in the counterattack, responded well to her treatment.

"The Lieutenant is feeling better, today," said Marguerite.

"Much better, ma'am. Thank you for your concern and your excellent care," he said.

"A broken leg is easier to treat than dysentery or typhoid," said Marguerite, checking the man's splint as she spoke.

"How did you break it?" she asked.

The soldier explained that he slipped on a patch of ice while pushing a horse-drawn wagon, stuck in the mud.

"My leg was under the wagon when the horses decided to cooperate. I am fortunate that only my leg was crushed," said the officer.

Marguerite inquired about the Lieutenant's assignment in Montreal.

"The governor and the intendant are in Montreal," said the man. "I served as a Lieutenant of the Guard for headquarters," he said.

Marguerite jerked and took a quick breath. *If Bigot escaped to Montreal, after the English victory at Quebec, Lezard must be with him,* she thought. Although angry with Captain Dauphin, she despised Captain Lezard with a passion. She vowed that the French traitor would pay a steep price for ruining her life.

"I visited the intendant's warehouses when I lived in Quebec City," she said, as she busied herself with the man's bed sheets.

"He has many warehouses," said the soldier, a slight frown crossing his face.

"I know a captain who worked for the intendant. I cannot recall his name, but his face was badly scarred," said Marguerite, pretending to make idle conversation.

"I do not recall such a man," said the Lieutenant.

Marguerite's mind raced as she tidied the bed once more. Her patient noticed.

"Thank you, ma'am, thank you," he murmured. His eyebrows furrowed as he stared at the woman.

Marguerite, as if in a trance, walked away without saying a

word.

The English Army, unwilling and perhaps unable to engage the reconstituted French Army, pulled back to St. Foy, and then to the fort's walls.

Antoine could barely contain his excitement. He, like most of his comrades, sought revenge for their humiliating defeat, on the Plains of Abraham. But Antoine also harbored an infatuation with the thrill of war. The battle on the Heights, almost over before it started, and the fatal wounds suffered by General Montcalm, disappointed the ambitious warrior. Antoine's regiment barely engaged the enemy and the hand-to-hand combat he excelled at, never occurred.

"Why do they retreat, before we fight?" asked Alemos, overhearing the others.

"They wish to be close to the fort. A retreat behind the walls makes our job more difficult," said Antoine.

Alemos did not wait long for the fighting to begin. By 6:30 the next morning, Murray's troops could be seen marching from the St. Louis gate to the Plains of Abraham. Antoine, Alemos, and most of the Royal Roussillon regiment, gathered in and around the blockhouses on the Heights, newly built by the British, above Anse-au-Foulon.

When de Levis realized that Murray launched the entire English army, he ordered French troops to fall back into the nearby forest. Their orders were to remain hidden in the trees, until French soldiers held in reserve could also be summoned. From Murray's perspective, however, it appeared as if French forces decided to retreat. Murray immediately launched his attack.

"Get ready, my friend. Those green jackets are Roger's Rangers," Antoine shouted to Alemos, their position now under constant fire from British musketry.

Alemos fired as quickly as he could reload and grinned triumphantly each time a green jacket fell onto the snow-covered ground. He took no notice of the British bullets that whizzed by his head. The Rangers moved closer and closer to the block house.

"Fall back," yelled Antoine, motioning violently for Alemos to retreat in the direction of the woods.

As he looked to ensure that Alemos did as ordered, Antoine's left hand flew off his musket. The captain spun to the ground.

"Run, Alemos, run," Antoine yelled, grimacing in pain while trying to staunch the flow of blood from his lower arm.

Alemos refused to leave the wounded man's side. He crouched low and ignored the musket balls that buzzed near his head.

"I help you," he said, using a leather strap as a tourniquet and pulling it tight enough to make Antoine flinch.

Together, they ran and stumbled into the deep woods.

The green jackets, now in possession of the block houses, could be heard cheering their apparent victory. But the Rangers' celebration lasted for minutes only. When the French troops in reserve, arrived on the scene, a thousand French guns, firing from the safety of hundreds of trees, rained both musketry fire and the occasional artillery round onto the Rangers.

Green jackets fell onto the ground like rain and those that didn't, appeared shocked and confused. The green coats fell back. When Antoine heard a loud order for 'Hazen's troops' to retreat, the Captain and his men abandoned their positions in the woods and led the counterattack. Antoine ignored his flesh wound and moved forward with Alemos at his side. English troops, now on the run but firing as they fell back, surrendered the block houses. The English army, fleeing in full retreat, spiked and abandoned their artillery pieces. The French forces erupted in a joyous roar. Antoine and Alemos dashed through the mud and bloody slush to fell a few more green jackets. Antoine laughed as the adrenalin pumped through his veins and fueled his exultation. He shouted to Alemos.

"The field is ours, my friend. We have won a great victory."

Alemos, reloading one last time, grinned at the captain and stood rigid, with his eyes opened wide. The boy continued to smile, as a small, red stain on his chest grew larger and larger. Antoine, yards away, stepped forward. Alemos fell face down into the pink slush. Antoine rushed to the boy's side and rolled the Indian boy onto his back. His chest, looking more like a British Redcoat, heaved one last time. The boy's eyes remained open.

He no longer smiled.

Antoine absentmindedly fingered the bandage on his lower arm.

The brief, graveside ceremony for Alemos, lasted a few minutes and ended when Antoine tossed the Indian boy's tourniquet into the shallow grave. As two soldiers shoveled dirt and mud, laced with chunks of blood-stained ice and snow, onto the boy's body, Antoine's eyes settled on the white handkerchief which covered the dead boy's face. As a member of the king's regiment, Captain Dauphin never questioned the call of duty, the risks of mortal combat, or the horrors of war. It never occurred to him that death could be so personal, so gut wrenching, and so sad. Until now, Antoine suffered the loss of mostly nameless soldiers, faceless enemies, and a handful of brief acquaintances whose true worth rarely extended beyond the field of battle. Alemos' death, perhaps because of his relationship with Marguerite, perhaps because the Indian boy fought fearlessly despite his young age, triggered a new and strange reaction in Antoine's heart. Instead of celebrating the French victory, Antoine struggled with guilt, anger, and frustration.

And he dreaded that day when Marguerite learned of her young friend's violent death.

Blaming the still bitter winds of spring in Quebec for the moisture in his eyes, Antoine nodded his thanks to the grave diggers and walked to General de Levis' temporary headquarters. He learned that the defeated English troops took refuge behind the fort's walls. The French, given no choice, launched an immediate siege on the fort. Whether the French bombardment succeeded or not depended on how long the English could sustain themselves, with the necessary foodstuffs, supplies, and ammunition. In the late spring, there would be English reinforcements. Ships would be carrying hundreds of troops, fresh supplies, and the weapons of war.

The French victory on the Plains of Abraham could easily be reversed if the British held on till mid-May.

When Mother Nature melted the snow and ice, the trees, bushes, and fields which surrounded the Ursuline monastery in Three Rivers burst forth in a carpet of brilliant colors, on a lush background of green.

Marguerite neither cared nor noticed the change of seasons. She desperately sought passage to Montreal, where she hoped to locate and then eliminate Adolphe Lezard. Lezard attacked her and he betrayed the man she loved, and Lezard vowed that he would kill Marguerite, if given the opportunity to do so. The former nun decided that the fifth commandment, "Thou shall not kill," did not apply in this instance. The twin principles of justice and self-defense required that Adolphe Lezard be put to death. Hers was a just war.

Until such time as she could travel to Montreal, her entire world consisted of an endless supply of dirty dishes and piles of bloody bandages. She took no notice when a soldier's hard, leather boots announced a man's presence in her hot and humid kitchen.

"You wish passage to Montreal?" said the man.

Marguerite spun in the soldier's direction.

"Yes, but I have no money," she said.

"I need a wife," he said, the man's unsmiling face revealing the seriousness of his request.

"You cannot help me," Marguerite snapped, returning to her pile of bandages.

The stranger explained. He served as a French Regular in the Bearn regiment but recently deserted. The French Army would have nothing to do with him. In addition, the new English government intended to ship all French soldiers back to Europe.

"But if I am a native or married in Quebec, I will be allowed to remain. I need only sign an oath of allegiance to the English king," he said.

"A coward does not require a wife," she replied.

The man's face blushed pink.

"New France is lost. Must I die to prove that I am not a coward?"

Marguerite released a long breath of exasperation.

"No. Your death, like so many before you, is unnecessary," she said.

"You will be my wife in name only. On this, I give you my word," he answered.

Marguerite closed her eyes and slammed a wad of bandages into the wooden bucket. Her jumbled thoughts of Antoine, Lezard, and the obvious dangers of accompanying a total stranger on a two-day journey to Montreal, reduced the woman to confusion and frustration. She looked up.

"You will require the clothes of a peasant farmer," Marguerite answered, unwilling to verbalize her tacit approval of the scheme.

"You will help me, yes?"

Marguerite nodded.

"I will be your Quebec wife."

"My name is Jean-Pierre, he said, smiling his gratitude.

"The Royal Roussillon regiment will proceed to St. Jean," the Chevalier de Levis, announced.

Antoine closed his eyes, struggling to remain silent in the face of the French general's formal retreat from Quebec City. The general correctly anticipated that British ships, laden with troops and supplies, would soon appear on the horizon. No one quarreled with de Levis' decision. It was the French Army's only reasonable alternative. And, although unspoken, the general and his officers viewed the orderly retreat, as the beginning of the end. New France would soon belong to the English.

The days-long journey to St. Jean occurred without incident. But the Royal Roussillon shrank steadily, their ranks constantly depleted by sickness and desertion. Once at St. Jean, the situation worsened. Dozens of men abandoned their post each week. By the end of August, the order for all troops to proceed to Montreal yielded only a few handfuls of the king's most loyal troops. Antoine, unwilling to admit the end of his military career, listened intently as de Levis addressed the remainder of his forces. The general and his officers doubted whether or not the city of Montreal could be successfully defended. A three-pronged attack by the British, now underway, would bring thousands of Redcoats to the island of Montreal. The French Army could not survive such an onslaught. There remained one tiny sliver of hope. The commander would appeal to their Indian friends.

General de Levis met with the Indians at a meeting in La Prairie. He never finished his persuasive speech. An unexpected visitor forced de Levis to pause the meeting. An Indian messenger announced that the native tribes, once loyal to the French, successfully negotiated a truce with the British. As a result, the French Army would receive no help from their native friends. French forces, now numbering 2000 men, could not possibly defend the city against more than 15000 English troops.

Governor Vaudreuil called for a Council of War, in Montreal.

Marguerite's journey to Montreal with her "husband," went well.

Jean-Pierre, as promised, conducted himself as a gentleman. Marguerite cooperated fully, when the former soldier met with authorities, swore his oath of allegiance, and received written permission to remain in Quebec. And while Marguerite hardly needed a reminder of the other gallant soldier in her life, the stranger-turned-friend, prompted memories of her time with Antoine, good and bad.

When the couple parted company, Jean-Pierre thanked her, and Marguerite kissed him on both cheeks.

Despite several attempts, Marguerite's repeated visits to the governor's mansion, in Montreal, produced no results. French guards regularly denied her access.

A small gift of funds from Jean-Pierre, long since depleted, forced Marguerite to beg on the streets, for her sustenance. When desperate, she stole from the street vendors. She often recalled the young Ursuline nun of long ago, that prayed daily and worked constantly but never went to bed hungry. Marguerite yearned for those days and prayed for relief.

After several days, she found work as an aide at the hospital and a place to stay. When rumors of the imminent British invasion reached Montreal, Marguerite surrendered to reality. Her love and her nemesis might never be found. She wrote to her father, requesting funds for the journey back to France.

"I tell you it's true. A Council of War has been convened and the French Army will soon surrender," said a nurse, surrounded by mostly female hospital workers.

Marguerite pushed her way into the small group.

"Where? Where is the Council of War?" she asked.

Marguerite walked and ran, as she navigated the streets of Montreal, in route to the governor's mansion. On that particular day, the ornate building enjoyed a colorful addition to its normally impressive edifice, now surrounded by hundreds of uniformed soldiers, from various regiments in the French Army. She wandered through the crowd, generating curious and, at times, lurid stares. Eventually, Marguerite discovered the object of her search, a member of the Royal Roussillon regiment.

"I am in search of Captain Antoine Dauphin," she announced.

Yes, madam. But you must wait for him to exit the building. He and the remaining officers are in a Council of War, with General de Levis, Governor Vaudreuil, and Intendant Bigot," said the soldier.

The news triggered a jumble of emotions. She stood within yards of the man she loved but her stomach churned at the thought that Lezard too, could be in the building. She remained as near the entrance as she could, her view of the large, wooden doors unobscured.

And she waited.

"Gentleman," Bigot shouted, calling the Governor's meeting to order.

The intendant waited patiently while his guests grew quiet.

"I will read the terms and conditions of capitulation and then the Governor will speak," announced Bigot.

Antoine observed the proceedings from the rear of the room. Bigot appeared without Captain Lezard at his side. The Council of War included all French officers, with the rank of captain and higher. Governor Vaudreuil sat quietly behind his ornate desk. As Bigot read aloud, Antoine's anger and disappointment grew. Before anyone could react, de Levis recited the details of their plight and announced his recommendation to sue for peace.

Their first entreaty to British General, James Murray, would be a simple request to cease all hostilities, for a period of thirty days. This request, delivered immediately, prompted an immediate response from the English General—no. A second proposal, which included a lengthy list of specific requests, received a similar response. The English also insisted that French soldiers surrender their weapons and their regimental flags. The long-standing practice of allowing a vanquished army to retain their weapons and military regalia would be denied.

Howls of protest could be heard, Antoine's objections, some of the loudest. The Chevalier de Levis proposed that they retreat to St Helen's Island and fight to the death. Antoine cheered General de Levis on. When the room grew quiet, Governor Vaudreuil labeled the proposal as unrealistic and argued for yet another entreaty to the British, for more reasonable terms of surrender. The British refused to compromise. They argued that previous atrocities committed by the Indians were provoked by the French Army. Accordingly, the Honors of War would be denied French troops.

As the discussion continued, Antoine took note of two British demands in particular. They directly affected Antoine. No protections would be given anyone who deserted the French Army. In addition, all French officers would be forced to return to

France as prisoners on English ships. The one exception, soldiers who married in Canada, required such men to swear allegiance to the English crown. Those officers could remain in Quebec.

Antoine scratched his head and rubbed his unshaven face. Neither of his choices appealed to the man. Marry Marguerite or return to France. In the midst of his anxiety, Antoine noticed Bigot exiting the chamber. He scurried to the intendant's side.

"The intendant returns to France with his governor and his riches?" asked Antoine, tugging at Bigot's arm.

Bigot paused, a frown crossing his face.

"I do not recall the Captain's name. Please forgive me," said Bigot.

"This is the second time you have abandoned me to the English Army," said Antoine.

Bigot's face blushed red when he realized the Captain's identity. He hesitated before responding, pursed his lips and fixed his gaze on Antoine.

"I had no choice but to comply with the English general's request for a hostage," said Bigot.

"And why did you choose me as your hostage?" asked Antoine.

"I chose no one. Captain Lezard offered to find a volunteer," said Bigot.

"I was ordered to surrender," said Antoine.

"Of this, I was not aware," said Bigot.

"And Captain Lezard? Does he return to France with you?" asked Antoine.

"No, Captain Dauphin. Unlike you, who served General Montcalm with honor, Captain Lezard remains in Quebec City. He is now a friend to the British," said Bigot.

"A friend to no one," growled Antoine.

"The Royal Roussillon leaves for France in a few days," said Bigot.

"I have married in Quebec and will exercise my right to remain in New France," Antoine lied.

"And why not? These are the accepted terms of our capitulation," said Bigot.

"The English government exiled me to France, months ago. If I am discovered in New France, I will be executed," said Antoine.

"And yet, you wish to remain?"

"There is no honor for a soldier defeated in war, when he returns to the mother country. This is my new home," said Antoine.

"I cannot help you, Captain Dauphin."

Bigot made a perfunctory bow and left the room.

Before leaving the governor's mansion, Antoine learned that the ceremonial surrender of the French Army would take place in two days.

At that time, French troops would march from their fortifications on the water's edge and lay down their arms. From there, the French soldiers would be easily corralled and carefully observed, until it was time to board the English ships. Antoine could not risk the exposure to English officers. His mind raced, desperate for a solution. He recalled that a member of the militia, who wore no uniform, might once again escape notice.

Surrounded by white uniforms, trimmed in blue, Antoine slipped out of the room. He wandered through the mansion, unsure as to what he searched for but certain that a return to the fort would only worsen his predicament. A rear exit offered the last chance of escape into the Montreal streets.

As Antoine resigned himself to failure, the exit door opened. A large man, wide enough to block the entire hallway, cocked his head and grinned. He wore a food-stained, white apron, a white shirt, and grease-covered boots. He carried an empty cooking pot.

"If you wish to leave, I too must leave," said the oversized man, his large belly shaking, as he laughed at his own wry observation.

"I seek to leave the building, but I wish to remain in New France," said Antoine.

"I do not understand," said the cook.

"Permit me to explain," said Antoine.

The captain and the cook enjoyed a lengthy discussion and reached a satisfactory solution.

"Then it is settled. I will be your assistant," said Antoine.

"But you do not wear the clothes of a cook's assistant. And we rarely use a scabbard or a musket in the kitchen," said the man. His oversized belly jiggled once again.

"This, I can remedy," announced Antoine.

He removed his jacket, used his shirt to wipe a greasy pot, and stirred the ashes in the stove, with his boots. Antoine tossed his tricorn hat into the fire, ripped his breaches in several places, and rolled in the mud-tracked floor. In moments, he took on the appearance of a filthy local.

"And I surrender my weapon to you, not the English," said Antoine, bowing to the wide-eyed cook. He placed his sword and scabbard into the man's outstretched arms.

"The musket remains with me and I with you, at least until nightfall," said Antoine.

The cook nodded.

"When you leave the building tonight, use the door which leads to the stables in the back," said the cook.

Antoine nodded and searched for a hiding place in the large kitchen.

Marguerite, standing vigil at the governor's mansion, concluded that neither Antoine nor Lezard attended the Council of War.

When darkness fell, she trekked back to the hospital for a night of restless sleep. The next morning, she traveled back to the water's edge. One more search for Antoine might yield results, she thought. When the formal ceremony began, the French troops carried no flags to be surrendered. In his last act of defiance, de Levis ordered that all flags be burned. The French regulars, now disarmed, immediately marched to an area near the docks. Marguerite studied every face and every uniform, but to no avail. She decided to approach several of the men in Antoine's regiment, as they gathered dockside. None recalled seeing him at the fort when the troops prepared for their formal surrender. Several recalled seeing Captain Dauphin at the Council of War, but no one knew where he might be. She retraced her steps to the governor's mansion. After repeated knocking and no response, she started to leave but stopped when she heard the door open.

"Everyone has left. I am the cook and soon I too shall leave," said the fat man.

"Thank you. I look for a Captain in the Royal Roussillon Regiment. He has disappeared, I'm afraid."

"What does he look like?"

Marguerite provided a detailed description. The cook nodded.

"You look for a soldier, but he is now a cook's assistant," said the man, his large belly erupting in laughter.

Marguerite scowled.

"Antoine Dauphin is a Captain in His Majesty's Regiment," she announced, unsmiling and with her hands perched on both hips.

"Wait here," he said.

After a brief moment, he returned to the door brandishing a scabbard with a sword plus a spotlessly clean coat with a captain's insignia.

"He refused to surrender his weapons to the English," the cook reported.

Marguerite scampered up the steps and threw her arms around the man's neck. The cook wore a startled look.

"You have described my friend perfectly," she said, grinning broadly, as she dabbed at the tears in her eyes.

"He left last night," said the cook.

"Did he say where he was going?" she asked.

"Only that the abandoned fort included a large kitchen and many hiding places," said the cook.

Marguerite flew down the street remembering to thank the man only after she disappeared from his sight.

At the fort, and safely ensconced in a dark, kitchen storeroom, Antoine plotted his next move while seated on the floor and leaning his back against the door.

The staff had abandoned their posts when the soldiers left. They took with them all of the foodstuffs and most of the useable hardware normally found in a kitchen. Without food or a horse and a limited supply of ammunition, a trip to Three Rivers to retrieve Marguerite would be impossible. And yet, if he remained in Montreal, he might be recognized and captured.

A noise in the kitchen area interrupted Antoine's mental machinations. He tiptoed to a dark corner of the room, raised his musket, and carefully pulled the hammer back. The door handle rattled. Antoine stopped breathing. Initially, the sudden sliver of light blinded him, and he panicked, uncertain of his target. The door, now fully open, exposed the dark shadow of a woman's curves. Antoine's index finger twitched.

"You do not look like a Captain in the Royal Roussillon and you smell," said the shadow.

Antoine recognized Marguerite's voice, took a deep breath, and lowered his weapon.

"I am assistant to the cook and deserving of your respect," he said, a grin of relief on his face.

CHAPTER EIGHT

Savages

Adolphe Lezard made regular trips to Governor Murray's office.

Although the English governor barely tolerated the man's hideous appearance, he decided that Lezard could, on occasion, be useful. Murray did not, however, rely on the French turncoat as the sole source of his intelligence. Instead, he used Lezard to confirm what he already knew or suspected. And Lezard did not require a large amount of money for his "services." Despite the surrender of French forces at Montreal, the governor's constant need for information on "*les habitants*" remained.

"We have defeated the French Army, but we may never conquer the French people," said Murray.

"The Governor is wise to be concerned about the French people and I will do my best to assist you," said Lezard.

"What do the French people want from their new government?" asked Murray.

"Like your loyal servant, they desire English currency, food, and supplies," said Lezard, eying the cash box on Murray's large desk.

The governor rolled his eyes, wondering to himself, if Lezard was worth his time, much less his largesse.

"What information do you bring today that might interest me?" asked Murray.

"Captain Dauphin is rumored to have remained in New France," said Lezard, a slight smirk crossing his face.

Murray scowled.

"I am not interested in the whereabouts of this Captain Dauphin. He no longer poses a threat to His Majesty's army," said Murray.

Lezard squirmed in his chair and his eyes darted furiously. He spoke as fast as his accented English allowed.

"French Seigneurs will not swear allegiance to King George and they do not trust the English to respect the titles to their lands," said Lezard.

"And this is of importance to the governor, why?" asked Murray, as he frowned his frustration.

"They own large tracts of land. And almost all of the properties enjoy access to waterways. These tracts can now be purchased for a paltry sum. You can reward your best officers for their brave service or perhaps, the governor himself would like to profit from the foolish decisions of these French businessmen," Lezard reported.

The governor leaned forward in his chair, eyes narrowed and rubbing his chin.

"A rather delicate matter, don't you think?" asked the governor.

"I can be of great help, your Excellency, and I will exercise the utmost discretion," Lezard promised.

Murray reached for the metal box which contained a large number of British notes.

"We cannot stay here," said Antoine.

"There is a place near the hospital where I sleep at night," said Marguerite.

Soon the couple found themselves alone. They described to

each other the events of their immediate past. Marguerite cried when Antoine recounted Alemos' last moments.

"You should not have allowed him to go with you," she said.

"A man, even a very young man, cannot ignore the spilled blood of his family," said Antoine.

Marguerite paused, her anger wilting in the face of Antoine's dejected look.

"My Ursuline friends would argue that he is now with his family in paradise," she said. "But at least you are safe," she added.

"A brave soldier is willing to perish in battle. Only a coward survives in defeat."

"You are not a coward," she argued.

"Because you say so?" he asked.

Antoine rose to his feet and paced the floor in anger.

"I have failed my king and now I must choose–return to France as a coward or remain here as a British subject," he said.

"The war is over. What will you do?" she asked.

Antoine explained that when he first arrived in New France, a fellow officer persuaded him to purchase a portion of a Seigneury in southern Quebec, near the boundary line.

"For what purpose?" she asked, a surprised look on her face.

"We were friends. He said it was a good investment. But I think he needed the money," said Antoine.

"Where is this property?" she asked, her mind racing.

"It is a small tract on the waters of the Richelieu, but it is all I have."

"And you? What will you do?" he asked.

Marguerite looked away and cleared her throat, stunned by his response and needing time to compose herself. Clearly his question contemplated a future without her. She assumed that her feelings for Antoine were reciprocated. Perhaps she assumed too much.

"I am no longer welcome in the Ursuline community. I will return to France. My parents have arranged for the funds," she said.

"I have no money, no horse, and no supplies," he grumbled.

"But you can work the land, build a home," she said.

He glared at the woman.

"I am not a farmer. Don't you understand? I am a soldier," Antoine growled.

Marguerite blinked and leaned back.

"Can you be a soldier without a war?" she asked.

Antoine pounded his fist on a nearby table.

"No. I cannot. And I do not welcome this new life where my artillery piece is a horse-drawn plow and my regiment is a battlefield filled with cornstalks," he said.

Marguerite's eyes opened wide. Antoine's angry desperation filled the room. She required a moment to think and chose her words with great care.

"But neither a soldier nor a farmer is required to live alone," she said.

Antoine jerked in her direction. Marguerite managed a weak smile.

"There was a time when you prayed for my safety but not my return," he said. "What has changed?" asked Antoine.

Marguerite stared at the far wall, searching her mind for the answer to his question. She loved this man. Why did he not love her in return? It surprised and confused Marguerite. In the past, every man she ever encountered, lusted for her or professed their love for her—or both. Antoine was no different, she thought. There was also a time when he did not care that her oath as an Ursuline nun prohibited such feelings. And now that she lived unencumbered by her sacred vows, Antoine barely acknowledged her and mourned the loss of his military career, instead. She could feel the frustration, even anger, rise in her chest, but smothered the bitter words that came to mind.

"I have changed," she said.

"You no longer wear the veil," he said.

"You no longer wear the uniform," she countered.

"But I have not changed. I am, and always will be, a soldier."

"You love the military more than a man loves his wife," she said, daring to risk his wrath, once again.

"You are correct. It has been a blessing. And now, it is a curse."

"Will there be a day when you are no longer cursed?" she asked.

"I do not know," he said.

"Very well, then. You require a business partner and nothing more," she said. "I can be your business partner. The funds from my father are yours, if you wish."

"You would do this for me?" he asked.

"Yes, *Mon Capitaine*, I would."

Despite the crashing value of French livres, Antoine and Marguerite, using almost all of the money she possessed, accessed a horse and enough supplies to enable the couple's trip to Lacolle.

The journey included a number of dangers. In addition to the English Army, there might also be marauding savages and wild animals, on their trek to the boundary line. The couple exchanged few words in route to their destination. Antoine, especially quiet, contemplated this new chapter in his relationship with Marguerite. He wrestled with the idea of a woman as his business partner. He knew of no other man who had done such a thing. He also questioned whether Marguerite's largesse came with expectations. Marriage at this time in his turbulent life was out of the question.

Their first night on the long trail to the border, posed no

problem for the young couple. They agreed to take shifts. While one stood guard, the other would sleep. Antoine sensed danger. Marguerite, warmed by the small fire, slept soundly, bundled in several wool blankets, on a bed of tree branches. They spent their second evening a few yards from the trail, but still miles from the boundary line. It did not go as well.

The sharp blade of a scalping knife at his neck woke Antoine from a predawn slumber. His focusing eyes saw Marguerite in a death struggle, with a Mohawk savage. The Indian easily overpowered the woman. The warrior flipped her tiny body, face down, and tied the woman's arms behind her back. Antoine noticed three more savages and decided to fight back. The struggle did not last long. A blow to his head, with a Mohawk club, sent the soldier crashing to the ground. A scalping knife glistened in the morning light, as the Indian approached Antoine's unconscious body. A sudden war hoop, emanating from the forest, sent the Mohawk cabal running in the opposite direction, dragging Marguerite as they left.

Antoine's rescuers, a band of two dozen Indians, also Mohawk, proved what the captain learned long ago. During the war, members of the same tribe fought for both the French and the English. And they fought amongst themselves.

They threw Antoine over his own horse and traveled to a nearby Mohawk settlement. When Antoine came to, he focused his blurred vision on a young Mohawk squaw, ministering to the large bump and bloody laceration on the back of his head. She showed no emotion when Antoine caught her gaze, rising instead, and returning with a wooden bowl filled with a hot liquid. She fed it to the man and Antoine murmured his thanks.

"You are welcome," she responded, her skill with the English language, near perfect.

Antoine struggled to sit, but the chamber went dark.

Marguerite traveled on foot with hands tied behind her back, for most of the day.

When she stumbled and fell, her Indian captor kicked the woman and spit on her until she rose. At one point, the savage urinated on her head, laughing as he did so. Marguerite, although exhausted, rose and kicked the savage in the groin. He doubled over in pain as the other warriors laughed. The angry Indian swung hard with a closed first, loosening a number of Marguerite's teeth and sending her back to the forest floor, unconscious.

When Marguerite awakened, she did not move, and used the first moments of consciousness to survey her surroundings. She recognized the frame of branches and the elm-bark-covered interior of the Mohawk longhouse from her exposure to the Abenaki settlements. The long, rectangular chamber included several fires, around which mostly women and children gathered. She guessed that several families occupied the long house and wondered why her captor chose to keep her alive. The grisly possibilities made her stomach turn.

Marguerite closed her eyes again for some badly needed rest but a sharp kick to her side brought the woman back to consciousness. The same warrior who mistreated her for most of the trip motioned for her to rise. With both hands still tied behind her back, Marguerite struggled to comply. A long and violent pull on her hair brought Marguerite to a standing position. He brandished a knife, spun her around and, with a quick jerk, cut her ties. As the blood rushed into her sore and numb hands, Marguerite dared to stare at his face.

He stood almost two heads higher than his prisoner. Most of

the Indian's hair, plucked, left his scalp bare except for a large tuft in the back, decorated with a few black feathers. He wore a breech cloth and leggings, both made of leather. Ankle-wrapped moccasins, arm bands, and a necklace made from shells completed his fierce look. The one piece, hand-carved club he constantly carried, included a three-inch ball at the end of its two-foot handle, designed to fracture a man's skull.

His head swiveled, catching the gaze of an older, Indian woman perched in a chair, at the far end of the longhouse. She nodded her permission and the young warrior pushed and pulled Marguerite into a nearby wigwam, shoving her onto a blanket. When he left the tent, she immediately began to plan an escape. Darkness enveloped the camp and the blue sky she saw through the opening at the top of the structure, became a starlit gray. Marguerite searched for a way out and learned that the edges of the tent, securely fastened to stakes, could not be loosened. Her only path to freedom lay in front of her, the open slit through which she arrived. She slipped out of the wigwam and took a few steps. A violent blow to her stomach sent the woman back into the tent, gasping for air.

Marguerite fell onto the blanket and quietly wept.

Antoine required days to recover from his concussion and the young squaw remained at his side for most of that time.

"You speak the white man's language," he noted.

"Yes, our chief demands it of his wives, she said.

Antoine's eyes grew wide as saucers.

"You are the wife of a Mohawk chief?"

"I am no longer his wife," she replied, unsmiling and examining Antoine's injury, now almost healed.

"I don't understand," he said.

"The chief requires a son. I am without children," she said.

"What will you do?"

"The clan mother says I do not belong in her longhouse. I must leave," she said.

Antoine swallowed hard, uncertain if he should say anything at all. After several moments of silence, he announced his intentions.

"I too must leave."

"You look for Marguerite?" she asked.

"How did you know?"

"The white man speaks even as he sleeps," she said.

"She is with the Mohawk," he said.

"She is dead," said the squaw, showing no emotion.

"I must find her."

"You will not find the Mohawk. They will find you."

"I will leave in the morning," Antoine replied.

Marguerite woke to the smell of alcohol and sweat.

A large hand grabbed at her bosom and another hand pulled at her dress. Although the darkness hid his face, she knew that her attacker was the same savage that mistreated her earlier in the day. She resisted, biting at his ears and face, because the brute pinned both of her arms to the ground above her head. He lifted the long dress and ripped her undergarments, using his knees to separate the woman's limbs. She stopped struggling when he penetrated her and, after a few violent thrusts, the savage rolled to one side. He left the tent without saying a word. Marguerite stared at the bark-covered walls, as a lone tear rolled down her cheek.

She vowed to escape or die trying.

When Antoine rose, the dawn's light barely visible, he looked around him, expecting to see his nurse maid, but no one stirred. He rolled the blanket, tucked a few items inside the fabric, and tied it with a leather strap. He stepped outside of the tent. The squaw, with Antoine's horse in tow, came into view.

"You will ride, I will walk," she announced.

Antoine shook his head.

"No. I travel alone," he answered.

"I have nowhere to go," she begged.

He looked away, biting his lip and shook his head again.

"I thank you for your care and attention, but you cannot come with me. I'm sorry," he said.

The squaw's eyes narrowed.

"You cannot stop me," she said.

The squaw stepped forward, reached for Antoine's roll and pulled. He resisted but only for a moment. She fastened the rolled-up blanket onto the horse and handed the reins to Antoine. He hesitated, mounted the animal, and squeezed the horse into a slow walk. The horse and its rider trotted through the opening in the wooden palisade which surrounded the Mohawk camp. Antoine twisted in his saddle.

The squaw followed.

Marguerite recovered from the warrior's original attack and made several more attempts to elude her captor.

She waited until after his violent molestations when he fell asleep at her side. Each time she slipped away, the monster seemed to sense her intentions. He deliberately waited until she left the tent, dragged her back, and pummeled her with his fists. On one occasion, he used the wooden handle of his club.

Her face and body were bruised and swollen; Marguerite prayed for death. She searched the wigwam for a weapon with which she could end her suffering. Weeks passed since her arrival, the days and nights now much warmer, but bringing no comfort to the suicidal prisoner. More recently, she suffered from nausea, mostly in the morning. She constantly foraged for food, including scraps, nuts, berries, and almost anything to satisfy her pangs of hunger. As she nibbled on the scraps left behind by her assailant, Marguerite slowly connected the morning sickness, her constant hunger, and the absence of her monthly cycle. The overheard and usually hushed conversations of older woman in her mother's household came rushing back. Those women described such symptoms as being in a "motherly way." She shook her head, struggling to stop the flood of tears.

The monster stole her innocence and now, she carried his child.

Antoine Dauphin and the Mohawk squaw traveled south, in route to Lacolle, near the southern border of Quebec.

She called herself Ojistah, her tribe's word for "star." Several attempts to rediscover the camp where Marguerite disappeared, produced nothing except a series of disapproving looks from Ojistah.

"You will not find her. She is dead," said the squaw.

Antoine clenched his teeth, kicked at the sides of his mount, and forced the squaw to follow behind, at a considerable distance. He scoured the deep forest on either side of the narrow trail, no longer caring if his presence alerted unfriendly Indians. Guilty thoughts overwhelmed his common sense. He failed in his duty to protect Marguerite and she died a horrible death as a result. Antoine wanted to scream.

Ojistah caught up to Antoine when he stopped for water and a brief rest.

"You are angry with Ojistah, but I speak the truth," she said.

Antoine, sitting on the forest floor with his back to a large pine tree, toyed with a pinecone and studied the harmless squirrel that scurried to avoid the man's fingers. He refused to acknowledge his unwanted companion. The woman moved closer and reached for the scar on Antoine's head. He pushed her away.

"Don't touch me," he yelled, throwing the pinecone into the woods.

Antoine rose to his feet, mounted his horse, and trotted down the path.

Marguerite, her pregnancy now obvious, no longer dreaded the nights.

Her child's warrior-father ignored the woman, his lustful attentions now focused on a younger squaw living in the long house. Marguerite enjoyed her new-found freedom, regularly leaving the Iroquois community for short walks, in the deep forest. Her thoughts drifted constantly to Antoine and her last memory of him, laying in a pool of blood on the forest floor. She considered the possibility that he succumbed to his wounds but ended each of her miserable days, by dismissing such a horrible scenario.

Marguerite also worried about her unborn child. This would be her first time with an infant. She didn't know what to expect and wondered whether anyone in the camp would be willing to help a white woman give birth to a Mohawk child. Nor did she know how to care for a baby. As another harsh Quebec winter approached, her fear of the unknown grew.

On one particularly cold and snowy evening, Marguerite rested, her advanced pregnancy sapping most of her energy. A sharp kick to her side forced her to rise. Her rapist, with the young squaw in tow, motioned for the pregnant woman to leave the tent. Marguerite grabbed a blanket and walked out into the cold, wet snow. She shivered uncontrollably as she contemplated her options. She walked to the longhouse where several fires kept the occupants toasty warm. Her presence in the entrance triggered an instant reaction. Several of the older squaws rushed to the white woman's side. They shoved her back into the falling snow and yelled in a tongue that Marguerite did not understand. With nothing more than her blanket for protection, she wandered into the deep forest and took shelter under the overhang of a large rock. She broke off a series of small tree branches which allowed some protection from the cold, hard ground.

A few more branches, pulled onto her blanket, increased the warmth of her temporary shelter.

Marguerite rose at first light and began an immediate search for food.

The ground, covered in inches of snow, surrendered none of the forage to which she had become accustomed. She made no noise as she walked back to the Mohawk camp site. The lack of any smoke from the roof of the longhouse, prompted her to enter. Several well-chewed bones, almost entirely devoid of meat, lay near one of the fire pits. Those scraps, plus a leather pouch filled with nuts and berries, quickly disappeared in her blanket roll. Marguerite also liberated a few ears of dried corn, which hung from an overhead pole. She focused on the sleeping bodies as she exited the way she came and grabbed a second blanket drying on a tether strung between the long house and a tree. She entered the deep woods and used the rising sun to keep her bearings.

Marguerite walked south in search of the trail that she and Antoine last traveled.

A NOVEL BY MARK BARIE

Antoine discovered a single farmer, occupying a plot of land on his friend's Seigneury.

Like most of the long, narrow tracts, Antoine's portion included frontage on the west bank of the Richelieu River. He paced off the perimeter of his lot based on the neighbor's documents and advice. Antoine did not regret his decision to purchase the property from Colonel Beauleu, but deeply resented the unexpected turn in his life—from victory in battle, to ignominious defeat, from dedicated soldier, to lonely farmer.

Antoine's neighbor also loaned him the tools required to construct a lean-to made of logs. The captain and Ojistah shared the makeshift shelter, several blankets, and foodstuffs—but nothing more.

Antoine worked from sunup to sundown, ensuring that he had everything necessary for the survival of winter, in the Richelieu river valley. Despite his daily exhaustion, he could not escape the anger which consumed him. He fumed about the British government which flipped his world upside down, about the renegade Mohawks who killed Marguerite, and the terrible circumstances of his new life. He vowed retribution against all of them and vented his anger and frustration by focusing on the preparations for winter. Antoine rarely spoke to Ojistah and ate his meals in silence.

"You are angry," she said.

Antoine shook his head, focused on the small fire in their midst, and said nothing.

"She is dead. I cannot give you children, but I can give you comfort," she whispered.

Ojistah moved closer, reaching for Antoine's hand. He pushed her away. She persisted. He leaned in the opposite direction of her entreaty but did not resist. When they both lay under the blankets, she reached down and removed her leather garment. He marveled that the naked woman did not tremble in the cold. She pressed her body against his, with her head resting on his chest. He reached for her breasts, the smooth skin, soft and warm to his touch. She tugged at his shirt.

"No," he barked.

Antoine threw off the blankets, scrambled to his feet, and stood in the opening. The cold wind whipped at his face and his chest heaved. She watched and waited. Antoine's head drooped and he rubbed his eyes. She approached him again, naked, but warm to the touch. Ojistah led him by the hand back to their sleeping place.

He resisted no more.

Antoine, perched on a fallen tree in the woods, enjoyed a rare day of sunlit skies.

He mentally checked off the items required for the upcoming winter and absent mindedly jerked his head yes when he reached the end of his list. Ojistah deserved much of the credit for making their shelter, now fully enclosed, both habitable and comfortable. She worked alongside Antoine as would a full-grown man. She did as he did—cleared the land, dragged logs, and cut wood. She also cooked, cleaned, prepared, and stored foodstuffs, for the winter. She made their meals and, in the evening, whether she lay exhausted or not, Ojistah never refused his advances. The two of them became frequent lovers.

Antoine's thoughts strayed to his previous life, as an officer in His Majesty's army. A twinge in his heart, reminded the man of those days when he led soldiers into battle and the inevitable rush of adrenalin which followed. He reached down for a small branch and flung it into the woods, his anger still palpable.

His mind wandered to Marguerite, her face, her hair, still fresh in his memory. He remembered the woman's laughter at the captain's table and recalled, with a frown, that day she prayed for his safety but not his return. Ironic, he thought, that she would succumb to the ravages of the red man's war while the warrior himself remained alive and well. Her death did not come quickly, he concluded, and for that, he mourned. He deliberately reassured himself, that Marguerite could not and would not ever be a soldier's wife. Their violent separation occurred for a reason.

Antoine's stream of tortured thoughts came to a quick halt when the sound of rustling branches and snow crunching underfoot pierced the air. His alarm grew, as he reached for his musket and searched the forest around him. He made no noise, as he tiptoed in circles and wondered if it was man or beast that threatened his solitude.

All was quiet and then, another noise. For an instant, he thought a wounded animal cried in the wilderness. A second scream sounded human, like a female in distress. He took a few hesitant steps and strode deeper into the woods, until the object of his search became visible.

The woman, her back to Antoine, faced a small tree. Both of her hands clutched the bark as she crouched in a sitting position, her knees spread apart. She screamed again and when her pain seemed to subside, she peered through the brush, in his direction. The blanket, wrapped around her shoulders, fell to the ground. Antoine could see the bulge in her dress. He stopped, reaching for a tree to steady himself, his eyes wide open and unblinking. The black and blue bruises, evidence of numerous beatings, hid the delicate features of her face but he recognized the flaming red hair. She appeared soaked to the skin, her hair tangled and covered with twigs and dry leaves.

"Antoine," gasped the woman, falling to the ground, unconscious.

He carried Marguerite to the shelter, covered her with blankets and, when she regained consciousness, brought her a cup of hot tea.

Ojistah, usually helpful, sat in the corner, eying the red-haired woman but turning her head whenever Marguerite looked up. In time, Marguerite's contractions subsided, and she recovered enough to speak.

"Who is she," she asked Antoine, but eyeing the squaw.

"Her name is Ojistah. She nursed me after the attack. She is Mohawk, abandoned by her community for being unable to produce children."

Marguerite squeezed her eyes shut.

"I have not been so fortunate," she said.

"Marguerite, I thought they killed you," Antoine said, stopping short of explaining that Ojistah did more than nurse him back to health.

"I wish they had killed me. Death would have been easier," she replied.

Ojistah walked to Marguerite's side. The two women examined each other, their thoughts, unspoken. Marguerite, filthy and disheveled, her appearance neglected after weeks in the wilderness, looked away in shame. The Indian woman appeared unblemished, almost resplendent, in her simple deerskin attire and long, black, shoulder-length hair.

"You carry the child of a Mohawk warrior," said Ojistah, pointing an accusing finger at Marguerite.

Marguerite's eyes opened wide, surprised that the squaw spoke English.

"It is true, what you say. But I am not a mother by choice," said Marguerite, wincing at the arrival of yet another contraction.

"You are weak, and you are undeserving of such an honor," said Ojistah.

She left before Marguerite could respond.

Antoine, now alone with Marguerite, questioned the woman with his searching look. She spoke in a monotone, a distant look on her face.

"The Mohawk warrior who kidnapped me took me as his squaw. He attacked me almost every night. He found another squaw and threw me out. The other families refused to let me live in the longhouse. I was forced to leave. That was weeks and weeks ago."

"Will the child come soon?" asked Antoine.

"I don't know," she replied.

Antoine looked toward the open side of the lean-to, now covered with deer skins, as if expecting Ojistah to return. Marguerite noticed his anxious look.

"Will you too demand that I leave?" she asked.

Antoine's head jerked in her direction. He blushed.

"No. You and the child may remain," he answered.

And your squaw, will she approve?

"She will do as I say."

Marguerite eventually surrendered to her exhaustion and fell asleep as Antoine watched.

When her breathing became regular, he went in search of Ojistah. Her eyes burned into Antoine's face.

"The baby will not be white or Mohawk," said the squaw.

"We will welcome both mother and child," said Antoine.

"A half-breed is welcome nowhere," she announced

"You will do as I say," he replied.

Ojistah's eyes narrowed as she scowled at the man.

She folded her arms and stormed off into the woods.

Their first week together, as a trio, wore on forever.

Antoine fished or hunted as the weather permitted. Ojistah accomplished most of the chores, as Marguerite now spent her days resting and eating. Ojistah chose a quiet moment alone with Marguerite, to confront her.

"The white woman eats too much," observed the Mohawk squaw.

Marguerite shoved another handful of nuts and berries into her mouth and sneered at her accuser.

"Your Mohawk brother raped me, left me with his child, and then abandoned me. And now you object to my hunger?" said Marguerite, her voice rising.

The white woman's eyes flashed, and she threw the leather pouch, still partially filled with edibles, in Ojistah's direction. Ojistah did not move, the small pouch missing her head by several feet.

"I saved the captain's life," she snapped.

"And your Mohawk brother took mine," said Marguerite.

"The white woman cries like baby," said Ojistah.

Marguerite doubled over in pain. She fell to her knees and assumed a fetal position. Ojistah refused to budge, until she noticed a growing wet spot on Marguerite's blanket.

"It is time," said the squaw.

For two hours, Marguerite labored in vain. When Antoine approached the camp, he heard screams and rushed to the lean-to. Other than holding her hand, he could do nothing, as the squaw who saved his life now ministered to Marguerite.

Ojistah barked her commands for Marguerite to push and to bite down on a hand carved wooden spoon. The device did not lessen the pregnant woman's pain; it merely reduced the yelling to loud grunts and groans. After hours of labor, the small shelter echoed with the screams of a newborn child. Ojistah wrapped the tiny infant in a small piece of deerskin. She presented the child to Marguerite, still tethered to its mother by the umbilical cord.

"Chaska," said the Mohawk woman.

"I don't understand," said Marguerite, holding the child close.

"It means, "first born son," said Ojistah.

Antoine grinned as Marguerite counted fingers and toes.

Ojistah busied herself with the soiled animal skins and used them as an excuse to leave the tiny enclave. Once outside, she threw them to the ground and ran into the woods. Ojistah did not stop running, until her lungs screamed for a rest. She leaned her back against a young pine tree and slid to the ground, gasping for air. As her breathing returned to normal, Ojistah drew circles on the forest floor with a small twig.

Her eyes remained dry, but her heart overflowed with anger.

Chaska's arrival, two months early in May of 1761, coincided with the long-awaited spring.

Most of the snow in the forest melted and drained into the swollen Richelieu River. Antoine used the mild weather to begin construction on a large, log home. A traveling Jesuit, staying with Antoine's neighbors, reluctantly baptized the fatherless child and triggered Ojistah's wrath.

"The father of Chaska is Mohawk warrior. White man's religion make no difference," she argued.

Antoine and Marguerite ignored her admonition and together, checked on the sleeping child. Ojistah rolled the blankets she and the captain once shared and collected her things.

"I leave," she announced. Antoine did not object to her departure and Margaret welcomed it.

In the weeks that followed, Antoine paid little attention to the Indian child.

He expected Marguerite to complete all of the chores, previously accomplished by Ojistah, plus the tasks associated with a newborn baby. Marguerite did not complain and thought to find some clumsy humor in their predicament.

"His Majesty's soldier has become an unwilling farmer. And the Ursuline nun has become an unwilling mother. But still, we are together," she remarked. Antoine frowned.

"God's punishment," he observed.

Marguerite bit her lip and brushed at the imaginary dust on her work dress. The couple, grateful for a rare moment of silence as Chaska slept, sat outside on a pile of logs, destined for use in the new house. Antoine stole a glance at the woman he lived with but did not sleep with. He noted to himself how much she had changed, since they first met, seven years ago. Her face, no longer angelic or innocent, bore the evidence of her twenty-four-year old life. A few wrinkles at the corners of her mouth and dark circles under her eyes were the price of bringing a child into the world, thought Antoine. In addition, some of the weight that accompanied her pregnancy could be seen when her profile came into view. Pregnancy aged the woman.

Antoine's observations prompted a question.

"Did you try to escape?" he asked her.

"Yes, of course. Repeatedly. I was beaten each time," she answered.

He did not respond.

"What are you asking? Do you think I submitted willingly to this savage?"

Marguerite rose to her feet and glared at Antoine. He looked away.

"Your silence says everything, Captain Dauphin," she whispered.

"Marguerite, I accuse you of nothing," said Antoine.

He rose and reached for her. She pushed his hand away.

"I understand now. You have no desire for a woman who has been used by a Mohawk savage," she said, her voice shaking.

"Marguerite, please," he begged.

She stormed into the forest, forcing him to run after her.

Neither of them remembered the sleeping child.

Antoine, unable to find Marguerite, trudged back to his partially completed house and trimmed a few more felled trees.

After an hour, Marguerite appeared at the edge of the forest and walked past Antoine to the enclosure. When she pulled the animal skin door open, she yelled to Antoine. He ran to the enclosure. The scene inside, sent him staggering backwards. He stood in a large pool of blood. Ojistah, her wrists slit wide open, lay motionless on a blood-soaked deerskin, a large hunting knife by her side. The squaw still held the child in the crook of one arm but he too, wore the marble white color of death. When Marguerite noticed the thin crimson necklace of blood which circled the infant's throat, she fell to the ground and opened her mouth to scream. Her eyes filled with tears and her face lost its color.

But she made no noise.

CHAPTER NINE

A New Life

The spring thaw made it easier for Antoine to dig the grave.

Marguerite insisted that Ojistah and the infant be buried together. She constructed a crude crucifix, from two small pine branches, and mourned quietly as Antoine used a spay to hammer the cross into the ground. They sat on handmade chairs, in front of the unfinished home, under the glow of countless stars and an exceptionally bright moon. But the beauty of the evening sky could not eclipse the small mound of dirt which rose above the ground, yards from their shelter.

The murder-suicide did not erase the angry words they exchanged on that fateful day. But for a while, Antoine and Marguerite effected an unspoken truce. Antoine worked on the new home, almost every day. Marguerite helped in any way she could. Several months passed and the couple continued to live as brother and sister, each of them nursing the wounds that death and suicide inflict upon the survivors.

"I would have loved him as one of my own," she announced one night.

They lay on deerskins, a respectable distance apart.

"I would have tried. But can a man predict his success as a

father?" said Antoine.

His response quieted her troubled soul. She reached for his hand. He squeezed her fingers in response.

"I am sorry, Marguerite. I should not have spoken to you that way. Please forgive me," he whispered, a reference to the question that triggered her anger.

Marguerite pulled herself closer and studied his eyes. She leaned forward and kissed him on the cheek. He hesitated and kissed her on the lips, pulling back almost instantly, as if she might object. She welcomed his attention and caressed his cheek. He reached for her trembling body and for a moment, neither of them moved. The would-be lovers kissed again, and she rolled on top of him. He pulled at her night clothes. In moments, passion conquered their grief and lust overpowered their loss.

They made love and fell asleep in each other's arms.

Adolphe Lezard used a letter from Governor Murray's office to affect his entry into the offices and parlors of French Seigneurs.

The letter tasked Lezard with the identification of large tracts of land that might be of interest to Governor Murray. The French Seigneurs, unwilling to live under English rule and now anxious to sell their holdings, welcomed Lezard's entreaties, despite his horrid appearance.

In the course of his travels, Lezard learned that a former officer in the English army, conducted a similar search for properties once owned by French aristocrats. Lezard used his letter of introduction to arrange a meeting, with the former officer, Lieutenant-Colonel Gabriel Christie.

Antoine and Marguerite approached the traveling priest and

married, shortly after they became lovers.

For the first time in years, Marguerite did not feel as if the Lord despised her. He no longer punished her, she thought. The happy circumstances of her new life with Antoine evidenced her Creator's approval. She required nothing more. And for now, Adolphe Lezard faded from her life. Antoine's passion for the military, waned in a similar way. Without an army, much less a war in which to fight, Antoine the soldier, grew smaller and smaller. Antoine the husband and farmer, grew larger and larger. He did not resist the inevitable results of a peaceful coexistence with the beautiful woman who truly loved him.

Although neither of them broached the subject, both of them wondered about the prospect of children. She wanted to present Antoine with a son and he secretly hoped for the same, viewing the possibility as an exciting opportunity to raise a child in a way that he saw fit.

When the months became more than a year, Marguerite announced her conclusion.

"The Lord has not seen fit to bless us with children," she said.

"Perhaps it is too soon after . . ."

Antoine's voice trailed off.

"I carried the child of that savage. Why can't I bear the child of the man I love?" she asked.

Antoine, at a loss for words, resorted to humor.

"To be an expert marksman, one must practice. As often as possible," he said, a smirk on his face.

She began to undress.

He fixated on the beautiful woman and scooped her up in his arms.

"Are you not well?" Antoine asked.

In response, she ran from the newly, completed home to a nearby stand of trees. She took a deep breath, stooped over, and wretched.

"Marguerite, you are not well. Please rest for a while," he said, a look of concern crossing his face.

Marguerite blurted her news.

"I am with child," she whispered, almost afraid to say it out load.

"What did you say?"

She stepped forward.

"I am with child. Your child," she announced.

"I am a father?" Antoine asked, his eyes and mouth wide open.

"Yes," said Marguerite, her face beaming.

Antoine shook with laughter.

"Well, it is long overdue don't you think?"

"How is it that a French man works for the English governor?" asked Christie.

With the natural suspicion of a former soldier and a successful businessman, Lieutenant-Colonel Christie studied Lezard's appearance. He repeatedly fixated on his visitor's disfigured face and beady, black eyes.

"You suffered wounds in the war," said Christie, thinking it rude to openly ask a question about Lezard's hideous appearance.

"Yes, my friend, but you will forgive my reluctance to discuss the matter," said Lezard, using a morsel of truth to disguise a lie.

"I understand," said Christie.

"I am at your service, Mr. Christie, much like I am at the service of Governor Murray. Surely you have an interest in the French Seigneurs who are now desperate to sell their lands," said Lezard.

"I have purchased a seigneury south of the city and near the boundary line. I am contemplating another purchase in nearby Sabrevois," said Christie.

"I will report my findings," said Lezard.

"No, you will meet with my partner, first," said Christie.

His directive, a natural result of years as an officer in the English Army, could not be ignored.

"His name is Moses Hazen, a retired lieutenant in His Majesty's army.

"And where do I find this Moses Hazen?" asked Lezard.

"He is in route to the boundary line, tomorrow morning. There is only the one trail; I am sure you will find him," said Christie.

"You will not be disappointed, Your Excellency," Lizard purred.

Christie faked a smile and extended his hand.

Moses Hazen marveled to himself that a man, riding a few hundred yards behind, would neither approach nor overtake a fellow traveler, on the same trail.

Hazen, a former officer with Rogers' Rangers, did not like to be followed. He decided to take matters into his own hands. When Hazen rounded a bend, he quickly tethered his horse behind a stand of trees and waited in the bushes for the stranger to pass. Hazen calmly stepped out of his lair and pointed a musket at the stranger's back. He cleared his throat, pulled the hammer back, and waited for the stranger to stop.

"You will raise your hands, or I will shoot," said Hazen.

"I am an unarmed man, *mon amis*," said Adolphe Lezard.

"You are French, and you are a dangerously stupid man," Hazen replied.

"I have been sent by your business associate, Lieutenant-Colonel Christie," said Lezard, stuttering and shouting.

Hazen hesitated and lowered his weapon.

"You may dismount."

Beads of sweat now decorated Lezard's scarred face. Lezard reached for the sky with both hands and slowly pivoted in Hazen's direction.

"Adolphe Lezard, at your service, Your Excellency."

"I am in no need of assistance," said Hazen.

"Do you speak French, my friend?" asked Lezard.

"No, and I am not your friend."

Hazen refused to take his eyes off Lezard, even though the French man appeared unarmed. He motioned Lezard to a fallen log and the two awkwardly exchanged the amenities required by their mutual ally. Hazen, tugging at his chin, overruled his gut feeling about the strange Frenchman.

"I go to Lacolle. You may travel with me if you wish," said Hazen.

Lezard scrambled to his feet and took a few steps forward, his hand outstretched. Hazen flinched but retuned the Frenchman's gesture.

"My name is Moses Hazen."

Marguerite, her status as an expectant mother now obvious, studied the well-dressed man who knocked on her door.

"My husband is in the field. You will have to . . ."

Marguerite jumped back. The color in her face drained and her unblinking eyes grew wide, with fear. She slammed the door shut and pulled the wooden slat into place that barred an unwanted visitor's entry. She scurried to the back room and retrieved Antoine's pistol.

Hazen, standing alone on the porch, faced Lezard.

"Mr. Lezard, until today I have not seen this woman, but she obviously knows you," said Hazen.

Lezard, his scarred face, red, pushed past Hazen and, when the door refused to yield, kicked and pounded on the wood. Hazen, a foot taller than Lezard and of muscular build, grabbed the collar of Lezard's coat and yanked with all of his strength. Lezard fell down the steps and on to the ground.

"Mr. Lezard, you will restrain yourself or I will do it for you," Hazen demanded.

Lezard pulled a long knife from his boot and rose to his knees. Hazen's well-placed kick sent the knife flying. A second kick to the man's head, rendered Lezard unconscious and sprawled face down on the ground. When he stepped forward to retrieve Lezard's weapon, the distinct sound of a musket, when a man's thumb pulls the hammer into firing position, forced Hazen to stop. The experienced soldier knew what came next.

"I should like to know your name before I kill you," said Antoine.

Antoine brought the barrel of his long musket to the back of Hazen's head and used the cold, grey, steel to reinforce his threat.

Hazen drew a sharp breath and raised his hands into the air.

"My name is Moses Hazen and I am unarmed.

Antoine paused when he heard the familiar name. He stared at Lezard but responded to Hazen.

"You fought for the English at Saint Foy. Rogers' Rangers," said Antoine, slowly circling Hazen, his rifle now inches from the man's face.

"And there is a large scar on my leg as evidence of your fellow countrymen's hospitality," said Hazen, a grin on his face.

Antoine laughed, impressed with the man's calm manner. Hazen, his hands still in the air, grew somber.

"We are no longer at war with the French, my friend. The treaty was signed months ago," said Hazen.

Antoine jerked his head toward the unconscious man.

"And him, how do you know him?" asked Antoine.

"His name is Adolphe—"

Antoine, his eyes on fire, shoved the gun barrel into Hazen's midriff.

"I know who he is. How is it that you know him?"

Before Hazen answered, Marguerite stepped onto the porch, a pistol in her hand, aimed at the man's head. Hazen shoved his hands higher into the sky. His eyes darted from the woman's pistol to Antoine's musket. Drops of sweat formed on his forehead.

"He was sent to me by Lieutenant-Colonel Christie, the owner of this Seigneury," said Hazen.

"Christie is not the owner of this property," barked Antoine.

He yelled to Marguerite.

"Tie their hands behind them. Lezard first."

Marguerite rushed into the house and returned with several leather laces. She pulled the material especially tight around Lezard's wrists. Lezard regained consciousness and struggled to free himself. Marguerite spit in Lezard's face and reached for Hazen's raised hands.

"This is most unnecessary, sir," said Hazen, wincing, as Marguerite tested her handiwork with a sharp yank.

"My name is Antoine Dauphin, formally a Captain in the Royal Roussillon regiment of His French Majesty's Army. I purchased this portion of the Seigneury, years ago, from Captain Daniel Beauleu, also an Officer in the French Army," said Antoine.

Hazen, staring down the barrel of Antoine's musket, spoke in a measured tone.

"Captain Beauleu was killed at Fort Duquesne, in 1755. My associate purchased the entire plot from Beaujeu's widow and his daughters."

Antoine, startled by Hazen's report, glanced at Marguerite and checked on Lezard. He returned his darting eyes to Hazen. Antoine exhaled sharply and lowered his rifle. Hazen saw his chance.

"May we talk?" asked Hazen.

Antoine's head jerked in Lezard's direction.

"The monster stays where he is. Marguerite, if he moves, shoot him," barked Antoine.

Antoine reached for the knife at Hazen's feet and, with one hand, sliced the leather which bound the prisoner's hands. Hazen, rubbing the red lines on his wrist, sat on the porch. Antoine chose a nearby tree stump, affording him a view of both Hazen and Lezard. Marguerite glared at Lezard; her weapon pointed at his chest.

Hazen explained his work for Christie. In return, Antoine recounted his purchase of a portion of the Seigneury from Beauleu. He also related Marguerite's history with Lezard, including the unprovoked attack when she sailed as a passenger on the *Leopard*. He did not recount the manner in which Lezard's face became seriously disfigured.

"Clearly, the widow and her daughters were unaware of Mr. Beaujeu's business transactions," said Hazen.

"I will not pay for the same land twice," Antoine announced.

"I understand completely, Captain Dauphin."

"And I am not a captain anymore," said Antoine, as if the minor correction would help his cause.

Antoine grew silent. For a brief moment, the sound of a slight breeze in the nearby trees, imposed an eerie calmness on the two retired warriors. Antoine's eyes softened and he abruptly looked away, as if to hide the frustration in his voice.

"I am just a soldier trying to be a farmer," said Antoine.

Hazen scratched his scalp and brushed back his unkempt locks.

"Forgive me, Captain, but I must ask. Are there any documents to evidence your purchase?"

Antoine shook his head and stared at the trees.

"Lost in a fire, long ago," said Antoine.

"Nevertheless, you shall be allowed to stay," said Hazen, his demeanor now cheerful. "I will explain this to Mr. Christie and strongly recommend that you be allowed to remain on the property."

"Thank you, Mr. Hazen," said Antoine.

Marguerite interrupted the two men.

"And what about him?" she asked.

She stepped in Lezard's direction, her weapon, perilously close to Lezard's bruised and sweaty face.

"He will return to Montreal with me. Mr. Christie and I are no longer in need of his services," said Hazen.

Antoine walked toward Lezard, knife in hand. The prisoner cowered and begged for mercy.

"Please, Captain, please," said Lezard.

Antoine yanked on Lezard's scalp, pulling the man forward and exposing the prisoner's neck.

"If I ever see you again, you will not escape the death you deserve," said Antoine, as he cut the leathers.

Lezard glared at the woman who tied him up and rubbed his bloody wrists. Realizing that he would soon be released, Lezard winked at Marguerite. His suggestive leer gave Marguerite the excuse she needed. She lowered her pistol, aimed at the ground in front of Lezard, and discharged her weapon. All three men jumped back in fear. Lezard scrambled to his waiting horse.

"Look, he runs like a rabbit," said Hazen.

Antoine laughed. Hazen grinned and Marguerite smiled.

"Thank you, Captain Dauphin. You are a warrior with wisdom," said Hazen.

Antoine grew serious.

"You cannot trust Lezard. Be careful," Antoine advised.

"I hope to meet both of you, once again, under more pleasant circumstances," said Hazen.

Adolphe Lezard did not attempt a return visit with Lieutenant-Colonel Christie, opting instead for a preemptive visit with Governor Murray.

He explained to Murray that Christie acted as a competitor to the governor and purchased the best Seigneuries for himself. The governor, with no word from Christie, focused on more important matters. He explained the situation to Lezard.

"His Majesty, the King, is pleased with the administration of His colony in New France, but He is very frustrated with events in Massachusetts and elsewhere on the American side of the line," said Murray.

Lezard, all ears, leaned forward in his chair.

"How may I be of assistance, Your Excellency?"

Murray tapped his fingers on the desk and cocked his head.

"I wish for you to go to the northern colonies, learn what you can, and report back to me."

Lezard cleared his throat. Murray, knowing what Lezard was thinking, reached for a handful of English bank notes, and handed them to his visitor.

"There will be more, depending on the value of the information you gather. I must be able to advise His Majesty's government on the proper way to govern the American colonists," said Murray.

Lezard understood perfectly what his beneficent leader wanted, grabbed the money, and bowed.

As Lezard walked out of the governor's mansion, he remembered that the trail to the international boundary line would lead him to Lacolle.

Antoine, planning a trip to Montreal, begged Marguerite to accompany him.

"I do not wish to leave you alone for days at a time. Come with me," he pleaded.

Marguerite refused to budge.

"It is a difficult journey. Too difficult for a woman with child," she said.

"Please?"

"I will manage just fine," she answered.

Antoine arrived in Montreal days later.

His first view of the city shocked him. Although the fire that destroyed more than a quarter of the city occurred months ago, (May of 1765), evidence of the devastation appeared everywhere. A large portion of the business district sat in ruins. The stone walls, designed to protect city residents from attackers, did nothing to protect them from the flames. Flying sparks and embers left an irregular pattern of total destruction interspersed with unscathed buildings. Hundreds, now homeless, wandered the streets in search of food and shelter. Antoine surveyed the devastation, in a state of disbelief.

A sign in front of one building, charred but not destroyed, caught his attention.

Moses Hazen, Justice of the Peace

Antoine stepped through the unlocked door. Moses Hazen swept dust, debris, and ash into a small pile at the center of the room.

"Mr. Hazen or shall I say, Justice of the Peace Hazen?" asked Antoine, a grin crossing his face.

Hazen, frantically wiping his filthy hands against an even dirtier shirt, scurried to welcome his guest and apologetically extended a hand.

"Captain Dauphin, please forgive the mess."

"I received word of a fire, but I am shocked by the devastation," said Antoine.

"We have appealed to Governor Murray and are hoping for assistance from his Majesty, the King," said Hazen.

"Until then, there are no supplies?" asked Antoine.

Hazen explained precisely where in the city Antoine might find what he required. They exchanged news of the seigneury in Lacolle and updated each other on the details of their respective families. Both men wore disgusted looks when the subject of Adolphe Lezard surfaced.

"I have not seen him or even heard of his whereabouts, since we visited with you," said Hazen.

"Perhaps he returned to France, said Antoine.

"I do not know," said Hazen.

The discussion morphed into current political events.

"There is talk of rebellion in the colonies," noted Hazen.

"The colonists bristle under British rule," Antoine responded.

"They object to the new taxes, first on molasses and now on paper. And before a man can gamble in the colonies, he must first pay the tax on his playing cards," said Hazen, chuckling to himself. Antoine shook his head.

"The American rebels have no army. King George need not worry," said Antoine.

With a shake of his head and a serious frown, Hazen disagreed.

"The situation will only worsen," he said, retrieving his broom as he bid Antoine good-bye.

Adolphe Lezard traveled in September, in route to Albany, New York.

Before he crossed the boundary line, he took a short detour to spy on the woman who left him permanently disfigured. When the homestead came into view, Lezard's jaw dropped and his eyes grew wide. The fenced-in pasture had no horse and Marguerite wandered from chore to chore, with no one to help her. Lezard's evil heart leapt for joy. Marguerite Valtesse was alone.

Lezard licked his lips and forced himself to stay hidden behind a large clump of trees and bushes. He must do this in a carefully planned manner, he thought. He tugged at his misshapen ear and ran his fingers across the scars which Marguerite inflicted on him, years ago. They served as a reminder that she could not be underestimated.

The woodpile would serve as a distraction. Lezard torched the dry wood and lay in wait. Marguerite smelled the smoke and ran to the wood pile. She extinguished the fire, with her apron and a nearby shovel. As she stood there, desperate to catch her breath, a blow to the head sent the woman falling to the ground in a crumpled heap.

"And how is Sister Marguerite this morning?" asked Lezard, as he flashed his evil grin.

Marguerite, her head pounding, opened her eyes and recognized Lezard. She struggled in vain to loosen her ties.

"You are a snake," she replied, trying to rise.

Lezard took a few steps in Marguerite's direction and kicked the pregnant woman in her stomach. The force of the blow sent her backwards wheezing and gasping for air. After several moments, Marguerite reached a kneeling position once again. A wicked smirk flashed across her face.

"Your scars are healing nicely, she said.

Lezard kicked her again and continued to land blows on her head, chest, ribcage, and back. Marguerite stopped moving. He reached into his boot for the knife he carried and brandished it over her body.

"And now, Sister Marguerite you will receive your just reward," he growled.

He reached for her right ear, yanked his blade, and threw the severed flesh in the air. Lezard, mesmerized by his long-awaited revenge, did not hear the sound of an approaching horse. Nor did he expect the explosion of a musket. He did hear the buzz of a musket ball as it flew past his good ear. Antoine did not hesitate. He immediately began to reload, an instinctive maneuver he could accomplish, with his eyes closed.

Lezard ran to his horse, mounted, and galloped off. A second shot from Antoine's rifle, spooked the inexperienced horse. Lezard nearly fell but managed to regain his balance when he grabbed at the animal's long mane.

Marguerite did not move.

Antoine carried Marguerite into their home and rushed to locate blankets, bandages, water, and a ration of rum.

After several hours, the woman regained consciousness. She fingered the bandages which surrounded her head.

"You have been injured. The bleeding has stopped but do not remove your bandages," Antoine instructed.

"Lezard. He was here," Marguerite cried.

"Yes," said Antoine. "Lezard was here."

After barricading the door, the couple collapsed onto the bed. Hours later, Antoine woke to the sound of Marguerite weeping, her head no longer bandaged. Antoine replaced the head bandage and covered the woman with a blanket. He sat with her, until she cried herself into a deep sleep.

Weeks passed and Marguerite, except for hot tea and a small piece of bread, rarely ate. When not in bed, she occupied the rocker and stared into the flames, dry eyed and deathly still. Antoine, unwilling to leave her, used his friendly neighbor to report the incident. But Justice of the Peace Hazen could do nothing. In a lengthy missive, Hazen reported that Lezard had traveled to the colonies, apparently at the request of the governor.

Antoine threw the letter into the fire.

Chapter Ten

Life and Death

Marguerite, still suffering from Lezard's vicious attack, rose from her stupor in pain.

"Antoine," she gasped and immediately the former soldier sprung to his feet.

"It is time," she said, through clenched teeth.

By previous arrangement, Antoine agreed to fetch help from the neighbor's wife. But Marguerite would be suffering alone, during the one hour required for the round trip.

"I will return as quickly as possible," promised the nervous father.

Marguerite endured a series of long and painful contractions. After less than an hour, she no longer resisted the urge to push. She wanted it out. Now.

When Marguerite spied the growing pool of blood, on her night shirt, she screamed in anguish and pain.

Her eyes closed and remained that way.

Antoine hurried the horse drawn wagon over the trail and onto the path that led to his home.

The neighbor's wife reassured the man, but her words did little to calm Antoine's fears. At that moment, he welcomed the prospect of musket fire, artillery fire, and an enemy in overwhelming numbers, rather than face the terror of his child's birth.

When he scrambled up the stoop and flung the door open, Antoine fell to his knees. Marguerite, a deathly white on her face, lay unconscious on the bed. Their child, his skin blue and gray, lay motionless between the mother's legs. The helpful neighbor rushed to Marguerite's side and yelled for hot water and clean skins. She shook the infant boy and vigorously rubbed the child's entire body. She pleaded with the infant.

"Breathe child, breathe."

Finally, she laid the child on the nearby table and covered the infant's face and body with her shawl.

The neighbor lady, unable to face the father, cried openly.

"I'm sorry, Captain Dauphin. I am so sorry," she said.

Antoine backed into the nearest wall and slid to the floor.

With his head in his hands, he sobbed.

Antoine assumed that viewing the dead child would make it more difficult for Marguerite.

He chose a spot, adjacent to the graves of Ojistah and Chaska, to bury the child. When he returned to her bedside, and broke the news, Marguerite grew violent. She flung the nearby basin, filled with dirty water, in her husband's direction.

"You buried my child? Am I not allowed to see my son just this once? You are a heartless bastard," she screamed.

Marguerite flung her bedcovers to one side, intent on leaving her sickbed, but fell on her knees, instead. Antoine dropped to his knees and struggled to embrace the hysterical woman as she pummeled his chest with clenched fists and issued a series of gut-wrenching screams that sounded more like a dying animal.

Antoine wrestled his angry wife back into bed. He stayed at her side, until fatigue closed her eyes and she slept. While she rested, he exhumed the child, still carefully wrapped in a woolen blanket. He placed the lifeless form in the handmade crib which lay in front of the fireplace. Hours later, when she awoke, he escorted Marguerite to the dead child. She held the lifeless form, kissing its cold flesh and counting the child's fingers and toes. For hours, she refused to surrender the dead child, screaming in anger each time Antoine approached. But she didn't cry. Not once. When fatigue forced her eyes shut, Antoine made yet another attempt.

"May I hold him," he asked.

She handed the child to her husband, rolled over in her bed, and fell asleep.

As the New Year dawned, Marguerite and Antoine exchanged only those words necessary for the accomplishment of their daily chores.

Antoine made a number of attempts to engage his wife in a conversation about their loss, but Marguerite refused. She spent hours rearranging her hair to cover the scar of her missing ear. Mostly, she sat in the rocking chair and stared into the flames of their fireplace.

"Must we mourn the loss of our son for the rest of our lives?" he asked.

Marguerite continued to focus on the far wall, as if the rough-hewn logs held the solution to her manic depression.

The impasse remained unchanged for months more. On a particularly cold night, Antoine chose to open a bottle of rum. After imbibing several rations, his liquid courage prompted an offer.

"A drink for the fair lady?" he asked Marguerite.

"No," she answered, staring in the opposite direction.

Antoine continued to drink and closely watched her, as she prepared for sleep. He staggered to the bed and joined her under the covers, fully dressed. He reached for her nightshirt and gave it a playful tug. Marguerite responded by pulling the blankets tight around her arms and neck. He repeated his entreaty.

"Leave me alone," she snapped.

"No."

Antoine yanked the blanket to one side and, with little effort, straddled his wife, pinning both of her arms to the bedcovers. She spit in his face and growled her thoughts.

"You are no better than the Mohawk savage," she hissed.

Antoine, using one hand to restrain both of her arms, slapped the woman. The blow left a large handprint on the white skin of her cheek.

"Damn you woman. You are still my wife," he said through clenched teeth, as he ripped her nightdress from collar to waist.

She no longer resisted and turned her head to one side. Her dry eyes betrayed no emotion and she said nothing while her husband satisfied his drunken lust. She lay there, motionless, as Antoine's heavy breathing slowed. He released her arms and made a clumsy attempt to cover Marguerite's exposed body.

"You will not see me again," he said, as he shut the door behind him.

Days later, Marguerite paced the floor like a mad woman.

She cleaned every room in the house and did it again. She searched for Antoine, in and around the house, and repeatedly called his name. He did not answer. Several times, she heard the screams of a tiny child and inspected every room in the home.

Nothing. She retrieved the handmade crib that once held her dead child and placed it in front of the fire. Her anxiety worsened.

She continually reassured herself that Antoine would return, and have with him, their infant son. A fearful panic took hold in the woman's mind. She could hardly breath and that throbbing in her head grew louder and louder. She consumed large quantities of water, in a vain effort to moisten her dry and swollen tongue. The house got smaller. The walls closed in. She felt trapped. Lezard might return. He might harm the child. She must leave.

Now.

Marguerite did not remember the overnight horse ride from her Richelieu river home to Montréal.

She thought only of the infant child in her arms, swaddled in blankets, completely covered, and deathly still. She held her precious cargo close, whispering to the baby that he would soon be fed. After tethering the horse, she wandered the streets and alleyways in search of a merchant who sold fresh milk. A small country store on the outskirts of the city, with a large sign offering fresh eggs, caught her attention. As she waited behind several customers, an older woman approached.

"A son or a daughter," she asked.

"My son, said Marguerite, clutching the bundle a little closer to her bosom.

"May I see him?" asked the old woman.

"He's sleeping right now. I'm sorry," said Marguerite, unsmiling and stepping forward in the line.

"I understand," said the old woman, a disappointed look on her face.

When Marguerite reached the counter, she placed the child on the hard surface and reached for her handbag.

"Do you have fresh milk?" she asked the clerk.

"I'm sorry, ma'am, sometimes in the early morning, but not today," said the clerk.

"May I see the little one?" he asked, reaching for that part of the blanket wrapped around the child's head.

Marguerite pounced, shoving the man's outstretched arm to one side and whisking the child off the table. In her haste, she collided with a large man standing behind her. The impact of the collision caused Marguerite to lose her grip and the infant fell to the floor, with a dull thud. For one brief moment, the only sound in the room came from outside, as horses and pedestrians passed by.

The motionless bundle of blankets made no noise. Several of the onlookers gasped and the large man dropped to his knees, repeatedly apologizing, as he reached for the child. When the baby's face, now partially decomposed, came into view, the man recoiled.

"It's dead," he screamed, now moving away from the baby and sliding backwards on all fours. "She's carrying a dead baby," he yelled.

Marguerite stood motionless, eyes wide, and spoke in a soft whisper.

"Please, he's sleeping," she said.

Another woman stooped to cover the tiny remains and made the Sign of the Cross. The stricken man on the floor rose to his feet and ran from the store. The clerk, now on Marguerite's side of the counter, escorted her across the room to several chairs positioned near the wood stove.

"You must be tired, ma'am. Please sit down and rest a while," he said.

Marguerite did not resist and watched as several women bundled the dead child and laid it to rest on a nearby table.

"Could someone fetch the doctor?" asked the clerk.

Antoine spent the night in the deep woods, his only companions, a bottle of rum and a curious squirrel.

Tonight, he would move back into the lean-to, his home away from home. He walked to the large pile of firewood on the side of his house. He made no noise but stopped when he noticed that the horse no longer grazed in its pasture. Antoine's unobstructed view of the small cemetery, inside the forest, also distracted the man. The flowers, the wooden crosses, and the terrain itself looked disturbed and disheveled. A closer look sent Antoine running.

"No, no, please no," he cried.

The stones and crucifix that identified the grave of Ojistah and Chasta no longer decorated the burial site. The vandal threw them in every direction, leaving the forest floor sprinkled with the debris of death. An attempt to exhume the body of the Indian squaw, partially completed, transformed the woman's burial site into a series of shallow holes and uneven mounds of dirt and pine needles. A shovel, pushed deep into the ground, replaced the hand-made crucifix which lay on the ground, splintered into pieces.

A gaping hole marked the resting place, for Antoine's stillborn son. It no longer contained the child-sized coffin made of pine. The box, its cover removed, lay empty, under a large maple tree. A child's knit mitten brought Antoine to his knees.

He fell to the ground in tears.

Marguerite, questioned and examined by the doctor, agreed to a forced relocation.

The Gray Nuns of Montreal, a Religious Community, regularly

took in the ill, old people, and the homeless. The doctor directed that Marguerite be sent to the Order's convent, at their Chateauguay Seigneury. Their previous location, the General Hospital at the center of Montreal, lay in ruins, one of the many casualties of the great fire of 1765.

At the Seigneury, the still able-bodied Marguerite, would be expected to work hard for her room and board. The woman's diminished mental capacity did not excuse her from work at the Order's newly rebuilt mill, their acres of cornfields, and their apple orchards. And when the winter months arrived, the Grey Nuns and their boarders engaged in sewing, needlework, candle making, and laundry services.

Marguerite, catatonic and rarely communicating with her caregivers, did as she was told. She reverted back to those early days when she served the Ursuline nuns at their monastery in the French countryside—strict obedience, long days of hard work, and daily prayer. When the months became years, she began to communicate and recounted her past; her time as an Ursuline nun, as a victim of rape, and as a grieving mother. Despite her missing ear, no one believed Marguerite. She told the stories to anyone who would listen. Most of the nuns thought her wound to be self-inflicted. The community considered her tale of woe interesting and tragic, but untrue. No woman could survive such hardships. They dismissed her as mildly insane and Marguerite secretly wondered if her memories were real.

"I am telling you the truth," she once complained to a senior nun. But to no avail.

"Marguerite, there will be no mention of this, today. We have important visitors and your job is to serve the luncheon. Do you understand?" asked the senior nun.

The woman did not wait for a response and left the kitchen. Marguerite, still fuming, busied herself with preparations for the meal. The visitors, a delegation from the Ursuline convent in Quebec City, represented a separate and distinct Order, within the Catholic Church. Marguerite knew them well. As a former member of their community, she recognized the habits, but she did not recognize any of the attendees, including the newly installed Mother Superior. Mother Mary of the Nativity, the one person who could verify Marguerite's stories, retired or died. Marguerite did not know. And although questions about her former colleagues burned in Marguerite's mind, she said nothing. She finished her only task—to bring food to the table and clear the dirty dishes, in complete silence.

"The lunch was delicious, but I was hoping for a tarte made with eel meat," said one of the Ursulines, reaching for Marguerite, as she passed by with a full tray.

Marguerite stood motionless, staring at the Ursuline. The middle-aged nun looked familiar. Marguerite suddenly recognized the novitiate who worked in the Ursuline kitchen. The woman, now a full member of the Ursuline Order, grinned. The dishes on Marguerite's tray began to rattle, her eyes welled up, and her face blushed red.

"Sister Josephine," said Marguerite, smiling through her tears.

The other Ursuline nuns grinned, as the two old friends hugged and cried and hugged some more. The Gray nuns frowned their disapproval, viewing Marguerite's antics as inappropriate. When she noticed their obvious displeasure, Marguerite recovered and apologized.

"Please forgive me," she said, but tears of joy and a wide grin on her face, betrayed the woman's true feelings.

She did not suffer from insanity. The tragic memories of her horrible past were real. A lifetime of horror, love, violence, and tears, flashed before her eyes. She recalled everything with clarity, sadness, and joy. Sister Josephine and her tarte made with eel meat, triggered Marguerite's memories and proved her sanity. Marguerite decided she would leave the cloister.

CHAPTER ELEVEN

Searching

Antoine searched for Marguerite for months after her disappearance.

In the spring of 1766, he approached Moses Hazen.

"I've searched the countryside and most of the city. I fear she is dead," he reported to Hazen.

"Clearly, she lost her mind, after the death of your son," Hazen said.

"I have made a decision about the Seigneury," said Antoine, announcing that he wished to sell his portion of the land.

"Where will you go?" asked Hazen.

"Boston," said Antoine. "If there is a rebellion against the British, it will start there."

"You wish to be a soldier, once again?"

"I am not a farmer," said Antoine.

Hazen expressed frustration, with his own state of affairs, and recounted for Antoine a recent spate of legal problems plus his growing list of grievances with the British government.

"My own loyalties are very much in doubt," said Hazen.

Antoine, although sympathetic to the man, did not linger. He requested half of the proceeds from sale of the Seigneury, in advance.

"The remainder should be set aside in case she returns," said Antoine, biting his lip and looking away.

The political unrest in the American colonies worsened.

The Townshend Acts, implemented in November of 1767, taxed British china, glass, lead, paper, and, most importantly, tea—a common staple in most family's diet. A number of protests and a series of widely distributed circulars strongly urged the colonists to boycott all British goods. A secret society of American business leaders, the "Sons of Liberty," railed against "taxation without representation" and a general unrest spread through the colonies.

By 1769, the British installed more than 2000 troops in Boston, a town which contained no more than 16,000 people. In the spring of 1770, an angry mob confronted a handful of British troops. Before the night was over, five American colonists lay dead in the streets. The "Boston Massacre" inflamed the colonists like nothing before. In 1773, the Americans, dressed as Indians, dumped a shipload of British tea into the Boston Harbor. In September of 1774, the colonies organized and convened their first meeting of the Continental Congress.

Antoine Dauphin found work on the docks in Boston. As the years drifted by and the colonists grew more militant, his enmity for the British festered and grew larger in his mind and heart.

Armed conflict would be a welcome alternative to the mind-numbing work of a dockworker, he thought.

Flyers and literature from the American colonies covered the top of Moses Hazen's desk.

Before plowing into the pages of narrative, he took the precaution of locking the office door. It would not be good if word leaked that he read such stuff. In fact, he sympathized more and more with his fellow British subjects south of the borderline.

Several "Letters from a Farmer" caught Hazen's attention. They appeared in a number of colonial newspapers and the intent of the writer was clear. American colonists should boycott British goods and resist taxation without representation. He reached for a missive from the first Continental Congress to "the inhabitants of the province of Québec." A loud knock on the door forced Hazen to gather the documents into a disheveled heap and cover them, with several nearby ledgers. He scurried to the door and opened it.

"Mr. Hazen," said the red-haired woman.

Hazen did not immediately recognize Marguerite, her natural beauty partially hidden by the effects of age. His eyes grew wide.

"Mrs. Dauphin?" asked Hazen, opening the door and motioning the woman into the office chamber.

He locked the door behind them and gestured to a chair.

"The years have treated you well," Hazen lied.

In fact, the years that passed, since the death of her unborn child, appeared etched in the dark lines and wrinkles of Marguerite's once glowing face. Her red hair, now showing a tiny hint of gray, could not hide her gaunt frame or the wretched look, in her green eyes. Marguerite spoke in a barely audible voice, constantly stroking her locks to ensure that no one saw her hideous wound.

"Where have you been for all of these years?" Hazen asked.

Marguerite recounted the diagnosis of insanity and her years-long confinement at the Gray Nuns' cloister. She related the details of her chance encounter with the Ursuline novitiate, and the decision to strike out on her own, despite opposition from the Gray Nuns. She found work at a boarding house and managed to save some money.

"I have been, shall we say, indisposed, for a very long time. But my situation has changed and now I search for Adolphe Lezard," said Marguerite.

"The captain also searches, but without success," said Hazen.

Marguerite's head jerked up, her eyes wide and unblinking.

"You have heard from Antoine? I mean Mr. Dauphin,"

"You have not communicated with your . . . ?"

Hazen's inquiry trailed off into an awkward silence. Marguerite shook her head, blinking back tears. The woman blamed the entirety of her wrecked life on Lezard. She spoke in a whisper, as if to herself.

"Mr. Lezard is responsible for many, many scars, seen and unseen," said Marguerite.

"He travels between Quebec and the colonies, spying for the English governor. Your husband works on the docks in Boston," said Hazen.

Marguerite stared into space, her face betraying no emotion. Hazen paused for a moment and reached for a cubby hole in his desk.

"He instructed me to give you this," said Hazen, handing the women an envelope filled with English notes.

"It is your share of the proceeds from the sale of the homestead on the Richelieu," Hazen said.

She shoved the envelope into her tiny bag and rose to leave.

"Thank you. I must go now," said Marguerite.

Hazen's eyebrows arched, surprised by the brevity of their visit.

"Where will you go?" he asked.

"To the colonies. I will search for this devil in the colonies," said Marguerite.

Adolfe Lezard grinned, as he surveyed the trappings of his new office in Albany.

He misled all who would listen, into thinking that the British forced his exile to the colonies, because of his well-known connection to the corrupt French intendant. In fact, Lezard regularly informed his British friends about the activities of Albany's openly rebellious citizens. In return, the English secretly provided a "stipend," generous enough to convince the Albany business community that Lezard made his living as a successful trader of exotic goods.

In truth, he acted as a British spy. Albany, New York, now a patriot stronghold, served as home to several organized groups of rebels. Their central purpose was to resist the English and root out the King's Loyalists among them. These rebel groups openly demanded support for the Patriot cause and expected Loyalists to remain silent or risk punishment. Lezard reported to his British superiors in Boston, New York City, and Montréal, by correspondence and special messenger.

Unknown to Albany's patriot community, a traitor lived in their midst.

Antoine collapsed onto his cot.

The small room he rented, in a large, New England house, served as home, since his arrival in Boston years ago. As he lay there, waiting for sleep to conquer his tired frame, Antoine's thoughts drifted to the circumstances of his new life. He lived alone, with no woman to stop him from returning to the battlefield. When Marguerite's face appeared in his mind's eye, he grimaced but quickly moved on. Tomorrow, he would meet with the rebels and join their cause.

After a restless sleep, Antoine would once again, share a large breakfast table with British soldiers, quartered in the same house. They served as a reminder to him, that English interlopers destroyed his country and destroyed his life. He vowed revenge and anticipated, with joy, his meeting with the Sons of Liberty, that evening. Antoine heard a great deal about the patriot organization, many of the locals crediting the group with last December's "tea party," in Boston Harbor. As the spring of 1775 unfolded, talk of rebellion filled the air. New Englanders viewed the Redcoats with suspicion. Their distrust was mutual, and Antoine held similar views.

When Antoine entered the boardinghouse dining area, he noticed two British soldiers, finishing their breakfast. The Redcoats, aware that Antoine was bilingual, ended their discussion when he strode into the room. But not soon enough.

"I am surprised that His Majesty's officers have an interest in the Sons of Liberty," Antoine observed.

The slight smirk on his face disclosed the fact that Antoine overheard a significant portion of their conversation.

"And what would a Frenchman know about this organization of rebels?" asked one of the soldiers.

"They rebel against a tyrannical king, unreasonable taxes, and unreasonable men, occupying their homes," said Antoine.

One of the Redcoats slammed his fist on the table, rose from his chair, glaring at the tall Frenchman. The second soldier restrained him. Antoine did not flinch.

"This is not the time or the place," said the second man.

Antoine grinned his ridicule, stuffed a cornbread muffin into his coat pocket, and left.

Despite her generous offer of English currency, Marguerite could not persuade a trader, businessman, or even a guide, to escort her to the colonies.

No one wanted to assume the risk of a dangerous trip, made more dangerous, by the presence of a woman. As she traveled once again to the office of Moses Hazen, the still beautiful woman thought back to the nightmare of her last journey through the wilderness. She understood their reluctance.

"Mrs. Dauphin, I did not expect to see you again," said Hazen.

"I am desperate, Mr. Hazen. No one is willing to accompany me to the colonies," Marguerite complained.

Hazen stared in silence at the woman and rubbed his scraggly face.

"Mrs. Dauphin . . ."

His voice trailed off. Marguerite leaned forward in her chair.

"Yes, what is it? You have a solution?" she asked.

"I have business in Albany. You could travel with me if you wish. But you search for the needle in a very large haystack," he said.

Marguerite's full lips transformed into a snarl and her large green eyes narrowed to slits.

"I will find this devil as God is my witness," she said.

"Of this, I have no doubt," he said.

The Sons of Liberty could not disguise their surprise when Antoine Dauphin introduced himself.

The former soldier spoke the King's English, but a French accent remained.

"I served in the Royal Roussillon regiment, as a captain," Dauphin announced.

A half dozen colonials leaned forward.

"Were you at the Siege?" asked one.

"Yes, for the battle and the burial of *Mon Generale*," said Antoine, looking down at his mug of beer.

"But the British ordered all French officers back to France," said one man, a look of skepticism covering his face. The room grew eerily quiet.

"I did not come to your meeting because I obey the English king," said Antoine.

Antoine's reply generated a round of wry smiles and approving murmurs.

The patrons inched closer to hear what the Frenchman would say next. Antoine found himself surrounded by farmers, artisans, shopkeepers, dockworkers and schoolmasters. One man introduced himself as a Methodist minister. The former captain spoke openly of the British Army, their tactics, and the French Army's defeat. The colonists learned much from this displaced soul, even if he talked funny.

One patron recounted a speech delivered by Patrick Henry, a week earlier, at a church meeting in Richmond Virginia. "Give me liberty or give me death," fell off the lips of many, in the Green Dragon Tavern that evening. Their militancy grew with their consumption of alcohol. Most of the attendees agreed. The British would soon launch an attack on Boston.

The rebels intended to fight back.

"You are needed in Boston," said the governor's messenger. Adolphe Lezard, sitting behind his desk, stared in disbelief.

"But it is the governor who installed me here in Albany," Lezard complained.

"The king himself has declared the colony of Massachusetts to be in a state of rebellion. Shall I tell his Excellency you have refused his request?" said the soldier.

Lezard shook his head in dismay and tossed his writing quill onto the desk.

"I will leave for Boston as soon as possible," Lezard replied.

"Very well, then," said the emissary.

Lezard stood, his arms outstretched with palms up, and cleared his throat. The emissary stared, a confused look on his face.

"There will be extraordinary expenses, of course," said Lezard.

"That is of no concern to me," said the soldier, as he left the office chamber.

Hazen and Marguerite traveled by horse to the boundary line.

From there, with two guides, they traveled the length of Lake Champlain. As part of their week-long journey, the small group portaged the land bridge between Lake Champlain and Lac Sacrament, (Lake George), and used a flat-bottomed boat, (bateaux) to travel the Hudson River to Albany.

They moored at one of the city's newly built docks, near Patroon Street, the Northern boundary of Albany. It was a popular gathering spot for fur traders, Indians, and English soldiers. British troops regularly patrolled the docks, for obvious signs of rebellion against the king.

At an eatery near the water, Hazen inquired about rooms and a meal. The travelers, exhausted from their days-long journey, decided to stay at the recommended boarding house. They lingered in the dining room for a bite to eat. Two nearby English soldiers could be heard above the din, talking about a Frenchman.

"He does nothing for the money he receives," complained the taller man.

"Why do they pay him at all?" asked the second.

"He served in the French government at Québec. Claims to have rebel friends in the colonies. I don't believe it."

The taller soldier continued.

"No matter. I gave him the good news yesterday. His presence is requested in Boston. There he will work for his money or be killed by the rebels," said the soldier, a large grin crossing his face.

"Do I know this scoundrel?" asked the subordinate.

The taller man laughed.

"No, but you would remember him if you did. His face is badly scarred, and he is missing most of his right ear."

Marguerite rose from the table and rushed across the room where the two soldiers sat.

Hazen stopped her before the woman's intent became obvious.

"Marguerite, you cannot approach these men," said Hazen, his desperate whisper giving her pause.

"But they talk of the devil, Lezard," said Marguerite.

Hazen refused to comment and instead forcibly escorted the woman to the door. He did not stop until they stood outside. The cool of dusk had no effect on the hot-tempered woman.

"You are my guide not my guardian," said Marguerite, as she yanked her arm from Hazen's grip.

"They are British soldiers. One is an officer. You are a Frenchwoman. They will ask you many questions, perhaps even detain you. Are you mad?"

Marguerite focused on the door to the tavern. She shifted her gaze to Hazen.

"You are correct," she mumbled, trying hard to show remorse.

Hazen breathed a long sigh of relief.

"When we get to Boston, I will make inquiries," said Hazen.

Without resistance, she followed the man to their rooms.

Marguerite waited until Hazen's room grew quiet.

She slipped out of the building without a sound and hastened back to the eatery. Two empty tankards on the soldiers' table sent Marguerite back onto the street, searching in every direction. The filthy street, filled with neat homes shingled in white pine, also served as a pasture for the homeowners' cattle in the evening.

Marguerite, forced to traipse through the muck and mud, saw two men walking in the distance. They appeared to be wearing red uniforms. She ran as fast as she could and stopped yards before reaching them, to catch her breath. The two men appeared ready to enter a large home. Marguerite pretended to slip and fell to the ground. She screamed in fake agony. It worked.

The senior officer, a captain, arrived on the scene first.

"Madam, are you injured?" he asked. The private, a few steps behind his commanding officer, arrived afterwards.

"No, I am just a clumsy woman. Please forgive me," said Marguerite.

The captain studied the beautiful damsel in distress and quickly dismissed the junior officer.

"I will accompany the lady to her destination. You may take your leave, private," said the officer."

The younger man, unseen by his superior, rolled his eyes. Marguerite focused on her target and beamed.

"I am most fortunate to have you at my side, Captain," she said.

"You are French," said the captain.

"My husband, a British captain, was killed at the Siege. We were married for less than a month," she lied.

The officer brought Marguerite to her feet and, after a brief exchange of formalities, headed in the direction of Marguerite's boardinghouse. When Marguerite noticed a nearby tavern, she winced in pain and announced she felt woozy. The captain walked into the tavern and promptly ordered two measures of rum. His prescription worked. In a few hours, both the patient and the captain forgot about the injury.

Marguerite easily cajoled the officer into a discussion of the "man with one ear." She also learned the exact location of Lezard's office. Neither party referenced Lezard by name, making the interrogation seem more like a harmless discussion. The redheaded beauty invited the inebriated man to escort her back to Marguerite's boardinghouse. The officer now required her support to remain upright. When they arrived, he stumbled through the door and the two of them landed on her bed. She reached to remove her wrap, he pawed at her dress. She pulled his hands to her lips and softly excused herself.

"Please forgive me, my friend. I shall return momentarily, as I would like to make myself presentable," said Marguerite.

The man's eyes glazed over, an alcoholic stupor, only minutes away. Marguerite did not leave the building. She waited silently in the hallway. In moments, she heard the man's loud snoring, through the closed door. She reentered the chamber, retrieved her belongings, and went in search of a place to spend the evening—alone. The woman did not sleep for most of the night, however.

Her plans for Mr. Lezard did not allow such luxuries.

Moses Hazen, unable to rouse his beautiful traveling companion, took breakfast by himself.

He remembered to return with a few cornbread muffins. Marguerite, exhausted from her journey, needed nourishment, thought Hazen. Repeated knocks, with no results, forced Hazen to try the door. When it opened, he hesitated for several moments, and announced himself. He knocked yet again. Still, no response. Finally, Hazen entered the room, muttering his surprise, after a few steps.

"Damn," said Hazen.

On the bed, lay a British officer sleeping in his uniform. A stench of alcohol filled the room. He could see none of Marguerite's possessions. On a small chair, draped carefully as it should be, hung the captain's holster. Empty. Hazen studied the snoring man's unshaven face.

He recognized the captain as one of the two soldiers who knew Adolphe Lezard.

Marguerite observed Lezard's comings and goings for most of the next day, stopping only for the occasional cup of tea and the need to relieve herself.

In the late afternoon, her target emerged from the building, with a crate and several backpacks. She concluded that Lezard's departure for Boston was imminent. She followed her intended victim, maintaining a discreet distance between them. He entered a large boardinghouse but emerged moments later to greet a man on a horse. The rider pulled another horse behind him. She watched as the man surrendered the second horse to Lezard, who paid for the horse in paper currency. Lezard tethered the horse and returned to the boarding house. Marguerite slipped into a nearby alley, enjoying partial cover, from a small tree near the street. She intended to use its lowest branch to steady the British officer's pistol.

Lezard, fussing over his already saddled horse, prepared to leave. He checked the girth and his saddlebags one more time. Marguerite scowled and slowly raised the officer's sidearm to eye level. She waited for the man to mount, closed one eye, and pulled the hammer back. She exhaled and gently squeezed the trigger. Her eyes opened wide when the full effect of her errant shot became clear. The horse, a bullet in its side, began to stagger and wobble. Lezard whipped the animal with the bridle, in a desperate attempt to escape his intended assassin. The stricken horse fell to the ground, pinning Lezard between the animal and the hardscrabble road. Horse and rider flailed but neither creature could move.

Marguerite ran from her perch in the alleyway and hid behind a building. A British soldier came to Lezard's rescue and, with the aid of several bystanders, freed Lezard from beneath the dying animal.

"It was a lady who shot him. I saw her," shouted a young boy.

His mother immediately scolded the child and pulled him away from the small crowd gathered around Lezard. A second British soldier, the captain who Marguerite abandoned at the boarding house, stopped the mother and son. The boy quickly pointed in the direction of the alley. The captain ran the distance of the alleyway and spied Marguerite, as she darted from the rear of one building to the next.

"Stop or I'll shoot," he said, pointing his newly acquired pistol at the woman's back.

Marguerite stopped to face the captain. She offered no resistance, as the officer escorted her back to the scene of the shooting.

Lezard, pointed an accusing finger at Marguerite as he limped in circles.

"She tried to kill me. I want her hanged," he screamed.

The British captain and his assistant, with a firm hold on each of Marguerite's arms, marched her down the street.

Moses Hazen paced the floor in his room.

Every few minutes, he stopped, leaned out his open window, and surveyed the scene, on the street below. He paced some more. The entire city buzzed with the news that General Gage deployed hundreds of troops to the Boston suburbs of Lexington and Concord. The turmoil in Albany grew by the hour.

Hazen's half-packed bags sat on the bed as a visible reminder of the indecision which plagued him. The situation could worsen and war between the colonists and the British might soon break out. He seriously considered the possibility of joining the colonists. Hazen objected to heavy handed British rule and their onerous taxation. On the other hand, his significant holdings in Canada, his indebtedness to the Englishman, Christie, and his financial dealings with the British, all required that he support His Majesty's government.

The street below now had a half-dozen small crowds of both men and women, informed only by rumors, innuendo, and the occasional "eyewitness" testimony. He even heard a gun go off. The locals talked loudly of rebellion and war. Several expressed their intention to go to Boston. Hazen shook his head and decided the chaos below did not bode well for the colonists or his business interests. He finished the packing, paid his host, and arranged for transportation back to the boundary line.

Marguerite, nowhere to be found, would have to manage for herself.

CHAPTER TWELVE

Prison

"The man you almost killed works for his Majesty's government," said the captain.

Marguerite struggled with the chain and iron manacle which tethered her left wrist to the leg of a large desk. The younger soldier, once again dismissed by his superior, left in search of their commander for instructions. Marguerite showed no remorse for her attack.

"He tried to rape me and then he tried to kill me, said Marguerite.

The captain snapped his head in the woman's direction, a puzzled look in his eyes.

"You know Lezard?" he asked.

"Yes," she said.

Marguerite described her short stint with the Ursuline nuns, Lezard's attack on the *Leopard*, and her rescue by Antoine Dauphin. When she described the knife attack, Marguerite pulled at her long hair and exposed the missing ear. The captain flinched and closed his eyes. As she repositioned her hair, the captain spoke in a barely audible voice.

"I rescued a man who deserves to die," said the captain.

He sauntered over to Marguerite, key in hand.

"I am Captain Charles Harrington and I am truly sorry."

"Marguerite Valtesse, and I too am sorry for the trouble I have caused."

You must promise not to escape," he said, releasing her from the manacle.

Marguerite, her face still pink from the humiliation of exposing her wound, nodded her ascent.

"You used me to get to Lezard. But is not for you or me to decide his fate," said the flustered captain.

Marguerite reached for both of his hands, holding them close to her chest.

"You must let me go. I will do anything you ask," she said.

She paused and whispered a single word.

"Anything."

For a moment, the captain froze in place, temporarily hypnotized by her fragrant, red hair and still beautiful face.

She looked up; her lips enticingly close to his. A loud slam of the office door announced the young officer's return. The captain and Marguerite, angry about the interruption, scowled at the inexperienced private.

"The commander says, 'lock her up,' announced the intruder."

The captain reached for the key and manacled Marguerite for the second time. She offered no resistance.

"I will bring you something to eat," said the captain, his tone, soft and apologetic.

"Why, thank you, Captain," said the junior officer.

"I wasn't talking to you," fumed the captain, as he charged out the door.

Antoine, roused by daylight streaming through the single window in his bed chamber, could hear people talking on the street below.

The sound of horses' hooves rushing by and the creak of wagon wheels, lots of them, caught his attention. He dressed quickly and searched for answers, in the boardinghouse dining room.

"Something has happened?" he asked.

Several boarders related the story in hushed and hurried tones. British Regulars crossed the Charles River last night. According to the locals, they marched to Lexington and Concord. The news came as a surprise to Antoine and he wondered if his new-found friends, in the Sons of Liberty, forgot their French-Canadian comrade.

Antoine returned to the Green Dragon Tavern, in the heart of Boston, in search of the men he encountered a few nights ago. An old man, by himself and cleaning the tables, greeted Antoine's entrance with a quick nod of the head.

"Where is everybody?" asked Antoine.

"Dozens of them have left for Lexington. Others have gone to their farms to prepare," said the old man.

"Prepare for what?" asked Antoine.

"The British attacked at Lexington and Concord, said the old man. "The war has begun."

Antoine, angry he missed the first battle in the American rebellion, headed to the docks. He needed time to clear his head and calculate the precise way in which he would support the rebel cause. He desperately wanted to fight the British, once again. But a former officer in the French Army may or may not be welcomed into the Patriot Army, he thought. There had to be a way.

The docks, strangely bereft of men, matched the harbor—empty except for one ship. The ship reminded him of the *Leopard*; it was especially old and decrepit.

"You are not permitted here," barked a male voice.

The order came from one of two British Regulars, patrolling the docks.

"I work here," said Antoine.

"Not anymore," said the Redcoat.

"I do not take orders from British soldiers," said Antoine, brushing his way past the two men.

"Halt or I will shoot," said the soldier.

Antoine ignored the order. Perhaps he secretly wanted them to shoot. His life as a soldier without an army made him miserable. And, for reasons he did not fully understand, Marguerite lingered in his mind and haunted him almost every day.

The soldiers charged after Antoine. He turned to engage his attackers, but one of them struck the Frenchman from behind. Antoine fell to the dock, bleeding from a large gash, in the back of his head.

His eyes fluttered and everything went black.

Four stonewalls and a thick, wooden door, with a small barred opening, greeted Antoine, when he regained consciousness.

He shouted for a guard, but the only response came from an inmate, in a nearby cell.

"Shut up. I'm trying to sleep," said the prisoner.

Hours later, a guard appeared, tossing a stale piece of bread thru the opening.

"Here," said the jailer, offering Antoine a pewter cup filled with dark, smelly water.

Antoine, ravenous, shoved the entire piece of bread in his mouth and swallowed the liquid in two gulps.

He drifted off to sleep shortly after his meal of bread and water. The guard interrupted the prisoner's nap.

"You are free to leave," said the British sentry.

Antoine took a sharp breath and jumped to his feet.

"And leave I will," he said, brushing past the guard and through the door.

"But I must ask, who or what is responsible for my freedom?" asked Antoine.

"All available men are being ordered to Bunker Hill," said the soldier.

Antoine concluded that another confrontation between the Rebels and the British might soon take place.

"If the British were victorious at Lexington and Concord, why would they gather at Bunker Hill?" asked Antoine.

The young militiamen pursed his lips, shook his head, and refused to respond.

Antoine, about to leave, stopped to face the lone guard.

"I am in need of a horse," said Antoine.

"I can't help you," said the guard.

"Is your horse for sale?" asked Antoine.

"No, sir."

"I will pay you well," Antoine said.

He reached into his trousers and pulled out a wad of English notes. Antoine counted out loud, struggling with numbers in English, as he placed each note on the desk in front of the private. The sentry gasped his surprise. The stack of notes represented much more than the soldier's horse could possibly be worth. The young soldier focused on the money. Antoine focused on the young soldier. The sentry blinked several times and then scooped up the money.

"Thank you, private. Thank you very much."

Marguerite smiled when the British captain returned, with a cloth covered basket.

She quickly swallowed the warm soup and tore at the piece of bread. She also drank water from the soldier's flask. The captain studied his beautiful prisoner as she ate. Marguerite smothered a burp and thanked her captor.

"Thank you, Captain Harrington. You are most kind," she said.

The younger officer echoed her words; a sarcastic smirk on his face.

"Yes, Captain, that was most gracious indeed," he said.

Harrington flashed a dirty look and growled.

"Go and get something to eat," he said.

The subordinate scurried from the room.

"You have been most gracious, my friend," she said.

"A jail is no place for a woman," said the captain.

"What will you do with me?" asked Marguerite.

"I am quartered in a large home near the Charles," he said.

"Is that an invitation, Captain Harrington?" she asked, batting her eyelids.

The officer blinked and looked down, partially hiding his pink face. When he recovered, he stepped in Marguerite's direction, his hands now gripping her shoulders.

"You will not leave me as you did before," said the captain, "Is that understood?"

"No, I will not," said Marguerite, her eyes downcast.

"What do you mean she is gone?" asked Adolphe Lezard.

Lezard's disfigured face grew red with rage. The flustered guard at the Albany jail, cleared his throat and stared at Lezard, visibly transfixed by the Frenchman's scars and missing ear.

"I'm sorry, Mr. Lezard, you will have to speak to Captain Harrington," said the British regular.

"And where, may I ask, is your incompetent Captain Harrington?" asked Lezard, through clenched teeth.

"I am sorry, Mr. Lezard, the entire army has been ordered to vacate. I do not know where the Captain is staying. He too will be ordered to leave."

Lezard flew into a rage, grabbing an inkwell off the desk and throwing it at the guard.

"She killed my horse and she nearly killed me. I demand justice," he shouted.

The British soldier, his face speckled with ink, shoved Lezard to the door.

"You will leave now, Mr. Lezard, or it is you who will face British justice."

CHAPTER THIRTEEN

Spying

Marguerite, still in bed with only a nightdress to cover her, watched as the British captain dressed.

She learned that her new paramour received orders in the middle of the night, to proceed to Boston, as soon as practical. A messenger knocked on the couple's door, forcing Harrington into the hallway, wearing nothing but his trousers. Although he shut the door, less Marguerite be seen, she rushed from the bed to hear the conversation. When Harrington informed her of his new assignment, she pressed him for details.

"When will you return?"

"I don't know," said the captain.

Marguerite's tryst secured her release. But now, she contemplated something more. If Lezard attached himself to the British Command, she might be able to find him. And a recklessly friendly captain in the British Army could prove useful to the rebel cause, she calculated. Marguerite dismissed a sudden pang of guilt, justifying her illicit activity as necessary and proper, given her self-assigned missions.

He returned to the bed and kissed her on the lips. She clung to him.

"I will accompany you to Boston," she purred.

"That is not possible," he replied, and pulled away.

"Please?"

In fact, the British army regularly supported "camp followers." But the married captain did not wish to advertise a French mistress to his brethren in the military. He stepped to the door.

"There are less than a dozen of us left here in Albany. We all go to Boston," said Harrington.

Marguerite ran to Harrington, cupped his head in her hands, and kissed him on the lips, with all the passion she could muster. When she released him, the look on Harrington's face told Marguerite that the man's lust easily overpowered his military discipline.

"I'm begging you, Captain Harrington," she said, reaching between his legs.

Harrington took a deep breath, unaccustomed to such aggressive behavior.

"Very well. We leave for Boston in two days," he said.

She nodded. They kissed once more.

"Couldn't we pack our things tomorrow," she asked, as she slipped the night dress from her shoulders and stood nude before the captain.

Harrington fumbled with the buttons on his jacket.

Antoine guided his expensive horse down a side street.

His plan, to join the colonists at Bunker Hill, seemed thwarted at every turn. British soldiers patrolled the streets of Boston and hundreds more quartered, in the homes of colonists. Antoine, certain they all stared at him, returned to his boarding house. He packed his few belongings, waited until sunset, and returned to the Green Dragon tavern. The building, empty of its usual customers, meant that Boston's colonists now prepared for a large-scale battle. Some of them evacuated the city, but a number of men stayed behind, intent on joining the fight. Antoine used the alley ways and empty backstreets to make his escape, from the mostly British-controlled waterfront. He slowly made his way to the Heights. Antoine could see feverish activity on Bunker Hill and nearby Breed's Hill.

The colonists like so many ants in the dirt erected barricades against the expected British onslaught.

Marguerite, now in Boston, spent most of her days at a boardinghouse on the waterfront.

She rarely saw Captain Harrington and decided to venture from her bedchamber, choosing a moonlit evening to do so. The British gathered at the east end of the city and the colonists occupied recently fortified positions in the south, north, and west side, of Boston proper. She wandered the city streets and alleyways unmolested, as large portions of the city stood vacant. After a series of inquiries, Marguerite managed to locate the tent which Harrington occupied.

"What are you doing here?"

The Captain, clearly irritated by Marguerite's unexpected, late night visit, forcibly marched her to the street.

"Captain Harrington, is this any way to treat your lover?" Marguerite asked, allowing her lower lip to protrude. The Captain grabbed the woman's arm and walked further away from his quarters, looking around as he did so.

"Marguerite, this is no place for a lady, please go back to the boardinghouse. You'll be safe there," said Harrington.

"Why can't I stay here? There are British troops everywhere. Surely, I will be safe," she cooed.

"Yes, and soon there will be more," he said, his head swiveling to ensure no one could hear their conversation.

Marguerite's mind raced. Her lover knew something. Something important. She faked her acquiescence to his demand.

"Okay, I shall leave. But when will you leave this forsaken place?" she asked.

Harrington surveyed his surroundings once more. He spoke in a hushed toned.

"I promise you, this will all be over in a matter of days. I will see you when it is finished," he said.

"Why? Tell me what you know," she said.

He shook his head and glared at the woman.

"Go! Now," he yelled.

She gave him a perfunctory kiss on the cheek and left.

Marguerite, determined to learn more and to contact the rebel command, devoted entire days to the streets of Boston.

As she explored the busy pathways, clogged with marching soldiers, horses, and wagons, the details of her previous life, returned with a vengeance. The voice, which narrated her checkered past, showed neither mercy nor understanding, and condemned her at every street corner.

The innocent Ursuline nun, of long ago, had become a harlot. Sister Marguerite's charm and grace disappeared behind a cold and calculating mask of cunning machinations, blind vengeance, and murderous intent. She lied constantly, stole occasionally, and regularly used her God-given charm and beauty, to ruthlessly manipulate everyone with whom she came in contact, including the kind-hearted Captain Harrington. She abandoned her lawfully wedded husband and selfishly spurned his loving attempts to lessen her emotional burdens. The former religious, had single-handedly smashed the tablets on which the Ten Commandments were inscribed. Worse, she had replaced them with a twisted version of God's proscription.

"Vengeance is mine saith Marguerite Valtesse."

But the ugly details of Marguerite's life story, did nothing to thwart her plans. She intended to find Lezard and kill him. She also hoped to inflict as much damage on the British Army, as possible.

The fact that she shared quarters with a British officer, allowed her access to places where most colonists could not go. Her natural beauty and her beguiling ways made it easy to charm a sentry, mentally disarm an officer, or enter a popular tavern patronized by British soldiers. She searched for anything that might lead to her quarry–Adolphe Lezard. She also took mental notes of the British military presence and activities. She intended to transmit the information to the American Army, her contempt for the British almost as virulent as her hatred for Lezard.

Marguerite noted a significant increase in activity at Long Dock and in the harbor, but she needed details. A precise location for British headquarters would be especially helpful. The Colonial army would like that, she thought. And, not coincidentally, Adolphe Lezard would likely be nearby. A tavern, not too far from the waterfront, gave her the opportunity she desired.

"You do not belong here," said a British lieutenant, as Marguerite did her best to look lost and confused.

"Me, I wish you to pardon," she whispered, faking her lack of skill with the English language.

The officer grabbed her arm, ready to escort Marguerite from the tavern.

"Me, I am lost," she said, clutching the man's arm and bringing her face provocatively close to his.

The young soldier relented and questioned her, wanting to

know where she lived. She intentionally misdirected him.

"Thirsty. *Si vous plait.* Please?" she asked and mimicked a drink from an imaginary glass.

The young officer, persuaded by her fragrant beauty, summoned a glass of water and showed Marguerite to an empty table. He chose a less crowded corner of the tavern.

"What is your name, Madam?" he asked.

Marguerite deliberately hesitated before she answered, arching her eyebrows for effect and looking questioningly at the man.

"Name? Yes. Name is Catherine," she said.

"Drink some water, Catherine. We will rest and then I will bring you home," he said.

In time, Marguerite's broken English improved, and the officer's initial resistance disappeared. While he chattered away, she could hear several conversations about a General Howe. Marguerite played dumb.

"You are general, yes?" she asked.

The lieutenant flashed a big grin, clearly flattered at the suggestion.

"No, not yet. But my commanding officer is a general," said the soldier, and he went on to explain that he served with the Marines.

"Marine? What is that?" she asked.

The compliant Englishman ordered more beer and more water. He disclosed that a large number of British reinforcements, recently arrived, would defeat the rebels. He served under General Burgoyne and offered a confident prediction.

"The rebels will soon be forced back into the hills from whence they came," he grinned.

Marguerite's eyes fluttered as she rested her head on the man's shoulder.

"*Je suis fatigue,*" she said.

He understood and immediately stood up. After a half-hour of wandering, Marguerite spied a street, with many large houses. She caught the soldier by surprise.

"*Voila! Ma maison,*" she yelled, and pointed to the end of the street.

Before the soldier had time to respond, she thanked him and kissed him on both cheeks.

"*Merci, merci, merci.*" she giggled, prancing down the street, looking back and waving her gloved hand. "*Au revoir,*" she said, waving her hand one last time.

It worked. He did not follow her.

Adolphe Lezard wandered from tent to building to boat and looked for an opportunity to ingratiate himself with British officers.

But the Redcoats, officers and regulars alike, hurried in every direction. Lezard interpreted the activity as a sure sign the British planned to attack the rebels.

"Lieutenant, where is your regiment moving to?" asked Lezard.

It was a stupid question to ask at a time when tensions ran high. And even the lieutenant looked askance. The cherub-faced officer stared suspiciously at Lezard's scarred face. He grew more skeptical when the man's French accent became obvious.

"My captain is over there, said the officer, pointing to a large tent.

Lezard strode into the canvas shelter, not bothering to announce himself.

"Captain, my name is Adolphe . . ."

Lezard's voice trailed off and his face blanched white. He stood yards from Captain Charles Harrington.

"I should run you through with my sword," said the Captain, scowling at the little man in front of him.

"Captain, I have done nothing wrong. She shot at me," Lezard said, but his voice shook with fear.

Harrington drew his sword.

"You attacked this woman, not once, but twice. She showed me the scars of your murderous intent. If I was not preoccupied with more important duties, I would see you hung by the neck, until dead. As it is, I have a war to fight. Now, get out," said the Captain, thrusting his sword to within inches of Lezard's heaving chest.

Lezard scampered to the opening but dared to stop and turn.

"Captain, I have information about the rebels. Surely you can put aside our differences, in the service of His Majesty, King George," said Lezard.

Harrington hesitated and lowered his sword.

"Speak," said Harrington.

"The rebels have gathered in Cambridge," Lezard said.

Harrington jerked his sword up and rested the sharp tip on Lezard's bobbing, Adam's apple.

"You tell me what we already know," he said, through clenched teeth.

"They are reinforcing the Heights," said Lezard.

Harrington moved his sword, using its flat side, to repeatedly tap Lezard's shoulder, as if conferring a knighthood. Sweat matted the hair on Lezard's scalp.

"How do you know this?"

"Breed's Hill. They work as I speak. And I know this because the rebels drink too much," said Lezard.

Harrington stepped back and lowered his blade.

"Why there? Why now?"

"They wish to prepare for your attack," said Lezard.

"How do they know we intend to attack?" asked Harringtom.

"They too have spies, *Mon Capitain*," said Lezard.

"I will inform the general. You may leave."

"You will give General Burgoyne and General Howe, my

182

regards?" asked Lezard.

Harrington looked askance and his eyes narrowed.

"You know them?"

"Well, not exactly, Captain, but I wish to know them."

"Leave and don't come back," said Harrington.

A knock at the door sent Marguerite flying from her bed chamber chair.

She flung the door open and threw her arms around Captain Harrington's neck. He forcefully removed them.

"Marguerite, I have only a moment," he said, unsmiling and obviously worried.

"But I have not seen you in two days," she cried.

"We attack in two days. And you should know that your friend is still looking for you," he said.

Marguerite grew silent and stepped back from the captain, pulling at her hair with both hands.

"You spoke with Lezard? Where is he?" she asked.

"He found me at our camp on the harbor. I do not know where he lives," said Harrington.

"I shall go to your camp," she announced.

The captain grabbed her by the shoulders and shook her, but only once.

"No, you will not. You will remain here. The real fighting will start soon. It begins on the Heights, but who knows where it will end," he said.

"And you? Where will you be?" she asked.

"We cross the harbor in two days. Moulton's Point. More than a thousand regulars," he reported.

Marguerite looked down, pretending to worry about the captain but secretly grateful she now knew Lezard's whereabouts. And the plans of British generals.

"Go with God," she said, kissing the captain on his lips.

He kissed her hands and shut the door behind him.

Marguerite walked the short distance from her boarding house to Cambridge Street.

Although repeatedly stopped by British soldiers, she soon stood on the banks of Charles River Bay. Marguerite scanned the horizon for a ferry, a whale boat, or even a rowboat that would deliver her to Cambridge where most of the patriot army now encamped. She approached the barge owner who carried mostly farm animals, back and forth, over the water.

For a smile and a single note, he became Marguerite's water taxi. Across the bay, Cambridge buzzed like a beehive, in the summer. The woman hastened to a gathering of officers near a large tent, raising eyebrows as she did so.

"I must speak to the general, at once," she said.

The officers and their aides greeted her demand with laughter.

"We have only colonels here. Now run along and leave us be," said a lieutenant.

Marguerite approached the officer, a bit shorter than Marguerite and, perhaps, half her age. She slapped him hard on the face. He stepped back, stumbled, and fell to the ground, stunned by the unexpected blow. The men who witnessed the assault laughed and pointed at the hapless soldier. The young officer blushed a deep shade of red and struggled to his feet.

"You will show me to your commanding officer, at once," said Marguerite, with her finger pointed at the young officer, like the barrel of a gun.

"General Putnam is not here, at the moment. I am Colonel William Prescott."

The deep voice came from behind her and forced Marguerite to swivel in the man's direction. He stood tall, even with his hat in hand, gaunt in his appearance but with a full head of jet-black hair. Marguerite recognized the calm and experienced look in Prescott's eyes. Antoine wore the same look.

"May we speak in private?" she asked.

The Colonel showed her into the tent and offered a chair. Marguerite declined, choosing instead to immediately relate what she had learned from Captain Harrington.

"These have been the rumors. How can you be so sure?" he asked.

"I learned this from a captain in the British Army," she said.

"And why would he disclose this information to a woman?"

Marguerite fixated on the canvas wall behind the colonel. She instinctively reached to ensure her hair covered the hideous wound where her ear used to be. She thought of Antoine, blinked, and took a deep breath.

"We are lovers."

The Colonel welcomed a return visit and promised a friendlier reception.

CHAPTER FOURTEEN

Casualties of War

A blade of light cut through the early morning sky as Captain Harrington stirred in his cot.

Seconds later, the loud explosions of a ship's cannon, sent the man running onto the cold, wet ground outside his tent. The twenty guns on board the British ship, HMS *Lively*, aimed at the Heights in Boston, woke everyone in the British camp.

A hastily called Council of War, at which Harrington listened but did not speak, announced shocking news. The rebels secretly constructed a redoubt on Breed's Hill. The small rectangular fort, no more than eight feet wide but 165 feet long, included six-foot-high earthen walls. The structure prompted the *Lively* to open fire. Harrington assumed he and his men would soon see the redoubt, up close.

Despite intentions to immediately launch an attack, Harrington and his men did not reach the other side of the bay, until two that afternoon. The captain did not respond directly to the soldiers' complaints, shaking his head instead and wondering, if the delay could be blamed on the tide or his commanding officers, or both.

"We're here now," he said to the men. "Get ready."

Harrington's men, a small part of the 1500 British troops now prepared to attack the rebels, hurried into position. They waited another hour, before an order to charge the hill finally sounded. The captain planned to charge the redoubt and engage the enemy in hand-to-hand combat when the rebels paused to reload. Their overwhelming numbers made a British victory almost certain.

The Redcoats moved in no particular hurry, up the hill. Harrington frowned, wondering why the rebels had yet to open fire. When he and his comrades in arms stood no more than thirty yards from the enemy fortifications, the rebels responded. Dozens of British soldiers fell and disappeared into the tall grass.

"Hold the line," shouted Harrington, tripping over crumpled heaps of writhing men, many of them screaming in agony.

The blaze of grapeshot and lead projectiles did not cease, even for a moment. As Harrington and his men retreated, struggling to regroup, the wisdom of the rebels became obvious. The colonists fired in shifts so as to deny the Redcoats even a brief opportunity to charge the redoubts.

When British Regulars charged the hill for a second time, their efforts produced similar results. When Harrington ordered the men to regroup, yet again, his booming voice disappeared into a scream of pain. He fell forward into the long grass, now streaked with the blood of his colleagues.

"Captain, your leg," said a private, mesmerized by the site of Harrington's blood spurting in an arc, a foot above the ground.

The captain, laying in the grass and propped up on his elbows, studied his left leg. Below the knee and above his ankle lay a mass of muscle, tendons, shattered bone, and blood—lots of blood.

"Help me get up," said Harrington, after fashioning a makeshift tourniquet, from the leather strap which held his sidearm.

As the soldier stepped closer, arms outstretched, the young man's head exploded. The captain's would-be savior lay motionless at Harrington's feet, most of the boy's head, now on Harrington's lap. The captain gagged as he pushed the bloody mess to one side and began a slow crawl to the bottom of Breed's Hill. He stopped at one point, to watch the Redcoats make their third charge. Fewer Redcoats fell wounded. The long, red line marched closer and closer to the enemy's fortifications. The rebels now fired intermittently. He crawled a bit more, surrounded by the sound of metal against metal, rifle butts smashing into bare heads, and the agonizing screams of men in mortal combat. As Harrington lay on his back, staring at a bright blue sky, he watched as the occasional puffy cloud drifted by.

He winced in pain, his eyes opened wide, and then, darkness.

"Captain Harrington requests your presence."

The knock and voice at Marguerite's door, came from a young private. The soldier struggled to catch his breath and his uniform appeared dirtied and bloodied. A grime of black powder covered his face, evidence that he had repeatedly fired his flintlock rifle, that morning.

"Is he hurt?" Marguerite asked.

"My orders are to escort you to the hospital tent," said the young man, explaining that Harrington lay wounded.

After a ride made longer by her imagination and two passengers on a single old mare, the red-haired woman surveyed the horrific scene of wounded and dying men. She hurried down the center aisle, her head swiveling, as she studied each pain filled face. She searched the mass of bleeding bodies for Captain Harrington. Most of the wounded lay on the ground, some with blankets, but many shivering in the cool air of a Boston evening.

"Marguerite."

The weak voice came from behind. She barely recognized the captain, his leg wrapped in a crude bandage, cut from a uniform, dyed red with blood. Harrington's face, black with dirt and gun powder, partially hid the officer's pain and suffering. Marguerite fell to her knees and the Ursuline nun of long ago, reappeared. She did as she was trained to do, in silence, while her patient mumbled words she could not understand. Marguerite refused to let her face betray the man's fate. It was the Ursuline way.

The captain's lower leg was destroyed and needed to be removed.

"You have done this before," said the surgeon, noticing the woman's handiwork.

Marguerite nodded. The patient, now clean and properly bandaged, continued to grimace in pain, as Marguerite exposed his wounds to the doctor.

"We don't have a choice," said the surgeon.

Marguerite nodded her agreement.

Harrington looked at the doctor and Marguerite, shaking his head and waving both hands.

"No. Please. No," he begged, through clenched teeth.

No one said a word, as the helpless man writhed in pain. Several attendants brought the captain to the operating table. One of them reached for some leathers with buckles. Marguerite strapped her struggling lover to the wooden slab and pulled on the leather as much as she could. Harrington winced and screamed his objections. She gave him a small shot of spirits. He cursed her and spit it out. She placed a well-worn, cigar-shaped piece of wood in his mouth but that too, he refused. Harrington shook his head and continued to writhe and squirm, trapped under the leather straps. Marguerite retrieved the wooden pacifier.

"Bite down as hard as you can," she instructed. "It will reduce the pain," Marguerite lied.

When the surgeon's scalpel cut an oozing red line into the flesh above Harrington's knee, the officer groaned. When the carpenter's saw began its work, the Captain screamed. As the teeth on the saw sliced into marrow, Harrington's teeth ground into the wood. The surgeon stopped briefly to verify his progress. Marguerite brushed away the bone dust and the surgeon resumed his work. The wooden cigar in the patient's mouth, fell to the floor. Harrington passed out. Marguerite and the surgeon breathed a sigh of relief and returned to their task. In less than two minutes, the surgery ended. The sound of lifeless flesh banging against a barrel filled with severed limbs, reminded Marguerite of wars past. She watched as the surgeon folded two flaps of skin over the open wound and sutured them in place.

Harrington's eyes remained closed.

Marguerite remained in the hospital tent, initially to administer to Captain Harrington.

When he slept, however, she wandered the aisleway and assisted when and where she could. She recruited a Surgeon's Mate, Benjamin, to assist with the heavy lifting and, at times, the restraint of patients who spasmed in pain. The young and inexperienced orderly watched in awe as the woman visited patient after patient, ministering to their wounds. When her limited supply of rum ran out, she offered words of comfort. Many of the men, spellbound by her beauty and angelic voice, struggled through their pain, anxious to please their beautiful caretaker.

Benjamin watched as she knelt by a patient and closed her eyes. When he realized she slept rather than prayed, he summoned several attendants and escorted the exhausted woman to a nearby cot.

Marguerite said nothing and, within minutes, fell into a deep sleep.

"The lieutenant-colonel will see you, now," said the sentry.

"Mr. Lezard, I am a busy man," said the officer.

George Clark, Commander of British troops, studied his unexpected visitor. The scarred face and missing ear prevented him from responding immediately to Lezard's self-introduction.

"Excuse me?" he said.

Lezard repeated himself.

"Ah, yes. Harrington mentioned your fay, I mean name," said Clark, blushing.

"Lieutenant-Colonel, I merely wish to congratulate you on your hard-fought victory at Bunker Hill," said Lezard, bowing his compliments.

"A few more victories like yesterday and His Majesty's army will cease to exist".

"The rebels got lucky," said Lezard, his voice oozing with gratuitous praise.

"No, they were clever and conniving," said the officer. Clark groused about the overnight construction of a redoubt, the late arrival of English troops, and the "ungentlemanly" manner, in which the colonial soldiers met their enemy, refusing to fight the British face-to-face.

"I will endeavor to keep you better informed as to their activities," said Lezard.

"You are a Frenchman, yes?" asked the Lieutenant Colonel.

"Yes, and I pass easily into their camps," said Lezard.

"And why do you help the British?" asked the officer.

"The French government treated me poorly after their defeat at Quebec," said Lezard, pointing to his face.

"Very well then, I will expect regular briefings," said Clark, avoiding Lezard's disfigured appearance.

"Of course," said Lezard, choosing another time to discuss his compensation.

"You are feeling better, *Mon Capitaine*," said Marguerite.

Captain Harrington focused on the single foot that made a small tent, in his woolen blanket. His angry eyes flashed in Marguerite's direction.

"You let them do this to me," he snarled.

The Ursuline nun, still hiding in Marguerite, suddenly reappeared.

"Don't be a fool. The surgeon saved your life," she said.

"What kind of life is that, Marguerite? I am a crippled soldier," Harrington muttered.

"Excuse me, madam, the surgeon is asking for you," said Benjamin.

"I have to leave," she said to her lover.

Lezard searched for the hospital tent.

Several officers suffered wounds, during the battle at Breed's Hill and Bunker Hill. It occurred to the cold and calculating Frenchman, that a kind word and, perhaps a drink from his rum-filled flask, would pay great dividends. If the officers did not recover from their wounds, Lezard would be out a swallow of rum. If the patient survived, Lezard will have recruited a few more friends within the British high command.

As he wandered the aisleway in the center of the canvas hospital, Lezard deliberately ignored the men who could not speak or appeared unlikely to survive. He managed only one conversation with an officer, a captain, and continued his search for more. Unfortunately, the highest-ranking officers rarely led their troops into battle and few of them suffered wounds.

As he turned to leave, Lezard caught a glimpse of the operating table, located in the far corner of the tent. The sound and sight of a patient undergoing an amputation did not appeal to Lezard. He stopped in mid-turn, however, when he spied the surgeon's female assistant and her long, red hair. Lezard swallowed hard and blinked, to confirm what he had seen.

"We meet again, Sister Marguerite."

"I pray for death."

Captain Harrington refused to leave the boardinghouse for weeks at a time. He announced his depression to Marguerite, as the exhausted woman staggered through the door of their bedchamber.

"I will soon kill you myself," she replied, falling into an overstuffed chair and glaring at her lover, as he sat in their bed rubbing his stump.

"You do not understand. I am a man no longer. I am a useless cripple," he said.

"Have I not cared for you and loved you and fed you and bathed you?" she asked.

He looked down and away.

"Yes," he murmured.

"Your comrades in the hospital tent are dying. They surrender much more than a leg. You are fortunate to be alive," she said.

Marguerite groaned when she rose from the chair. Every muscle in her body ached from overuse and lack of rest. She stumbled to the edge of their bed and reached for her lover's hand. He jerked his arm away and pulled the covers tight to his chest. His other hand lay hidden beneath the covers.

"Does the Captain wish for me to show him my love?" she

whispered.

Harrington's right arm moved. From underneath the blanket, he pulled a sidearm and wrapped his lips around the cold, steel barrel. Marguerite's mouth opened but the words did not come. She jumped from the bed and stepped back.

"What are you doing? Please. Put the gun down. I'm begging you," she cried.

Harrington's eyes grew wide. Marguerite spun and reached for the door. He pulled the hammer back. She heard the familiar click and squeezed her eyes shut. When Marguerite heard the explosion, she fell to her knees in the open doorway. She covered her face and sobbed into her hands, unable to turn her head and confirm what she already knew. A boarder in the room down the hall, came running. He surveyed the scene and pulled Marguerite to her feet, pushing her to one side and stepping into the room to close the door. Marguerite did what she didn't want to do. She peered into the open doorway. Chunks of blood-soaked brain matter and pieces of bone covered the far wall. The headboard supported Harrington's lifeless skull and he wore a blank stare.

His dilated pupils seemed to rest on Marguerite.

CHAPTER FIFTEEN

Hunter and Hunted

Adolphe Lezard hid behind rows of spectators as the new commander of American forces rode into the rebel camp at Cambridge.

He chose not to participate in the warm welcome given to General George Washington and slipped away, as soldiers and citizens alike greeted their new leader. The French traitor traveled back to the Long Wharf, noting with pleasure that British positions on Bunker Hill, Breed's Hill, and the Charlestown Peninsula now appeared visibly reinforced. The American loss of those strategic posts made Lezard happy and confirmed the wisdom of his decision to work for His Majesty's militia.

General Howe paced the floor and gestured wildly with his arms.

"Those rebel bastards killed or wounded half of my men," he complained.

Lezard chose his words carefully, ignoring the fact that British losses would be significantly less, had a frontal attack on rebel positions been avoided.

"The city is practically yours, *Mon Générale*. There is much to celebrate," said Lezard, hoping to placate the British officer.

Howe stopped and pivoted on one heel.

"You have word from their headquarters?" Howe asked.

"Their new commander has arrived. Washington," said Lezard.

"I recall the name. The French Army defeated this man on several occasions," said Howe.

"Oui, Mon Générale. And now His Majesty's army will do the same," said Lezard.

"We cannot attack with only 10,000 men," Howe snorted.

"The rebels have gathered in large numbers at Cambridge. I estimate 15,000 or more," said Lezard.

"I can neither leave nor attack. I am forced to remain in this rebel hellhole," Howe complained.

Lezard, unsure of what he should say next, changed the subject.

"It has been several months, since the unfortunate incident with Captain Harrington," said Lezard.

"And why should this concern me?" asked Howe.

"His mistress continues to associate with your officers," said Lezard.

"She is from your country is she not?" Howe asked.

"Yes, *Mon Générale,*"

"I am responsible for British subjects and American rebels. Nothing more. Now, leave me," Howe ordered.

As Marguerite walked to the boardinghouse, its owner willing to let her remain, despite the Captain's demise, she heard the sound of footsteps behind her.

She quickened her pace. Her head swirled in search of a building, with a light still burning. The late nights with wounded and diseased officers became a habit. At this moment, Marguerite prayed for daylight.

The footsteps got closer. Marguerite grew more desperate. The adrenaline pumping in her bloodstream made her more reckless. She stopped and spun in the stranger's direction. The slice of moon barely exposed the young man's face, but Marguerite quickly recognized him as her medical attendant.

"Benjamin, you frightened me half to death. Why are you following me?" she demanded.

"Please forgive me, Madam Valtesse. I follow only to protect you," he said.

Benjamin Church, a twenty-one-year-old lad, originally from England, once served as a deck hand on-board an English Man-of-War. When the ship came under attack, the captain pressed Benjamin into service as a surgeon's mate, to assist with the many casualties. The boy tended to the sick and wounded and helped the surgeons as requested. The ship's captain knew the boy's estranged father served in the colonies, as a well-known surgeon. He assumed Benjamin possessed similar talents. In fact, the moody lad sought adventure in the New World and harbored no interest in the medical field.

"And why must I have protection?" she asked.

"There is this man. He too comes from France. He asks about you. He knows where you are quartered and he claims to know General Howe," said Benjamin.

"His name?" she asked.

"His name, I do not know. Only his face," said Benjamin.

Marguerite leaned forward.

"Tell me," she ordered.

"He has many scars and is without most of one ear," said Benjamin. "Like you," he added, in a soft whisper.

Marguerite's face lost its color. She pulled more hair over her missing ear. For an instant, she refused to make eye contact with the young man, biting her lower lip and rubbing her temples with trembling hands. Finally, her head jerked up. Her eyes flashed in anger.

"He is the man who attacked me."

For a brief moment, the couple stood in silence. Each of them avoided the other person's gaze.

Marguerite spoke first.

"I will sleep at the hospital, until I find new quarters," she announced.

They walked back to the large hospital tent, constantly searching the horizon for her assailant.

Marguerite used the summer months to make regular sojourns to rebel headquarters in Cambridge.

She now carried a small dagger, given to her by a grateful patient. She worked hard to aid the rebel cause in any way she could—perhaps because her sworn enemy worked for the British or perhaps because Antoine's animosity for the English infected her thinking. Either way, she continued to pass intelligence to the rebel army.

Her conversations, and an occasional cryptic letter, allowed Marguerite sporadic access to one of General Washington's most trusted officers, Brigadier General Nathaniel Green. But she usually dealt with Washington's personal valet, William (Billy) Lee.

Lee, an enslaved black man, accompanied the Commander of the Colonial Army when Washington first arrived at Cambridge. "Billy" regularly laid out the general's clothes, brushed and tied the general's hair, waited on Washington's visitors, organized the general's papers, and tended to his owner's every need. But most important to Marguerite, Washington's man servant regularly delivered messages to and from the general. The fact that he regularly interacted with white folks, reflected Billy's status as one of Washington's most trusted and loyal aides.

Whenever she visited colonial headquarters in Cambridge, Marguerite made it a habit to call on Billy, even when she possessed little or no intelligence for the general's review. She wondered aloud why neither side in the war appeared willing or able to act on their stated intentions. Gage and Howe seemed content to rely on British ships for their army's required supplies. Similarly, General Washington, with most of Boston now under his control, took no obvious steps to evict the British.

On one occasion, Marguerite queried the black man about the American general's reluctance to pursue the British. Billy, more knowledgeable than most about the General's military strategy, smiled his discreet non-response and allowed Marguerite's question to go unanswered.

CHAPTER SIXTEEN

Northward Bound

In the weeks that followed, American colonists learned about the events at Bunker Hill.

During that battle, a ragtag army of farmers, artisans, millers, storekeepers, and amateur soldiers inflicted great damage on the army of General Gage. One young firebrand, in Connecticut, refused to wait for the next battle, and traveled at once to Cambridge. His small company of men, in full regalia, followed their captain, as he paraded through the streets of Boston. Benedict Arnold's entrance made a favorable impression and earned the young officer an audience with the Massachusetts Committee of Safety. The captain argued that a successful raid on Fort Ticonderoga, in upstate New York, would yield the ordinance that the rebel army so desperately needed. Days later, the committee agreed, and promoted Benedict Arnold to the rank of Colonel. They also authorized his recruitment of up to 400 men.

When Antoine heard the news, he saw Arnold's recruitment campaign as the perfect opportunity to join the rebel cause. Benedict Arnold's plans to travel north, hardly a secret, also held great interest for Antoine. A return visit to the boundary line might reveal the whereabouts of Marguerite.

Assuming she still lived.

"You fought for the French at Ticonderoga?"

The recruiter for Benedict Arnold did not disguise his skepticism. He sat back in his chair at the tavern and looked askance at Antoine.

"I served as a Captain in the Royal Roussillon Regiment for His Majesty, the King of France. We fought the English at Carillon, (Ticonderoga), and at the Siege of Quebec," said Antoine.

"You fought with Montcalm?" asked the recruiter.

"Yes. I had the great honor to serve under General Montcalm. At Ticonderoga, we defeated a British force five times the size of our own," said Antoine, almost indifferent to the significance of the French victory.

Within the hour, the recruiter escorted Antoine to Arnold's quarters. When the former French soldier recounted his experiences at Ticonderoga and Québec City, Arnold asked Antoine to accompany him to Fort Ticonderoga and beyond.

"You will have the opportunity to fight the British, once again," said the New Haven colonel.

"And, I pray, with better results," said Antoine.

Antoine traveled with Arnold and his men, first to Bennington, Vermont.

The reception given to Arnold, by the Green Mountain Boys, shocked Antoine. At a prearranged meeting, a back woodsman named Ethan Allen, paid lip service only, to Colonel Arnold's formal commission from the Massachusetts Committee on Safety. At one point, Allen, who stood a head taller than the prim and proper Arnold, announced to his men, that Colonel Arnold would be their new commander. To a man, Allen's men stacked their weapons and announced their intention to return to their farms. Arnold, given no other choice, reluctantly agreed to a "joint mission." On May 10, 1775, Allen and Arnold marched 200 men to the eastern shore of Lake Champlain.

"The Frenchman stays behind," Allen shouted, his distrust of the French, obvious.

"He knows the Fort, fought the British with Montcalm," announced Arnold.

Antoine ignored Ethan Allen's insult.

"We will all stay behind, without boats to cross the lake," Antoine observed.

The search for boats took most of the night. A large thunderstorm allowed only eighty-five men to cross the lake and reach Willow Point, a spot one-third of a mile from the fort. The colonial rebels faced a decision. They could wait until the next day for the balance of their men or they could achieve the element of surprise, with a much smaller force. They chose to attack at the first light of dawn, with all of their men.

After a hurried trip, through a thick forest, Arnold, Allen, and their troops could see the walls and bastions of Fort Ticonderoga, in the early morning light. The massive fortress, dotted with large cannon, inspired the two leaders to run up the hill. Much to their surprise, a wicket gate remained open and the lone guard stood slouched over his weapon. When stirred by the enemy's arrival, the sentry fired his musket. But the damp evening made the weapon useless. The click of a hammer on wet gunpowder sent the sentry running. Another British soldier, hearing the ruckus, arrived on the scene, but threw his weapon to the ground and fled, after a minor scratch from Ethan Allen's sword. Minutes more, and the entire American contingent stood in the fort's courtyard.

"Come out you damn skunk," Arnold yelled, as the men hooted

and hollered while waving their tomahawks and rifles.

A British officer, absent his trousers but wearing the famous British Redcoat, accosted Allen.

"By what authority have you entered His Majesties fort?" he asked.

"In the name of the great Jehovah and the Continental Congress," said Allen, towering over the British officer.

The invading force disarmed most of the British soldiers as they lay in their beds. The British officer in charge wisely surrendered. Antoine watched, as Ethan Allen and the Green Mountain Boys celebrated their bloodless coup. They consumed much of the ninety gallons of rum, which they discovered, in the British stores. Benedict Arnold, a professional soldier in appearance and demeanor, shouted one order after another, in an effort to restore order and decorum.

His words fell on deaf ears.

"A ship on the lake," announced a sentry, days later.

The ensuing panic did not last for long. Colonel Arnold grinned when he realized the approaching British schooner, stolen from a Tory and commandeered by one of Arnold's officers, delivered fifty of his newest recruits. In a few days, the boat, fitted with weaponry from the fort, allowed Arnold to abandon the Green Mountain Boys and search for additional victories against the British. His destination, the British fortifications north of the boundary line at St. John, lay thirty miles away.

"You're going home," one of the men shouted to Antoine.

Antoine nodded but said nothing, as the waves of Lake Champlain splashed against the ship. He planned to fight the British, in Quebec. And he secretly intended to resume his search for Marguerite.

Arnold's men encountered more good fortune when they reached the border. A seventy-ton sloop, armed with a handful of British soldiers, offered no resistance when the patriots caught them by surprise. The next day, when Arnold took his leave, towing all of the British rowboats behind him, Antoine announced his departure.

"I must remain here for a while," he said, delivering the sharp salute Colonel Arnold relished.

Arnold returned the salute and extended his hand in thanks.

Guy Carlton paced the floor, threw up his hands, and shook his head.

"I know about Fort Ticonderoga," snapped the English Governor of Quebec.

His guest, Moses Hazen, who clamored for their meeting, pressed his point.

"Did you know Arnold commandeered a British sloop at St. John's?" asked Hazen.

The governor stopped pacing. His eyes fixated on Hazen.

"Are you certain?" he asked.

"A seventy-ton sloop, with two six pounders. All of their rowboats, too," said Hazen, as if to rub it in.

"I must go to Montreal. Now," said Carlton.

"The danger of an invasion by the American rebels is real. I would recommend it," Hazen replied.

Antoine, hidden behind a small stand of trees, studied the home he and Marguerite built, more than a dozen years ago.

Two small children played on the porch, their mother keeping a watchful eye. He swallowed hard and quietly cleared the emotion from his throat. The 39-year-old man wallowed, in bitter memories. He thought of his service in the French Army and of his time with Marguerite. He thought of Alemos, and the loss, of his stillborn son. For all of that, he blamed the British. Antoine's decision to return to New France and fight the British there, rather than the colonies, partially satiated his anger, with the country that ruined his life. But his decision to return to the Richelieu river valley brought him closer to Marguerite and her memory.

As he traveled north, the road which took Antoine by Hazen's Manor House included a shocking surprise. British soldiers now occupied Hazen's mansion and milled around the grounds. Before completing his journey to Montreal, Antoine made surreptitious visits to several other British strongholds.

He memorized much of what he saw, calculating that such intelligence would prove useful in future battles.

Antoine did not bother to knock on Hazen's office door.

Instead, he greeted his old friend with bad news.

"The British military occupies your home on the Richelieu," said Antoine.

Moses Hazen looked up from his desk, grinned widely, and rose to meet his French friend.

"I know this already," said Hazen, grabbing Antoine's outstretched hand, with enthusiasm.

"It is my reward for warning the governor that American rebels now threaten Quebec," said Hazen, rolling his eyes and grimacing.

"I believe I have become one of those so-called "American rebels," said Antoine.

Hazen's head jerked up. A puzzled look covered his face. Antoine continued.

"I accompanied Ethan Allen and Colonel Arnold at Ticonderoga.

And I was with Colonel Arnold when he captured the British sloop at St Johns," and Antoine.

"Why do you fight for the rebels?" asked Hazen.

"Because New France belongs to its people and not King George," said Antoine.

"And because you blame the English for the loss of your wife and your military career," said Hazen.

Antoine winced. The truth hurt. He took a jab of his own.

"And where is your good friend, the governor? Antoine asked.

"He is not my good friend," said Hazen, shaking his head. "He left for Quebec City."

The two men chose to dine at Sutherland's eatery in Montréal, discussing Guy Carlton's decision to return to Québec city.

"The governor's campaign to enlist loyalists, in the fight against the rebels, did not go well?" Antoine asked.

"No. He hopes to organize the Indians, instead," said Hazen.

"A dangerous mission with great risk," noted Antoine. "The savages cannot be trusted."

"A few of my neighbors oppose the Americans, but most of them side with the rebel colonists or no one at all," said Hazen. "I am greatly troubled by the choice that I must soon make," said Hazen.

"I will fight with Schuyler. If he will have me," said Antoine, handing Hazen a missive written entirely in French.

Hazen could not decipher Major-General Schuyler's appeal to 'les habitants.'

"I can't read this," he said, handing it back to his friend.

Antoine explained the general's appeal for recruits from Quebec, in the Americans' fight against the British.

"Use caution, my friend," said Hazen. "The governor seeks to strengthen British fortifications, in Chambly, along the river, and up to the boundary line," said Hazen.

"He will not succeed," said Antoine.

"And you, who will you fight for?" asked Antoine, pressing Hazen for a commitment.

"My purse is with the British. My heart is with the Americans," said Hazen.

"I served in the Royal Roussillon. I wish to speak with the general," said Antoine.

Antoine Dauphin, forced to explain his intentions to a sentry at Philip Schuyler's encampment, scowled, as he stared down at the squirming, teenaged rebel. The rising, September sun temporarily blinded and confused the young soldier.

"You are French," said the guard, his bayonet still inches from Antoine's chest.

"Yes, and you are a fool," said Antoine, brushing the young man's rifle to one side as he stormed past the sentry.

"Halt or I will shoot," yelled the sentry, attracting the attention of several American rebels milling around a campfire.

Three of them rushed to stop the tall Frenchman. Dauphin easily lifted one soldier and threw him into the bushes. A second man, fell to the ground, unconscious, after a single blow to the chin. The third soldier charged with his bayonet. Antoine stepped to the side, wrested the weapon from his attacker, and shoved the man to the ground, holding him at bay, using the soldier's bayonet.

"That's enough," said an officer, emerging from his tent.

Antoine recognized the uniform as belonging to an officer in the Patriot Army.

The two men introduced themselves and General Philip Schuyler quickly ushered Antoine into the officer's tent.

"Captain Dauphin, I command this militia in name only," said Schuyler, a less than flattering reference to the undisciplined, twelve hundred American rebels, under his command.

"And yet, your numbers are superior to those of the enemy," said Antoine.

"I have been told otherwise," said Schuyler.

"I have seen the British preparations, with my own eyes," said Antoine.

"I have the testimony of my American friend who lives here," said Schuyler."

"Then he lies."

"Perhaps you know of him. Moses Hazen."

Antoine's head snapped to attention.

"This is most unfortunate. I too know Mr. Hazen. His heart is with the rebels, it is true. But his purse lies with the British," said Antoine.

Antoine recounted the details of his observations. The fort now included redoubts on both its north and south sides. The defensive structures included tunnels which connected each redoubt to the fort. The bastion housed approximately 700 fighting men.

"There are also several small boats to protect the river," said Antoine.

"Very well, then. We will attack, shortly. Your assistance would be appreciated," said Schuyler.

"I will fight the English anywhere I can."

CHAPTER SEVENTEEN

The Red Door

Marguerite, still in Boston, made her rounds in the sea of sick and dying.

She said little to any of her patients, save an occasional instruction or terse words of encouragement. Many of the men suffered from the fever, dysentery, or smallpox. She marveled that her own health remained good. But an empty heart gave little reason for her to live. She survived each day by promising vengeance on the man who mutilated her. And she swore revenge on the country that ruined her life, with Antoine. Until then, however, she remained in the safety of the hospital tent, having abandoned the quarters that once belonged to Captain Harrington.

"There is a sick soldier quartered a short distance from here. Your assistance is requested by the surgeon," said the young man.

Marguerite did not recognize the attendant and questioned him.

"You do not work in the hospital tent. Who are you?" she asked.

"I am new here, transferred from the *Lively*.

Marguerite recognized the ship's name as the sloop that fired on the rebels at Breed's Hill.

She walked with the orderly for a few blocks and stopped when he pointed to a large, two-story structure, with a bright, red door.

"Ma'am," he said.

"Thank you, soldier."

Marguerite climbed the porch steps, raised the large, wrought iron doorknocker, but did not release it. She silently replaced it against the door and looked in the direction of the medical attendant. He disappeared. A cold shiver rose from the nape of her neck, triggering a smattering of goosebumps. Her breathing quickened. Her chest tightened. She stepped away from the door.

The large, red door flew open and two men rushed forward. In her haste to descend the stairs, Marguerite fell forward onto the street. The men, dressed as civilians, rushed to her side. They picked her up by the arms and legs. She flailed and screamed and kicked her legs in an effort to loosen their grip.

"Quickly, bring her inside," said a voice from the still-opened, red door.

Marguerite recognized Adolphe Lezard's voice and screamed even louder. She broke the grip of one assailant and used her closed fist to swing at the other. Her blow landed harmlessly on the man's shoulder. A passerby stopped to stare when he heard the commotion. A window opened in the house next door and a cleaning lady shoved her bonnet-covered head into the opening for a better view. Marguerite's violent gyrations made it too difficult for the men to climb the steps to the red door. With one arm and one leg now loose, she forced her captors to release their hold. The angry woman fell to the ground and her captors ran down the street. As Marguerite struggled to stand, the red door slammed shut. Marguerite snarled triumphantly when she noticed Lezard peeking through a parted curtain.

And she vowed to return.

Philip Schuyler and his newest recruit, Antoine Dauphin, surveyed the fort at St. John's and its surroundings.

After a series of probing attacks, Schuyler began his siege on September 17, 1775. It did not go well. After an unexpected attack by Indians, allied with the British, Schuyler and his men retreated, to Ile aux Noix. The general, feeling decidedly ill, traveled to Albany, hoping to secure a treaty, with the natives. He left his army in the temporary care of General Richard Montgomery. When Schuyler's health showed no sign of improving, he indefinitely relinquished day-to-day control of his men to Montgomery.

Antoine's new commander resumed the cannonade, but the British defenders at Fort St. John showed no signs of giving up. An unexpected victory by the Patriots at nearby Fort Chambly, changed all of that. When Chambly fell, Montgomery replenished his supplies and ammunition, with English stores. The bad news for the British did not end there. The defenders at St. John, expected the imminent arrival of reinforcements. A large contingent of British troops, led by Governor Carleton, would soon come to their rescue. Unfortunately, Carleton and his men encountered stiff resistance from the rebels. Forced to turn back, the Governor's reinforcements could no longer aid British troops at Fort St. John.

Antoine recommended a flag of truce be used to inform the British, of their hopeless predicament. To ensure the message would be well-received, Montgomery and Dauphin included a British prisoner of war. The captured soldier verified the defeat of Governor Carlton's forces at Longueil. After several days of negotiations, the British garrison at Fort St. John, marched out of the bastion, grounded their weapons, and surrendered as prisoners.

Antoine, one member of a ragtag army of rebels, most of whom wore no uniform, could not hide his admiration when the British troops surrendered. The English soldiers, in full and colorful regalia, marched in strict formation, as music played and drums beat. Montgomery also took notice.

"Great men like you deserve an exception to the rules of war. Let the officers and volunteers take back their swords," Montgomery announced.

Once again, Antoine tasted the exhilaration of victory and the pomp and circumstance of triumph. He recalled the colorful regiment he once served and mourned the loss of his military career. The military life was and always would be Antoine's one true love. And now, his new-found friend, General Richard Montgomery, promised more of the same. As Antoine watched the last of the defeated British troops disappear over the horizon, he dreamed of more battles and more victories.

He gave no thought to Marguerite Valtesse.

Marguerite waited until the only sound in the hospital tent came from sleeping patients.

A sliver of moon provided enough light for Marguerite to navigate the streets of Boston. She took pains to walk in the shadows and avoided any building whose oil lamp or fireplace illuminated the walk. It took minutes for her to reach the two-story structure, with the red door.

After looking both ways for any sign of life, Marguerite crossed the street. She crouched low as she hurried to the side of the residence. She did not want to be seen through a window. The carriage house, at the rear of the residence, contained the handful of dry hay Marguerite required.

The small, metal tinderbox, stolen from the hospital tent, contained the flint and steel necessary for starting a fire. After a few attempts, the hay caught fire and, in moments, yellow and orange flames licked at the white clapboards. The dancing flames soothed the open wounds in Marguerite's heart. She crossed the street several houses away and again, remained hidden in the shadows. After a few blocks, Marguerite stopped to observe the glowing, red results of her arson.

The former Ursuline nun prayed that Lezard burned alive.

Antoine traveled with General Montgomery to Montréal where both men greeted, with great surprise, an unannounced visitor.

Moses Hazen related a long and sad tale of woe. It began when the Americans arrested him at his farm but immediately released him when a British detachment appeared on the scene. The British took him in as their prisoner. While in British custody, American fighters seized Hazen's farm. Everything moveable, including his livestock, grain, and tools, fell victim to the patriot army. Hazen, ordered to accompany Governor Carleton during their mission to rescue the English at St. John, continued to be a prisoner of the British. When American soldiers at Longueil forced Carleton to abandon most of his ships and supplies, Hazen used the distraction, to escape his British captors.

"This rebellion by the colonists has cost me dearly. And now I have no choice but to join your cause," he groused.

Antoine snarled.

"Perhaps your reports on British fortifications will, henceforth, be more accurate," said Antoine.

Hazen stared at his boots.

"I apologize to the general," said Hazen.

Montgomery extended his hand.

"You have suffered enough. Join us. We leave for Québec City, in days," said Montgomery.

The American general's announcement surprised both Hazen and Antoine.

"Winter approaches, *Mon Générale*," said Antoine.

"I will not be alone. Benedict Arnold is also approaching Quebec, as we speak," said Montgomery. "The invasion of Canada is not complete, until we have taken Quebec. We will take 300 men, the rest will remain in Montréal," he added.

"I know the city and the fort," said Antoine.

"And you, my friend, are especially important to this mission," said Montgomery.

Hazen interrupted, "And what of my situation? Must I now fight for the rebels who destroyed my farm?" asked Hazen, half in jest.

"You know the answer to that question. The British will see you hanged," said Montgomery.

Hazen grinned.

"Then we shall fight the British, together," said Hazen.

Marguerite returned to the hospital tent, as the early morning light slowly uncovered row after row of diseased and dying men.

"When I did not see you in your cot, I feared for your life."

Benjamin, the surgeon's attendant, searched her face for answers.

"I could not sleep. I went for a stroll," said Marguerite.

"You must not walk alone. It is dangerous," he said.

Marguerite gently placed her open hand on the boy's face.

"You are a loyal friend, Benjamin, and I am grateful," she said.

She resumed her duties at the bedside of a nearby soldier. Hours later, long after daybreak, Benjamin returned to her side. He focused on the woman but said nothing. She instinctively checked that her missing ear remained covered.

"Benjamin?"

Benjamin approached the woman.

"The rebels set fire to the general's quarters," he said, his unblinking stare focused on Marguerite's face.

Marguerite sat motionless, a bloody bandage in one hand and a small flask of whiskey in the other. Without thinking, she tossed both the bandages and the flask into a large bowl of pinkish water. Her eyes darted in Benjamin's direction as she retrieved the flask. His eyebrows arched.

Marguerite wiped the flask dry and refused to face her young attendant.

"Was the general injured?" she asked.

"General Howe is traveling. The home was empty except for a servant. She claimed she saw the rebel who done it," said Benjamin.

"Oh really," said Marguerite, absentmindedly wiping the flask once again.

Benjamin watched her every move.

"A woman. Can you believe it?" said Benjamin, moving closer to Marguerite and taking the flask from her trembling hands.

Marguerite exhaled and licked her dry lips.

"His quarters were mostly undamaged, but the old woman has a big mess to clean up," said Benjamin.

"At least you and I are safe," she whispered.

She stepped forward and gave the boy a hug.

Benjamin's eyes closed. He took a deep breath and reluctantly broke their embrace. He placed his hands on her shoulders and pulled her closer.

"You cannot remain here," he said.

Marguerite covered a yawn and slowly shook her head.

"I have no place to go, my friend."

"I quarter in a large home. My room can easily accommodate an extra bed," said Benjamin.

Marguerite stepped back, now wearing a suspicious frown. Benjamin rushed to respond.

"Please, Madam Valtesse, I mean no disrespect. I merely wish to ensure your safety," he said.

Marguerite looked away and reached again for the hair that covered her hideous wound.

"You were very nearly captured by Lezard's men. And he is still at large. Are you not concerned he will make yet another attempt?" asked Benjamin.

Marguerite began to tremble and used one hand to grip the other, to hide her uncontrolled tremors.

"It will be a temporary arrangement," she said.

Benjamin grinned broadly and shoved another log into the stove, his face glowing brightly in the firelight.

CHAPTER EIGHTEEN

Quebec City

Richard Montgomery and Benedict Arnold reconnoitered on December 3, 1775, eighteen miles from Québec.

Within days, they commenced a cannonade of the fort's occupants, but the British showed no signs of surrender. Arnold and Montgomery decided on a frontal assault.

"We will attack on the eve of the new year," said Arnold.

Their detailed plan of attack took days to assemble but the two men could not hide their excitement. Antoine sought to curb their enthusiasm.

"I believe that your plans are no longer a secret," announced Antoine.

Moses Hazen re-enforced the dark pronouncement.

"From their movements in the city and within the walls, I fear that deserters have leaked our plans to the enemy," said Hazen.

"We will change the plan," announced Montgomery.

The decision to reverse the attack meant the Americans' main thrust would be at the far side of the city. The walls at that end could be accessed, with much less difficulty. A diversionary attack would be staged on the Plains of Abraham. Montgomery and Arnold agreed to come in from opposite sides of the city. Hazen would accompany Arnold. Antoine agreed to stay with Montgomery.

"Just two shots and we will be without our leaders," observed Antoine, referring to the fact that both Montgomery and Arnold would lead the charge. The officers did not respond.

They reviewed, once again, their intricate plan, for the conquest of Québec city.

In the two days prior to December 31, 1775, the American rebels enjoyed clear and sunny weather.

On New Year's Eve, a vicious snowstorm surprised all of the combatants. Arnold and his men, forced to keep their heads down to avoid wind driven snow and ice, struggled to their destinations, on opposite sides of the city.

"Look. Fireballs," said Hazen.

The illuminating cannon fire, designed to shed light on a battlefield, appeared over the Heights of Abraham. Clearly the British believed that Americans troops formed on the Plains. The rebel ruse worked. Arnold swung his sword in exultation and charged forward. But he soon lost his way, confused in a maze of narrow streets, alleyways, and blinding snow. He waited for his men to catch up. They carried with them a small cannon, pulled on a sled. When the men finally arrived, empty-handed because the cannon lay stuck in a snowbank, every church bell in Québec City began to ring the alarm. The patriots' surprise attack surprised no one.

Musket fire rained down from the fort's walls, and from several of the houses. Many of Arnold's comrades fell to the ground and disappeared in the deep snow. Arnold kept running but he too fell forward into the snow. A sharp pain in his leg forced him to stop. He could no longer stand and struggled to the nearest wall, for temporary cover. Most of Arnold's men rushed past but Moses Hazen and a few others stayed behind. After much yelling, they persuaded Arnold to be dragged back to the rear.

"Rush on brave boys, rush on," shouted Arnold, as more men ran past their wounded leader.

The sky lit up with musket flashes and cannon fire as Arnold, one leg dragging behind him, slowly made his way to the General Hospital. A number of Catholic nuns tended to his wound. The bullet entered his leg below the knee but somehow lodged itself in the man's heel. As Arnold contemplated his injuries an officer rushed in.

"The rebel cause is lost," he reported.

"Men of New York, you will not fear to follow where your general leads," said Montgomery.

On the other side of the city, unaware that the rebel attack appeared doomed, General Richard Montgomery raised his sword and led his men forward. The first two, unmanned barriers posed no difficulty. The third barrier concealed an enemy surprise. The British waited, until the last moment, and responded with a torrent of musket fire and cannonballs. The volley felled two officers, eleven regulars and, worst of all, General Montgomery. He died instantly from his wounds. Antoine returned to the hospital and kneeled at Benedict Arnold's bedside.

"General Montgomery is dead."

Arnold, unable to stand and barely conscious, transferred his command to a lower officer and lapsed into a coma. Three days later, he resumed his command, but the news did not improve.

"We are outnumbered three to one and we are dangerously low in supplies," said Hazen.

"You must go to Congress. Tell them we need men, money,

arms, and supplies," said Arnold.

Benedict Arnold's instructions to Moses Hazen made it clear. The American siege of Québec city might not last beyond the winter months.

"I will go with you," said Antoine.

"I cannot overemphasize the importance of your mission to Philadelphia," said Arnold. He reminded his officers that disease among the troops, especially smallpox, reduced their fighting force to several hundred men. He also referenced the threat that came from warmer weather.

"The Almighty willing, our reinforcements and supplies will arrive, before the spring. British ships from England, filled with soldiers, will also arrive in the spring and our cause will be lost, if your mission should fail," Arnold said.

Weeks later, in Philadelphia, Hazen and Antoine celebrated their success.

"Congratulations General," said Antoine, as he extended his hand to Moses Hazen.

Hazen bowed slightly, acknowledging his recent promotion to General, by the Continental Congress.

"It is the money Congress has appropriated which we celebrate the most," said Hazen.

In addition to money, Congress also authorized Hazen to recruit an entire regiment, four battalions, of 250 men each. The ability to recruit new troops stood little chance of helping Benedict Arnold, however. Hazen and Antoine could not return to Quebec, in time. The wounded General, forced to give up his siege when British troops arrived by sea, in early May, made a hasty escape to the safety of Montreal. As a result, he left behind large quantities of munitions and supplies. The procurement of replacement supplies and additional munitions became Arnold's top priority.

Hazen, now in command of Montréal, greeted Arnold when the defeated General returned from Quebec. Hazen continued to experience little success in recruiting new men and securing more supplies. Quebec natives showed little interest in supplying, much less serving with, the American Army. The colonial government paid their bills with paper money, issued by the Continental Congress. Canadians viewed the American notes as worthless.

Hazen also informed Arnold about a recent visit, from three commissioners sent to the province, by the Philadelphia Congress. When Arnold discovered he missed the opportunity to greet such luminaries as Benjamin Franklin, Samuel Chase, and Charles Carroll, he fumed and resented Hazen's good fortune.

The relationship between Hazen and Arnold worsened, after a brief skirmish between rebels and the British. The conflagration, at The Cedars, forty miles northeast of Montréal, triggered Arnold's adamant call for a retaliatory attack. Hazen openly discouraged the idea. He argued that the element of surprise could not be achieved, because hundreds of hostile Indians surrounded The Cedars. In addition, such an attack might easily provoke a massacre of rebel prisoners, also controlled by the Indians. Again, Arnold fumed but eventually relented to Hazen's more reasonable approach. Ultimately, a temporary truce stipulated the exchange of prisoners.

Unfortunately, the enmity between Arnold and his subordinate general, continued.

Chapter Nineteen

Lovers and Soldiers

"You are here but you are not in the room," said Benjamin.

The young man and Marguerite, each in their own beds, remained awake despite the fall of darkness.

"I am very sorry, my friend. It is true, my thoughts are elsewhere," she said.

Benjamin moved to the woman's side, as she lay in her bed. He blew out the lone candle on her nightstand, leaving the room bathed, in the light of a full moon.

"Marguerite, listen to me," he whispered, as he reached for her hands.

"I know. I know. I must get my rest, but sleep does not come to me as it does to you," she said.

Benjamin pulled her hands to his chest and stared at the large, green eyes that reflected the moon's glow.

"It is I who cannot sleep, Marguerite. I think only of you," he said.

Marguerite yanked her hands from his. She grabbed at the blanket and pulled it to her neck. She took a deep breath.

"It is time to sleep, Benjamin," she announced. "Please, go to bed," she said.

Benjamin sat back but did not return to his bed. He waited for a moment, leaned forward, and whispered in her ear.

"The old, black woman described the rebel arsonist, as having red hair–long red hair," he said.

Marguerite bolted upright to a sitting position. She searched his face with wide eyes. Her heart raced and she gulped hard for her next breath.

"What are you saying, Benjamin?"

Benjamin ran his fingers through her hair and gently tugged at the shoulder of her nightshirt, exposing the creamy white skin above her breast. He gazed into her eyes.

"I wish to know *all* of your secrets, Marguerite," he said, his voice trembling with lust.

Marguerite didn't move. She pleaded with the boy.

"Benjamin. Please. Don't," she cried.

He touched his index finger to her lips.

"Say nothing, my love. And in return, I too will remain silent," he whispered, using the same finger to slowly trace the woman's lips, chin, throat, and neck, until he reached the top of her loose-fitting nightshirt.

Marguerite's lips moved, as if to speak. Benjamin scowled and yanked at the cotton fabric, exposing her bare breasts. She jerked and covered herself, with both hands. He pulled her hands away, leaned forward, and pushed her down on the bed. He kissed the heaving mounds of soft white flesh and used his tongue to caress her lips. Marguerite closed her eyes but did not resist. Her silent acquiescence told Benjamin that she clearly understood his unspoken threat. Submit to his lustful cravings or be hung by the British for arson.

Benjamin pulled off his nightshirt and threw it to the floor.

General Howe's new aide motioned Adolphe Lezard to a chair.

Lezard, unaccustomed to such hospitality, openly grinned, pulling his chair close to the soldier's desk.

"Tell me again, about the red-haired woman," said the aide.

Lezard recounted the circumstances that led to arson at the general's home. He paused for effect when he got to the part about the old, black maid and how she described the arsonist as a female, with long red hair.

"Marguerite Valtesse and the rebel arsonist are one and the same," announced Lezard, with a triumphant flourish.

The aide studied Lezard's scarred face; its capacity to shock the senses reduced, after each of the man's frequent visits.

"And what of this talk that the same woman confronted two men, in front of the general's quarters. A struggle took place and she escaped," said the soldier.

"Of this, I know nothing," Lezard lied, looking at the floor and tugging on the small portion of his right ear.

"Very well, I shall investigate," said the aide.

"But will the General . . . ?"

The aide interrupted.

"I shall investigate. You may leave now."

Lezard rose from his chair but did not turn for the door.

"Excuse me, my friend, but it is a well-known fact that General Howe and his men will soon sail for Halifax. I too would like passage to Canada. Would you inquire as to that possibility?" asked Lezard.

"I shall speak to the General," said the aide, using his hand to shoo Lezard from the room.

Marguerite waited until Benjamin slept soundly.

Their carnal embrace repulsed the woman. The inexperienced

boy-man pawed at Marguerite's breasts and required only moments to satisfy his animalistic urges. Her blackmailer wanted sex in return for his silence. She understood that. Nevertheless, Marguerite wondered if her hasty decision could withstand the test of time. Would the boy keep his mouth shut? Or would the blackmail continue?

As Marguerite starred at her blackmailer's closed eyes, distant memories flashed in her mind. She barely recognized the innocent child of Parisian high society. The Ursuline nun of long ago, wracked by a maelstrom of love, war, and savage violence, had morphed into a cold and calculating woman. Obsessed with revenge, devoid of love, and caring not if she lived or died, Marguerite made a radical decision.

The blackmail would end. Now. Marguerite's eyes narrowed. Watching the boy-man for any sign of movement, she rose from the bed and tiptoed across the floor. The bed groaned and the floor creaked but still, he slept. Marguerite walked to the opposite side of their bedchamber, naked, because her nightdress remained somewhere underneath the satiated body of her unwanted lover. She retrieved the straight razor, which the boy required every fourth day, and chopped at her long red hair in angry silence. As the unique evidence of her identity fell into the basin, she stole occasional glances in his direction. Marguerite finished her degrading task as the young man began to stir.

With hair now shorn to below her ears, Marguerite went to his side. She rested the sharp edge of the razor on the young man's throat. Benjamin's sleep-filled eyes grew wide as the short-haired woman sitting at his side, nude and unsmiling, came into focus. He blinked in disbelief when he felt the blade break the skin of his lily white, acne scarred neck. He lay motionless, barely breathing.

"Benjamin, what shall I do?" she cooed. "My secret is no longer a secret," said Marguerite, her grin mutating into a vicious glare.

Benjamin's breath grew rapid. His eyes brimmed with tears. But he dared not speak.

"Can I trust you, *ma Cherie*?" she asked, flashing a forced smile and pressing the blade against the white flesh a bit more.

"Yes," he whispered.

A rivulet of blood trickled down both sides of his neck and formed two, identical blood stains, on the bed covers.

"Are you certain, Benjamin? I must be certain," she purred.

Marguerite did not wait for his response.

"There are British spies everywhere," she hissed, intentionally exposing her clenched teeth.

"You have my word," he gasped, his pimpled face now red with fear.

She lifted the blade from his neck, yanked at her crumpled nightshirt, and used the garment to wipe it clean. She dabbed at the blood on his neck, as if nursing the wound of an innocent soldier. Her eyes locked onto his, even as she tossed the blade onto the floor. Benjamin took a deep breath. Marguerite used her index finger to replicate his attack of last night. She carefully traced his lips, his neck, and his throat, and paused when she reached the thin, red line that moved each time he swallowed.

He blinked and jerked when she suddenly yanked off the covers and pinned both of his arms to the bed. When she climbed on top of the boy, straddling his body between her long legs, he breathed a sigh of relief and the color returned to his face.

She waited only a moment for the boy's natural response and slowly engulfed her terrified lover.

"Our money is worthless and our promises, even more so. How are we to accomplish our orders?"

Moses Hazen did not respond to Antoine's angry inquiry. The

duo's weeks-long effort to secure men and supplies, in lower Quebec, ended in abject failure. The Continental Congress would be disappointed, and Benedict Arnold would be livid. General Arnold's adamant orders notwithstanding, both Hazen and Antoine saw no reason to continue their hopeless mission. Moses Hazen reached for his friend's shoulders and pulled Antoine close. He spoke in hushed tones.

"Listen to me, Antoine. I have been ordered to Chambly. The city of Québec is now controlled by the British. Soon they will march to Montreal. If we remain here, we are doomed. Come with me," said Hazen.

The two men left within minutes for Chambly. Days later, they watched in shock as load after load of foodstuffs, munitions, supplies, blankets, and clothing arrived, in their wake. Clearly, these items did not come into the rebels' possession, as a result of honest trading. Benedict Arnold and his men used worthless currency, empty promises, and unscrupulous methods to succeed where Hazen and Antoine failed.

"These are the ill-gotten possessions of my friends," said Hazen, kicking at the ground and shaking his head in disgust.

"We are no better than the enemy we fight," said Antoine.

A messenger accosted Antoine with a letter. The bad news forced Antoine's gaze to the ground. He closed his eyes and silently cursed. He hesitated and faced his friend, "They have torched your home, the barns, and all of the buildings at your farm," said Antoine, waiting for Hazen to react.

When General Hazen did not respond, Antoine continued.

"The home of your wife, in St. Therese, is also destroyed," said Antoine.

Hazen collapsed onto a nearby tree stump.

"The British?" he asked.

Antoine paused and shamefacedly muttered his response.

"No, sir. General Arnold's men. They destroyed everything. The General leaves nothing for possible use by the British."

The two men joined a growing procession of soldiers, wagons, women and children, sick, and wounded, as it slowly wound its way to St John's. They traveled by boat, to Ile aux Noix and on to Ticonderoga. Along the way and over several days and nights, most of the supplies were plundered by the travelers, destroyed by Mother Nature or abandoned on the trail. When Benedict Arnold discovered the meager results of his strong-armed tactics in Montreal, he blamed Hazen for the failure.

After reading an official looking letter, Moses Hazen flew into a rage.

"What is it?" asked Antoine.

"I will defend my honor," said Moses Hazen, shoving the document under Antoine's nose.

Antoine read the document that transformed his normally pleasant friend into an advanced state of apoplexy. He read the missive, twice, but the words did not change.

General Moses Hazen, at the behest of General Benedict Arnold, would soon be placed under house arrest and be court-martialed for the embezzlement of public monies and other misdemeanors.

"This is how General Arnold celebrates your country's Declaration of Independence?" asked Antoine, referencing the July 4, 1776, proclamation of several weeks ago.

A panel of thirteen field officers, convened at the end of July, did not require a great deal of time. They announced a unanimous verdict. Benedict Arnold's charges against Moses Hazen were without foundation. Hazen became even more inflamed.

"I will demand a Court of Inquiry into the aspersions against my character," Hazen announced to his officers.

Antoine pulled the irate officer to one side. He reminded Hazen that the inquiry must wait.

"We have only a few months in which to recruit more men, before the winter sets in," said Antoine.

Hazen frowned but nodded his agreement.

Marguerite's head rested in the crook of Benjamin's arm.

He dared not wake her, for fear of triggering the woman's white-hot wrath. He chose, instead, to use the few moments of quiet, to contemplate all that happened during the course of a single evening. He made love for the first time. And then, he made love for the second time. He grinned and used his free hand to pick at the dried blood on his neck. On the night he became a man, he very nearly became a dead man. The boy's body shuddered as a vision of him lying on the bed, in a pool of blood, flashed in his eyes.

"Where's my nightdress?" she demanded.

Benjamin lurched into a sitting position and tossed bed covers in every direction as he searched for her undergarment. He stared at her naked body, as she slipped the red-stained garment over her head. After examining the dark splotches, Marguerite looked up.

"You will not forget the first time we made love, will you, Benjamin?"

Benjamin shook his head.

"No."

"And you will not forget your vow of silence, will you, my friend?"

Her inquiry sounded more like an order than it did a question.

"No Madam. I am a man of my word," he said.

"You are not yet a man, Benjamin. Now, get dressed. There is something you must do for me," she said.

Marguerite instructed the boy to make inquiries of British officers and Loyalists, who might know the whereabouts, of Adolphe Lezard. Any other information, of potential use by the rebels, might also prove valuable. Benjamin refused. He searched for his missing boot, found it, and threw the item across the room. He glared at his first-time lover and paced the floor. His lopsided gait caused Marguerite to laugh.

"Are you finished?" she asked.

"I will not betray my country," he barked, falling into a chair and staring at her in an open act of defiance. Marguerite stepped forward and shoved a finger near his face.

"Your country has abandoned you. General Howe and his army have gone to Halifax and only a few hundred loyalists were allowed to board the ships. You have nowhere to go," she said. "And you will do as I say," she added.

Benjamin searched her face to confirm the seriousness of her threat.

"There is Canada," Benjamin said, his tone, much less confrontational.

Marguerite stepped back and placed both hands on her hips.

"I am determined to find Lezard. You will help me. Is that understood?"

"He could be in England for all you know," said Benjamin.

"I need you to inquire," Marguerite answered.

Benjamin's face twisted into a dirty look. Marguerite pulled the boy to his feet and reached for the boy's face.

"Please, Benjamin. I would be most grateful," she whispered, caressing his face and tugging at the ribbon which laced the front of her dress.

The boy leaned in and buried his face into her chest.

"Or, I could kill you in your sleep," she whispered, her hands pressing the boy's head to her bosom.

Benjamin stopped kissing the soft skin above her breasts. For a moment he stood in her arms, motionless and barely breathing. She pushed him away.

"It's time to leave," she said, reaching for the door.

He followed without objection.

Benjamin's lust blinded him to the fact that his English accent would be viewed with suspicion, in rebel-controlled Boston.

The British evacuated the city, days ago, and the remaining Loyalists feared for their lives. Nevertheless, the teenager dutifully made a number of indiscreet inquiries, at boarding houses, shops, and taverns.

"What's your name, boy?"

The large man quizzing Benjamin did not dress as a member of the Continental army, but he wore the air of authority.

"Benjamin Church. I'm a surgeon's mate," said the boy.

"You sound like a British soldier if you ask me," said the burly man.

Benjamin frowned and rolled his eyes.

"At the hospital tent, we accept the sick and wounded, British and rebel alike," he said, shoving his nose into the air.

"I ain't no rebel, boy. I am an officer in the Continental Army," said the man, as he shoved Benjamin from the tavern into the street. He looked to his companions and thrust an accusing finger in Benjamin's direction.

"Take him away."

The two men carried out their orders, each soldier taking an arm, pulling and dragging Benjamin down the street. Despite his loud protestations, they tossed Benjamin into a locked room with several other inmates. The building appeared to be a makeshift jail. A large, wooden plank across the closed door and boarded up windows allowed no possibility of escape.

Benjamin took the remaining spot on the floor, much too near the slop bucket used by inmates as a latrine.

Marguerite's young blackmailer did not appear for work at the hospital tent.

Nor did he return to their room that evening. She left early the next morning for General Howe's former quarters. The home with the red door, if it still housed the black servant, required a visit. Marguerite, with a bonnet to cover her shorn locks, decided a conversation with the old, black woman was necessary. She carried money and a dagger. The money could be used to silence the old woman. The dagger remained necessary, because Lezard might answer the door. As she walked, Marguerite considered her transition from innocent nun to cunning predator. She took no responsibility, for the precipitous decline in her moral standards.

She blamed God. And she blamed Lezard.

Marguerite knocked on the red door and scanned the street, in both directions, as she waited.

After a long and frustrating wait, she turned to leave. The sound of a key in its lock yanked her back to the door. The large, black woman standing in the open doorway wore a white kerchief, over her head, tied in the front. Her blue, checkered dress, covered by a gleaming white apron, looked worn and tattered. The servant also sported a swollen, upper lip and a large cut, over her left eye, visible but healing. She spoke in a harsh manner but swallowed hard and wrung her hands, as she talked.

"Iffin you here to see the general, he dun gone weeks ago," said the servant.

"I came to see you," said Marguerite.

"You bess leave," said the woman, as she stepped back and reached for the door.

Marguerite took a step forward, using her hand and one foot, to stop the door. Both ladies refused to budge. Marguerite reached for the ribbon which tied her bonnet. After a few desperate glances up and down the street, she exposed her shorn, flaming red hair. Despite its short, choppy appearance, the black woman recognized the stunning, red color. She shook her head and twisted in every direction, in search of spying eyes.

"You bess leave right now ma'am," she repeated, her voice rising, as she furiously smoothed the surface of her apron.

"Please," said Marguerite.

The woman hesitated and stole one more glance at the horizon. Marguerite did the same.

"Get in here, quick like."

"Thank you," said Marguerite, stepping into the home while feeling for the dagger, in her bag.

"Are you alone?" asked Marguerite.

"Yessum," said the servant.

Marguerite let the dagger drop.

"Girl, youz in a whole heap a trouble," said the servant.

Marguerite, her eyes downcast, spoke in a gentle whisper.

"Your silence is all that I require," said Marguerite.

"Listen to me wumen. Thay'z spies everywhere. And they be mean like a mama bear with chillun," said the black lady, pointing to her face.

"The British or the rebels?" asked Marguerite.

"Oh, he talk funny but he ain't no rebel and he ain't no Redcoat," she replied.

"What did you tell him?" asked Marguerite.

"I sez I saw a wumen with long, red hair runnin to the carriage house."

"Is he the one who beat you? asked Marguerite.

"Yessum, an I dun told him da Lawd's truth. But he be reel mean an I think he know you," said the black woman.

"What did he look like?"

"Oh, he look real bad. Been in a fight, I reckun. His face wuz cut and thaze scars all over him and he guts one ear."

Marguerite replaced her bonnet and leaned forward. She sympathized with the woman, each of them, victims of Lezard's cruelty. She pressed a few notes into the woman's hand, no longer believing the servant represented a threat.

The black lady nodded her appreciation but reached for Marguerite as she started to leave.

"Claims he gonna stay here. Dun it once before, when the general wuz gone. I dun told the rebels, but they ain't gonna bother with no niggah woman," said the servant.

Marguerite reached for the woman's arm, giving it an appreciative squeeze.

"Thank you," she said.

"You bess go now, honey, afore he cum back. An thank you. I needs the money."

CHAPTER TWENTY

Surgeons and Soldiers

"There have been too many fights. I want all the French soldiers in one company. Your company, Captain Dauphin," said Moses Hazen.

Antoine expressed his approval although the General's decision sounded more like an order.

"Those who speak English do not like those who speak French," said Antoine.

"Yes, and those who speak French do not like those who speak English," Hazen countered, adding, "Now they are your problem."

"I'm told that General Washington struggles with his own disciplinary problems," Antoine said.

"Yes, in New York city. They riot, pillage, and desert the army. But you are with Hazen's 'infernals' and when you arrive, you will distinguish yourself in battle," said Hazen.

"We are leaving?" asked Antoine.

"General Sullivan is planning an attack on Staten Island. He needs reinforcements. You and Lieutenant Antill will take three companies."

"And you?" asked Antoine.

"I will remain here. I do not believe that General Sullivan is as

241

competent as he believes," said Hazen.

"He is with Benedict Arnold's army, is he not? The same men who torched your property on the Richelieu," said Antoine.

"Yes," said Hazen, motioning Antoine to the door.

After days of searching, for both Benjamin and Lezard, Marguerite resolved to leave the Boston area.

Her repeated inquiries about a man, with a scarred face and a missing ear, generated strange looks, sometimes laughter, but never, results. She began to call Benjamin her son, hoping the ploy would garner sympathy and cooperation. One gentleman offered a suggestion.

"Have you looked in the jails?" he asked.

Marguerite frowned but thanked the man. After thinking about it, she started to search the jails in Boston. She soon discovered the rebels converted almost any structure into a jail. And they preferred to fill them, with anyone who spoke with an English accent or appeared to be a Loyalist. When she visited the various facilities, shouts and pleas for help from inmates who suffered in squalor, suggested the rebels did not worry about such things as inhumane conditions or the miscarriage of justice.

"I am in search of my son, he may be one of your prisoners," said Marguerite to a guard.

"Does he have a name?"

"Benjamin Church," she responded.

"You must know his father," said the soldier.

"Yes, I do," Marguerite lied.

"Then you too, must be a spy for the British," accused the guard.

Margarite hastened to explain that neither she nor her son had seen the notorious man in years. She added that Benjamin served as a surgeon's mate and that the two of them wanted to continue their work in the medical field.

The sentry glared and shook his head.

"You work for the Redcoats,' he argued.

"We do not refuse the sick and wounded. It matters not who we serve," said Marguerite, using the tone she once employed as an Ursuline nun.

The guard continued to stare at Marguerite. She removed her bonnet, using her uneven locks to discourage his lust and generate less suspicion. Marguerite covered her missing ear.

"Even now, we treat the sick and wounded at the hospital tent left behind by the British," said Marguerite.

"I should lock both of you up," said the guard.

"Please. We have done nothing wrong. Surely you want your fellow soldiers attended to," Marguerite pleaded.

"Who is this man your son searches for? Scarred face, missing an ear," asked the sentry.

Marguerite's mind raced. She stepped forward; her face so close to his that the man's breath nearly overpowered her words.

"A friend of the English General Howe. The man he searches for attacked me. The boy wishes to avenge my honor," said Marguerite, as she dabbed at an imaginary tear.

"Stay here," said the guard.

In a few moments, he returned with the prisoner. Marguerite worried there might be an unexpected and inappropriate display of affection. She turned away as the boy advanced.

"Benjamin, I am angry with you. Follow me," she barked.

The guard stepped between her and the door.

"You two ain't goin' nowhere. As of now, you're working for the Continental Army," he said.

Antoine and Lieutenant Antill, traveled to Hanover, New Jersey, with three companies of soldiers.

They would join the First and Second Maryland brigades plus a company of New Jersey's militia.

"I'm guessing, all told, there are about a thousand of us," said Antill.

"The question is how many Redcoats are on that island," Antoine replied.

"I'm going with General Smallwood's contingent. You stay with Sullivan and Hubert. Hubert is French, after all," said Antill.

Antoine agreed. General Sullivan's decision to form the men into two columns made the arrangement even simpler. On the afternoon of August 21, they marched, first to Elizabethtown, New Jersey, and, early the next morning, onto the island.

Initially, the American attack surprised the British. Within minutes, Antoine and his men herded more than eighty prisoners into a clearing.

"If they move, shoot em," Antoine shouted to his men, elated to be in the thick of battle, once again.

In a short while, Sullivan arrived with forty more prisoners. A half-dozen of the men stayed behind, to guard the captured Redcoats. The rest went on to Richmond, a small village at the center of Staten Island. The British, after their initial surprise, recovered in significant numbers. Sullivan, not wishing to engage with a superior force, ordered a strategic retreat. He yelled to Antoine.

"Cover us until we reach the boats," said Sullivan.

Antoine's men, pelted with a torrent of British grapeshot, soon ran low on ammunition. Several fell to the ground, wounded. A number of men threw down their useless muskets and surrendered. Antoine, with a few dozen soldiers remaining at his side, scrambled to the boats and joined the general. He searched the chaos for

Antill, but no one recalled seeing the officer. Several of the men speculated that Antill had surrendered, but no one offered an eyewitness account. Antoine shook his head and secretly blamed Sullivan's poor command for the fact that twenty-five men lay dead or wounded and more than fifteen soldiers remained missing.

Sullivan's plan for revenge against the British at Staten Island, ended in abject failure.

Marguerite and Benjamin learned on the second day of their unexpected journey that colonial troops traveled to Hanover, New Jersey, temporary headquarters for the rebel army.

The trip proved long and arduous. Benjamin's misery, made worse because he and his paramour traveled separately, also reflected Marguerite's foul mood. She blamed Benjamin for the delay in her search for Lezard and questioned whether her effort to find Lezard might ever resume. But her forced conscription, in service of the patriot cause, enabled Marguerite's second mission, resistance to everything British.

"You two. Report to the hospital tent," barked the sergeant who supervised their arrival.

The senior surgeon, busy with sick and wounded, dispensed with the usual amenities.

"I've got an amputation; come with me," he said.

He motioned the couple through a lengthy series of paths which separated row after row, of sick and wounded soldiers. Marguerite and Benjamin arrived at a small corner of the large tent where a crude operating table, several planks on a few massive barrels, served as the operating room. Marguerite's head swiveled when a soldier's French accent could be heard above the din, of groans and shouts.

"Do something, please," said the French officer, struggling with his wounded comrade.

The wounded soldier screamed in pain. His leg dangled by nothing more than a bloody strip of skin. When the French voice placed his wounded friend on the operating table, the injured man grew suddenly silent. The patient's eyes closed, and he groaned no more. The doctor motioned for the body to be removed. The French captain stepped into help. Marguerite could not move; her eyes fixated on the tall, handsome soldier in front of her. She mouthed his name but made no sound. When the French captain turned to acknowledge the surgeon, he spied Marguerite for the first time.

"Marguerite," he said.

"Antoine," she whispered.

Benjamin, distracted by the couple's reunion, dropped the carpenter's saw required for the surgeon's next patient, already lying in wait on the operating table.

"You clumsy fool," said the surgeon, slapping Benjamin on the back of the head.

"Sorry," Benjamin murmured, as he retrieved the saw and handed it to the doctor.

The incident with the carpenter's saw disrupted the reunion of husband and wife. If either of them welcomed the unexpected surprise, neither of them expressed their joy.

"After all of these years and still, you live to fight," she said.

Antoine exhaled and spoke as if to an errant child.

"I fight the British. You fight one man," Antoine said.

Adolphe Lezard spent most of the summer of 1777 trying to attach himself to British General Howe's command.

It did not prove to be a simple task. Howe variously occupied portions of New York City, New Jersey, and, by July first, Staten

Island. Most recently, Howe and his 15,000-man army made Philadelphia its target. A clash with George Washington's nearby army of almost the same size seemed inevitable. They would collide in the vicinity of Brandywine Creek. Lezard vowed to stay close to the action, so as to monitor both the enemy and his British friends.

The expected battle at Brandywine Creek forced Antoine to abandon Marguerite, once again.

Seeing her for the first time in years left the captain unsettled. He rejoiced that she survived but he also recalled, with painful clarity, why the two separated in the first place. Marguerite's obsession with Lezard continued to dominate every aspect of her life. The woman's need for revenge had risen to the level of an uncontrollable compulsion. Antoine did not want to be his wife's afterthought. He expected and deserved, to be his wife's first and only priority.

"After all these years and still you live to fight."

When Marguerite's clear-eyed observation echoed in his ears, Antoine squeezed his eyes shut and shook his head in protest. How could she equate his passion for battle with her zeal for revenge? His preoccupation with the military was justified. Her preoccupation with Lezard was . . . Antoine's troubled train of thought sputtered to an end.

He had a battle to fight.

Antoine rejoined his men.

With Antill still missing, General Sullivan ordered Hazen's regiments to the front lines, east of Brandywine Creek. On the afternoon of September 11, a thunderous clap of cannon fire signaled the beginning of the long-awaited confrontation between British General Howe and American General George Washington. Within an hour, the cannon fire, accompanied by prolonged musketry fire, enveloped Antoine and his men, in a low-lying cloud of dense smoke. Antoine struggled to see, much less direct, the movement of his troops.

When the order for a strategic withdrawal sounded, Captain Dauphin walked tall, knowing his men performed, with courage and effectiveness. As he gathered the men around him, a musket ball, hurled the captain to the ground. He laid there, his eyes open for a moment, studying the blades of lush, green grass which cushioned his fall and now appeared at eye level. He could feel a sharp pain in his lower stomach.

Antoine's eyelids fluttered and closed.

"Who is he?" asked Benjamin.

Marguerite, staring into space, spoke in a whisper.

"My husband of long ago."

"You never told me you were married," he complained.

"It is of no concern to you," she said.

"And now, he has returned," said Benjamin, throwing a ball of bloodied bandages into a nearby basin of water.

"Please leave me," she ordered.

Benjamin recalled the leverage he used to force Marguerite into his arms. He realized that informing the rebels of Marguerite's arson would only elevate the woman to hero status. But the boy's lust clouded his thinking.

"Do you love him?" he asked.

"I will tell you again. It is of no concern to you," she snapped.

"I am your lover. I have a right to know," he said.

"No. You are a blackmailer. Nothing more," she said.

Benjamin stormed out of the tent and found liquid solace in a nearby tavern.

"We have more wounded. Pack everything you can. We leave in an hour," said the doctor.

Marguerite acknowledged the surgeon. She gathered the instruments and stuffed bandages into several burlap bags. After a last-minute check on her patients, she climbed into the wagon that brought her, and several of the hospital staff, to the rear of the Brandywine battlefield. Benjamin, still at the tavern, did not join his colleagues.

At Brandywine Creek, the rebels' makeshift hospital had no beds and plenty of smelly evidence that its previous occupants walked on four legs. Today, the decrepit barn housed row after row, of wounded rebels. Many groaned in pain. Some stared into space, the look of imminent death in their eyes. A number of the wounded lay still, their pain and suffering, having come to an end.

Two barrels and several planks once again served, as the surgeon's operating table. For several hours, Marguerite assisted the surgeon, as he covered an empty stall floor with severed limbs. A break in the frenzied pace, prompted the doctor to acknowledge his helper.

"You are a very able assistant," he said.

Marguerite nodded her thanks. The doctor pointed to the dozens of sick and wounded that covered the barn floor.

"Do what you can," he said.

Marguerite stopped at each body, bandaging wounds when she could and offering a small sip of water to those men able to drink. She covered the dead, with their own jacket or a dirty blanket. Her next patient was lying face down. His shirt, thoroughly soaked in deep red blood, clung to the man's body, as if it were a second layer of skin. Judging from the gaping hole, Marguerite surmised the musket ball entered the soldier's upper abdomen and exited in the back. She stuffed wads of bandages into the wound and struggled to wrap the man's torso, in strips of the same material. When she rolled the soldier onto his back to tie her handiwork into a bow, the wounded man's ashen, white face came into full view.

She covered her mouth to smother a scream and squeezed her eyes shut. Her patient trembled uncontrollably, his breathing was shallow, and he was cold to the touch. Marguerite, familiar with such injuries, knew all too well, that Antoine Dauphin would not survive his wounds.

As she did her best to make the man comfortable, Marguerite could not quell the anger that rose in her heart. Antoine's obsession with the glory of battle would cost him his life, as she predicted. How could he compare her pursuit of justice, with his own zeal for the blood and gore of war? She expected and deserved to be treated as his wife and his first priority. The military served as Antoine's mistress and Marguerite could not tolerate his infatuation any longer.

"I fight the British. You fight one man."

When Antoine's last words interrupted her winning argument, Marguerite's eyes filled with tears.

She kissed him on the lips and moved on to her next patient.

CHAPTER TWENTY-ONE

Recovery and Escape

Benjamin waited several days before making his appearance at the barn-turned hospital.

He arrived, as the entire medical entourage packed to leave, yet again. A messenger notified the hospital unit that the newest battle line would likely be near Germantown, Pennsylvania. The medical team would follow.

Marguerite and her former blackmailer exchanged glances from a distance, but did not converse, as they made the day-long journey to Germantown. Their newest accommodations consisted of cots in the open air for the surgeons and his female staff. The rest of the workers slept on the ground, with only a blanket to protect them from the chilly air which announced Pennsylvania's oncoming winter. A nearby tavern would serve as their hospital.

The gossip spread that General Washington planned a surprise attack, on the British troops at Germantown. No one knew for certain, if and when such an attack would occur. Until that day arrived, Marguerite worked to ready the abandoned tavern as a makeshift hospital. Her frenzied effort, while appreciated by the surgeons, served as a needed distraction. Thoughts of Antoine and the chaos to come drove her wild with emotion.

"How long will you ignore me?" asked Benjamin.

The boy's unexpected appearance at the temporary hospital startled Marguerite, but not enough to hide her impatience with the boy-lover.

"You come and go like a spoiled child," she said.

"I'm a man and you will treat me with respect," Benjamin announced.

Marguerite, her head throbbing, reached for a nearby, metal basin and flung it at the boy. Benjamin used his arm to stop the projectile and it fell harmlessly to the floor.

"You whore. How dare you," Benjamin growled.

"Leave me or I will have the soldiers remove you," she ordered.

Benjamin's eyes narrowed and his lips quivered. He retrieved the bowl and flung it in Marguerite's direction, missing her by several feet.

"Your aim is as good as your lovemaking," said Marguerite, sneering at her would-be assailant.

Benjamin, his face now red with white-hot anger, vaulted over several cots and grabbed Marguerite by the neck with both hands. He choked her and yanked her head in a back and forth motion. A nearby woman rushed to Marguerite's side and struggled to loosen the young man's vice-like grip. Marguerite, gasping for air and unable to break free, jerked her knee in the direction of Benjamin's groin. The accuracy of her blow sent the boy to his knees, moaning in excruciating pain. Marguerite stepped back. He lunged for the skirt on her dress and yanked the woman to her knees. He swung hard with a closed fist hitting her on the jaw. She fell backwards onto the floor.

"Bitch," he growled.

Her eyes fluttered to the back of her head. The sound of booted soldiers forced Marguerite's attacker to flee.

Antoine screamed for water.

He flailed and thrashed wildly, as several women struggled to keep the man in his bed. Antoine lay drenched with sweat, and his wound emitted a foul odor. He summoned the strength to fend off his handlers, rolling onto the floor and crawling on his hands and knees to the doorway. The women watched helplessly as he tumbled onto the brown grass below. He landed on his back and relished the cold, October air.

A third woman, carrying a wooden bucket filled with water, stopped to assist the wounded man. Antoine reached for the bucket and tipped it over, drenching his torso, with the ice-cold water. He groaned from the shock but soon grew quiet. For a brief moment, he lay in the grass. In time, he summoned the strength to walk, stagger, and crawl to a nearby stream. He plunged into the water fully clothed, recalling the advice he once received from an experienced nun in Québec city.

"Fresh air and clean water will help you heal," Marguerite once said.

She also predicted his death on the battlefield, he recalled.

Benjamin ran into the woods, calculating that a thick grove of trees would hide his escape.

When the sounds of imaginary soldiers chasing him through the trees came to an end, the boy-man slowed to a walk. He followed Allen's Lane, from a safe distance, and followed the creek, south. Now close to dusk, hungry and exhausted, Benjamin rested where the creek drained into the Schuykill River. After a slow drink of icy water, he fell asleep behind a tall thicket of bushes, his head resting on a large moss-covered rock.

"We've gone far enough. Let's get back to the camp," said the soldier, speaking in German.

The soldier's loud command and the man's foreign tongue startled Benjamin, from a fitful sleep. As he scrambled upright, the snap of a dried branch beneath his feet, sounded like thunder, in the quiet cluster of dense trees. Before he could choose an escape route, four Hessian soldiers came into view, all of them with muskets. They held their weapons at eye level, prepared to shoot.

"Don't shoot! Don't shoot! I'm British," Benjamin clamored, praying his English accent would mean something to his would-be captors.

The senior Hessian, a lieutenant, approached Benjamin holding his weapon at chest level while speaking in broken English to the boy.

"You rebel, yes?"

Benjamin, almost too excited to speak, babbled a response and shook his head.

"No. No. No. I serve the King. Well, I was with the rebels, but only for a short while. But I was forced. I didn't want to go. I help the soldiers who are wounded or sick," said Benjamin.

When the lieutenant showed no sign of comprehension, the boy pantomimed a soldier, shot in the belly. The boy doubled over in fake pain. The Hessian soldier, unable to interpret Benjamin's actions, shoved the butt of his rifle into Benjamin's midriff. The Hessian watched, as Benjamin fell to his knees and struggled to breathe.

"Now you are wounded, yes?" asked the soldier.

His question sent the three, onlooking Hessians into a fit of belly laughs.

Two of the Hessian soldiers pulled the boy to his feet and guided him, at point of bayonet, to their camp in the woods behind enemy lines.

Marguerite could not stop thinking about Antoine Dauphin.

After several days, the captain most likely succumbed to his wounds. But she had to know, for certain. She inquired of visitors, patients, soldiers, and medical personnel. She also asked if anyone planned a trip to Hanover, New Jersey. Early one morning she heard a nurse shouting.

"The troops are on the move."

Marguerite ran to the door of the rebels' makeshift hospital and watched the soldiers form up. She could overhear several of the men talking, as they stood in line.

"General Washington has split us up. Some of the men are headed down the old York Road, some to Chestnut Hill, and we is going to the Kiln Road. I sure hope he knows what he's doing," said the young enlistee.

Marguerite, desperate for more information, thought to approach Antoine's colleagues, in 'Hazen's Infernals.' She learned they departed for the battlefield earlier that morning.

Marguerite returned to her workstation and whispered a silent prayer for the soldier she still loved.

Adolphe Lezard, hearing nothing from his friends in General Howe's camp, relied instead on local gossip, drunken soldiers, and the occasional return of men who served in the rebel army.

He traveled with relative ease and used his multilingual talents to convince suspicious patriots, they enjoyed the support of the French. As a merchant, he sought to assist the rebel army. Lezard's ruse allowed him to follow Howe's army, from a distance, to New York City, Staten Island, and Philadelphia. The French traitor realized, however, that his funds, now dangerously depleted, needed to be replenished.

An unplanned stop, at an inn in Bethlehem, presented Lezard with an unexpected opportunity. While eating his modest lunch, he watched two uniformed soldiers wander into the establishment. Lezard did not recognize their colorful uniforms but experienced no difficulty in understanding their perfect French. The soldiers wore navy-blue topcoats, waist length in the front, with tails in the back. Their military garb, festooned with gold buttons, also included gold cuffs and high collars. The men attracted everyone's attention but only Lezard could understand their conversation.

The soldiers, members of the French National Guard, served under the Marquis de Lafayette. The Marquis, recovering from a leg wound inflicted at Brandywine, enjoyed temporary quarters, at the home of a local businessman. The two men talked less about Lafayette's wound and more about his nursemaid, a young lady named Elizabeth. Her appearance impressed the two soldiers. Lezard sensed an opportunity and approached the soldiers, speaking in their native tongue.

"*Bonjour*, it is a pleasant surprise indeed to meet two of my fellow countrymen, so far away from home," said Lezard, bowing low.

Lezard introduced himself as a high-ranking member of the administration in Quebec, serving before those 'British scoundrels' took power in New France. Both officers, ignorant of the corruption which characterized the former French colony, invited Lezard to join them. They cheerfully ignored Lezard's horrible appearance, pleasantly surprised that a fellow countryman appeared in their midst.

Lezard quizzed the two soldiers, with subtle questions and discrete statements. They discussed Lafayette's recovery and speculated whether or not the wounded officer would recover in time to assist George Washington. The soldiers also opined on the rebels' willingness to attack the British at Germantown.

The guardsmen, with more than a few drinks to their credit, did not suspect anything nefarious, from their congenial host. Despite his meager funds, Lezard insisted on the purchase of several rounds of drinks. When the conversation lagged, the soldiers announced their intention to return to their boardinghouse.

"I must leave you here, gentlemen," said Lezard, as they stood in front of a large two-story home, on the main street of Bethlehem.

"You are leaving ush?" asked one of the soldiers, struggling to speak clearly. The inebriated officer staggered forward, forced to use Lezard's shoulders, as a means to steady himself.

"Yes, my friend, I must find lodgings for the evening," Lezard lied.

"*Non, non, non.*" said the drunken soldier. "You will shtay with ush."

Lezard effected a token resistance. He helped the more inebriated of his two companions, navigate the porch steps. A long flight of stairs led to their second story bed chamber. Lezard made himself busy, using a basin and pitcher of water to wash his face and hands. The two soldiers flopped onto the bed and, in moments, the room groaned with the sound of loud snoring.

Lezard stomped his boots on the wooden floor. The two men did not stir. He searched their pockets, their bags, and the balance of the room. The unconscious visitors carried only a small number of French livres on their person. But Lezard grinned triumphantly, when he discovered a small tin canister secreted beneath a blanket roll, in the armoire. The tin contained a large wad of French notes, which Lezard presumed belong to Lafayette.

The thief blew an imaginary kiss to his unconscious friends, as he shut the chamber door.

Benjamin, with his legs and hands bound, sat in a tent by himself, on the cold wet grass.

His only companions, a table, a chair, and a cot, decorated the otherwise empty enclosure. It grew colder as night fell and Benjamin fantasized about a warm blanket and a plate of hot food.

A British officer, accompanied by an aide, pulled the canvas door open and marched to Benjamin's side. He did not bring a plate of hot food.

"You are a rebel spy. You will be hanged in the morning," said the British officer.

The officer's aide smirked in Benjamin's direction, rolled his eyes, and left.

"I am not a rebel spy. I am a surgeon's mate, pressed into service, by the rebels," Benjamin whined.

"You were discovered very near our camp. You're a spy. Why else would you be so far away from the rebel lines?" asked the British captain.

Benjamin exhaled in frustration, paused, and resorted to the absolute truth.

"I was running away."

"Why?"

"I got into a fight. The soldiers were after me."

"You struck a superior officer?"

Benjamin studied the canvas wall opposite him. He could feel his face turn pink. The British officer took two steps forward and backhanded Benjamin with enough force to topple him onto his side.

"Answer my question, boy," said the officer.

Benjamin mumbled. The soldier kicked Benjamin in the ribs.

"I didn't hear you," said the officer.

Benjamin winced in pain and screamed his response.

"I hit a woman," he said.

The British officer paused. He reached for his prisoner, sat him up, and threw a blanket over Benjamin's shivering frame. The boy, puzzled by the captain's sudden change in attitude, studied his captor. The captain wore an impeccably, clean uniform and carried a well-polished sword, at his side. His clean-shaven face matched the hair, perfectly coifed and neatly trimmed. The captain stood close enough to place a hand on Benjamin's shoulder and squeeze.

"Ah yes. Women. A curse on us all," said the captain.

"Am I free to go?" asked Benjamin.

"I'm prepared to loosen your bonds and give you something to eat. But I need your word, as a gentleman, that you will not attempt to escape," said the captain.

Benjamin nodded.

"I promise," he said.

Antoine, now eating regularly and going for long strolls in the countryside, amazed the caregivers, with his stubborn refusal to remain in bed.

He insisted on daily outings, immersing himself in the ice-cold river, and leaving his wounds exposed. The man's stunning recovery amazed the medical workers who grew too accustomed to the inevitability of death and disease. It also made Antoine a popular patient. The wounded man used his celebratory status to quiz newcomers and visitors, about Washington's army. Antoine sought specific information about "Hazen's Infernals".

"Will you be going to Germantown?" asked a surgeon.

The doctor, himself in route to Pennsylvania, sought an escort. Antoine's response surprised even Antoine.

"I'm not sure," and Antoine.

For the first time ever, an officer's command in combat did not appeal to him.

The surgeon, a Deputy Director for the American's loosely organized Medical Corps, explained that a newly established hospital, in Bethlehem, required his presence.

"I'm Dr. Latimer. Moses Latimer," said the man, extending his hand to Antoine.

The two men chatted for a while and Antoine agreed to go with the doctor to Bethlehem.

"A military escort in exchange for medical attention," said Antoine.

"Agreed," said Latimer.

Antoine's day-long journey, with Dr. Latimer, left him exhausted, the effects of his wound still apparent.

"I will arrange for a room," said the doctor, leaving Antoine, with the horses, in front of an inn.

Moments later, when Latimer emerged, the doctor beamed.

"One room, one bed, but the food looks good," said Latimer.

Antoine, barely able to stand after an entire day in the saddle, grimaced his approval.

"I'm tired. I'm hungry. And I don't care where I sleep," said the soldier.

The dining area, mostly full, included the wonderful aroma of fresh bread and a soup or stew. The two men registered, scrambled to their room to dump their bedrolls, and returned downstairs.

Within minutes, the doctor and his recovering patient feasted on bowls of chicken soup and a large plate, of freshly made bread. The two men did not converse, until the bread disappeared, and the soup tureen lay empty.

"In the morning, I will go to the hospital. Tonight, we rest," said the doctor.

"Thank you, Dr. Latimer. I have not earned your hospitality," said Antoine.

Dr. Latimer reached into his vest pocket removing several silver coins.

"In truth, I required the company of a good man more than a military escort," said the doctor. "It is I who am grateful to you," said Latimer, as a grin crossed his face.

"Don't be flashing your money around here," barked a patron.

Latimer, a puzzled look on his face, twisted in his chair to locate the man's accented voice.

At a nearby table, two soldiers, in the process of leaving, nodded to the doctor and Antoine. They looked spectacular in their blue-and-white uniforms trimmed with gold. The junior officer spoke to Antoine and the doctor, as he walked by.

"We were robbed," he said.

"We were drunk," said the senior man.

The doctor raised both hands, palms facing up, and shrugged his shoulders.

"The evils of alcohol are many," said Latimer.

"Never trust a man with one ear," said the younger of the two soldiers.

A surge of adrenalin catapulted Antoine to his feet. The chair he sat on, scraped the wooden floor, as it careened across the room. He took two steps forward and grabbed the soldier, by the wide lapels on the man's uniform. All the diners in the room interrupted their meals, as the room grew silent.

"Describe the man with one ear," Antoine ordered, in his native tongue.

The French soldier hesitated but not for long, as Antoine stood at least a head taller. The soldiers described the man who plied them with drinks and absconded with their money. A scar covered face, jet black hair, a thin moustache, and an evil grin. Antoine stepped back and fell into his chair, speechless and out of breath.

"Captain Dauphin are you not well?" asked Dr. Latimer.

"He has seen a ghost," said one of the soldiers, grinning.

The second soldier laughed. Antoine, although seated, jerked his head up; his piercing blue eyes shooting daggers. The younger soldier no longer laughed.

"That ghost killed my unborn child, tortured my wife, and very nearly killed her," said Antoine.

A series of audible gasps and whispered words rippled through the dining area. Both soldiers removed their hats, the senior man now repentant and speaking low.

"Please accept our apologies, *Mon Ami*," he said.

Antoine's face softened, but only for a moment.

"Did he go south or north?" asked Antoine.

The soldiers looked at each other for confirmation.

"He came from the north, said the younger man, "heading south. Brandywine or perhaps Germantown. I cannot be certain."

The senior officer agreed; and Antoine thanked his fellow countrymen.

Adolphe Lezard made the journey to Germantown without incident, traveling west of the rebel encampment and east again, crossing the Schuykill River, twice.

Hessian troops stopped him, well before he reached General Howe's headquarters, but the traveler, with an air of superiority and plenty of name dropping, eventually received a friendly escort into the camp. General Howe recognized the name of his visitor but delegated the task, of a meeting with Lezard, to Lieutenant-General Wilhelm von Kynphausen.

The lieutenant-general listened patiently as Lezard revealed the precise whereabouts of George Washington's newly minted officer, the Marquis de Lafayette.

"I predict that Lafayette will come to Germantown," Lezard announced.

The high-ranking British officer looked skeptical.

"Mr. Lizard," he started.

"Please sir, it is pronounced 'Lee-Zard,'" said the Frenchman, unable to disguise the irritation in his voice.

"Very well, Mr. Lee Zard, if the French officer, Lafayette, is still recovering from his wounds in Brandywine, why would he travel to Germantown?"

"The enemy is within twenty miles of this camp. Surely you will be attacked soon, and I am confident that Lafayette will be at Washington's side." Lezard predicted.

"Even the rebels are not so foolish as to attack the superior forces of His Majesty's army," said the officer.

Lezard stared in disbelief.

"But sir," he said.

"I am a very busy man, Mr. Lizard. Thank you for your loyalty to his Majesty the King," said the lieutenant-general, mispronouncing Lezard's name, once again.

Lezard, now infuriated, stormed out of the lieutenant-general's quarters.

"Good day, sir," said Lezard.

CHAPTER TWENTY-TWO

Manacles

Benjamin's first evening in the captain's tent, passed without incident.

After formally introducing himself, Captain John Stuart proved to be a gracious host, engaging his prisoner, in long friendly conversations about medicine, war, difficult women, and politics. On their second evening together, he arrived with a plate of salted pork and several pieces of hardtack. Benjamin thanked the captain several times.

As the captain removed the iron manacles from Benjamin's hands, he frowned.

"I apologize. The leggings must remain," he announced, as Benjamin shuffled to the small table.

"Thank you, captain, you are very kind," said Benjamin, tearing into the food like a ravenous wolf.

While Benjamin ate, the captain talked some more. Non-stop, thought Benjamin. The sun disappeared into the evening sky and still, Captain Stuart rambled on, with little encouragement from his now tired but satiated prisoner. Stuart's long-winded soliloquy focused on the irritants in a soldier's life. The captain cursed the men under him and the Hessian soldiers especially, "Crude bastards, the lot of 'em," he said. And General Howe also earned the captain's ire because Howe remained unable or unwilling to capture and destroy the rebel army once and for all. Stuart barely tolerated his fellow officers and grew angry when he described the senior men whose wives had become "camp followers."

The captain ended his tirade when he spied the boy yawning, struggling to keep his eyes open. Stuart secured the opening of the tent and reached under his bed roll, a devilish look of mystery in his eyes. His hand emerged, with a silver flask.

"A measure of rum for my friend. Helps me to sleep," he said, placing the flask on the table, in front of Benjamin.

"Thank you, sir," said the boy, giving no thought to the officer's extraordinary hospitality.

Benjamin, with several measures of rum to his credit, did not object when the captain announced the sleeping arrangements. He rolled out a blanket on the ground near his own cot.

"You will sleep here," he announced.

"Thank you, sir," said Benjamin.

"But the manacles will stay, and I have to tie at least one of your hands to the tent pole. I'm sorry," said the Captain.

"I understand," said Benjamin.

The captain extinguished the candle and Benjamin closed his eyes, slipping into a deep sleep.

Captain Stuart, lay quietly, his eyes wide open.

Antoine, still in Bethlehem, wandered the streets, uncertain if he should engage the British, in their next battle with the Americans.

A wounded veteran with crutches, hobbled down the road, and caught Antoine's attention.

"I have seen you before," said Antoine.

The object of his long gaze, a young man, with a leg amputated below the knee, stared back.

"Hazen's Infernals," said the crippled man.

Antoine nodded. He pointed to the man's missing leg, still bandaged at the knee.

"Brandywine?" Antoine asked.

"Yes, sir. And who are you?" asked the soldier.

Antoine pulled at his shirt and nightshirt, to reveal a part of his scar, as he introduced himself.

"The British were victorious, but we lived to fight another day," Antoine said.

"I leave for Germantown, today," said the amputee.

Antoine leaned forward, as if he misunderstood the young soldier.

"You go to fight?"

"Yes sir. I will do what I can," said the soldier.

Antoine, awash in guilt, murmured his goodbye, as the crippled soldier brushed past and continued down the street. He studied the brave lad as he hobbled away. The limping soldier became a speck on the horizon. In Antoine's mind, however, the amputee stood eight feet tall and Antoine became the tiny speck.

His gut twisted and turned, with feelings of guilt, regret, revenge, and, for the first time, fear. Thoughts of Marguerite, Lezard, Alemos, the unborn child, and the blood and gore of yet another battle, collided in his mind like loose barrels, on the deck of a storm-tossed ship. His brain became a stubborn knot of confused thoughts. And while the scars on his body evidenced a recovery, the wounds in his mind and heart, remained.

As Antoine searched for the nearest tavern, he wondered to himself. When does the thrill of battle succumb to the love of a woman? Why must God and Country come before home and family? And must the fear of dying, transform a brave soldier into a frightened coward?

Antoine searched for the answers but discovered the nearest tavern, nothing more.

Benjamin awakened to the stale odor, of tobacco and rum in his nostrils.

The British captain, his face very near Benjamin's, straddled the tethered prisoner. Benjamin tried in vain to push the British officer away. The boy's arms and legs, now secured by iron manacles and ropes, made the prisoner helpless in the face of his captor's lurid advances.

"What are you doing?" asked Benjamin, thrashing and twisting to the extent his bindings allowed.

"Hush," murmured his attacker, "You will wake the camp."

Benjamin's response, to scream louder, forced the captain to shove a dirty, wool sock into the young man's open mouth. The boy's screams, now muffled groans, soon became tears of shame and fear. Captain Stuart groped the boy's private parts and undid Benjamin's trousers. Benjamin focused on the tent's canvas wall, as the captain's gentle ministrations had their inevitable effect. The boy entertained a series of distracting thoughts, desperate to thwart the predator's obscene intentions. Benjamin tried but he failed. The captain grinned in triumph and continued to caress his shamefaced victim.

"You are no longer my prisoner, Benjamin. Soon, you will be my lover," he whispered.

When Benjamin refused to respond, Captain Stuart grew somber.

"Remember. You are still a spy. If I say the word, you will be hanged. Now, you must not yell," instructed the captain, as he reached for Benjamin's smelly but effective gag.

Benjamin nodded, his face now red with anger and disgust.

Stuart removed the dirty sock and waited for Benjamin's prolonged silence. He tossed the gag to one side and ogled the boy's exposed body.

"Please, the blanket. Please," said Benjamin.

The captain pulled Benjamin's nightshirt to the boy's knees and covered him with a blanket.

"Until tomorrow," said the captain.

Benjamin closed his eyes and cried.

Antoine succumbed to an alcohol-induced night of sleep, in the hay mound of a nearby barn.

By morning, his mental fog lifted. The exhausted veteran left Bethlehem, for Germantown, that day. With a handful of silver coins, compliments of Dr. Latimer, plus his weapons and a bed roll, the French captain began the two-day journey. That night, he dined on dried meat and a single piece of hardtack, washed down with a measure of rum. His lengthy conversation with the stump of a dead pine tree, confirmed the wisdom of his decision and Antoine fell into a deep sleep.

"Hazen's 's Infernals. Where are they camped?"

Antoine asked the first person he encountered when arriving at Skippack, the small town, fifteen miles northwest of Germantown. Just days ago, the tiny enclave housed most of the patriot army, but now the place looked deserted. Antoine's question startled the soldier that guarded a handful of tents where there used to be thousands of canvas homes. The guard stood post near a large tent which contained foodstuffs and supplies for the army.

"They left with the rest of the troops, sir," said the sentry.

"Where?" asked Antoine.

"General Washington sent the whole army to Germantown, but they split up. I don't rightly know where Hazen's men went to. I know they marched under Sullivan. Probably leading the charge if I know Sullivan," said the guard.

Antoine nodded his appreciation and trotted his horse down the main street, wondering what he should do next. But an able-bodied man on the main road in a rebel camp, generated a number of long stares. Antoine quickened his pace to the edge of town. A creek and a road, also named Skippack, crossed each other, at the other side of the settlement.

He chose that spot to give his horse a drink and rest his weary frame.

Lezard paced the floor in his room, a tiny, second floor cubicle. The low, peaked ceiling forced the Frenchman, hardly a man of height, to pace in the center of the room, only.

Lezard's departure from the English camp and his desire to remain close to Germantown, forced him to seek shelter, in the small village of Skippack. The room's tiny window afforded him a view, of the street below. Lezard, grateful for that single comfort, spent much of his time in a small chair, leaning against the bed and staring out the curtain-less opening.

When his sleepy eyes caught the scene of a man, on a slow-moving horse, Lezard jumped to his feet. He cleaned the dirty window with his sleeve and focused again on the horse and rider below. Lezard moved his head to one side which allowed him to observe the street and still remain invisible to sharp-eyed pedestrians. He inched toward the sunlit square of dusty cobwebs so as to be certain. His pulse quickened and he took a deep breath, exhaling slowly, as if the man below might hear him.

The unmistakable profile of Captain Antoine Dauphin, trotting down the street, shocked the Frenchman into a motionless trance.

Benjamin's entire body stiffened, as the captain strode into the tent the next morning and set a plate of food on the small table.

Captain Stuart reached into his pocket, retrieved the key to Benjamin's iron leggings, and released the prisoner's feet. He reached for Benjamin's arms, thought better of it, and motioned to the food.

"Breakfast," he said.

"I'm not hungry," Benjamin growled.

"You should thank me for my hospitality," said the captain, a happy grin on his face. "I could have you hanged this afternoon."

"So, you said," Benjamin replied, using the bed for leverage, and rising to his feet.

When the captain took a few steps back, Benjamin ambled to the table, but ignored the food.

"I have coffee coming. Should be here soon. Eat up," the captain ordered.

Benjamin sat on the rickety chair near the table and watched, as the British officer guarded the opening. A voice on the other side of the canvas, announced the arrival of the coffee. The captain stood at the opening, thanking his aide for the hot beverage. Benjamin waited, until the canvas flap covered the opening and the voice departed. When the captain turned, a full cup of hot coffee in each hand, Benjamin pounced. Using the table like a plow, he plunged into the captain, scalding the man on his face and torso. Benjamin straddled the fallen soldier, using the full weight of his body, and pressing his knees into the captain's belly.

The chain which bound the boy's hands, fit perfectly around Captain Stuart's slender neck. The prisoner rolled to one side and pulled the captain on top of him. He yanked on the metal noose crushing the tiny bones in Stuart's neck. The captain choked. He gasped, as he struggled in vain to loosen Benjamin's death grip. For minutes, Stuart thrashed wildly, gurgling his screams, and jerking his limbs in protest. His red face turned blue. Eventually, the dying man's response consisted of no more than an occasional twitch. And then, except for the sounds of Benjamin's heavy breathing, there was total silence.

Benjamin loosened the captain's metal necklace and pushed the corpse to one side. The boy rushed to locate the key to his manacles, staring all the while at the captain's contorted face. The man's mouth, wide-open as if screaming, accurately pictured the captain's last moments of anguish and pain.

Benjamin freed himself, threw the manacles on the bed, and stepped to the door of his canvas prison. He stopped and spun around. The boy-man retrieved one of the metal restraints and, like a master whipping a stubborn animal, repeatedly bludgeoned the head and face of the British officer. After several dozen blows, the dead soldier could no longer be recognized. Gone were the perfect smile, the meticulously combed hair, the smooth complexion, and the proud profile of a British aristocrat. Benjamin dropped the manacles and slammed his boot into the porridge of bone, blood, and brain matter that used to be Captain Stuart's face. The boy snarled his approval when he noticed the canvas wall, nearest the captain's motionless body.

The dingy, white color now featured crimson raindrops and splotches of gray matter.

CHAPTER TWENTY-THREE

Shoes

"Excuse me, sir?"

Antoine jumped to his feet, a hand resting on his sidearm. A young recruit approached Antoine but stood motionless, as he stared at Antoine's holstered weapon.

"Yes, what do you want?" asked Antoine.

The soldier stammered, shifting his weight from one foot to the other.

"Well, sir, you speak with a French accent and I was wondering, sir, if you came from Québec, but if you didn't that's, well it's none of my concern I suppose."

Antoine stepped forward.

"Get on with it boy. What do you want?" Antoine demanded.

The young soldier explained that he had received a wagon full of supplies, addressed to 'Hazen's Infernals,' in care of General Sullivan. But Sullivan was about to attack Howe's forces in Germantown. If the captain served under Hazen, perhaps he could deliver the supplies.

A puzzled look crossed Antoine's unshaven face.

"I am under no formal obligation to General Hazen but tell me about these supplies," said Antoine.

The young recruit invited Antoine to the large supply tent where he regularly stood guard.

"There sir. The wagon," said the soldier.

Antoine inspected the shipment. His eyes grew wide as he realized the wagon contained a desperately needed commodity in Washington's army—shoes. Hundreds of them.

"There is a letter, sir," said the soldier, handing Antoine a small envelope.

Antoine grinned when he recognized the handwriting of Moses Hazen. He laughed when he read the note. The shoes would first be distributed to Hazen's troops. The balance would be given to the rest of Sullivan's men. Hazen also reported he could get his hands on 200 more pairs of shoes, if required.

"Thank you, young man. You and General Hazen leave me no choice," said Antoine.

"Sir?"

"I will deliver these shoes, myself," said Antoine.

Marguerite overheard several of the nurses and a surgeon's mate discussing a wagon loaded with shoes.

"What are you talking about?" she asked.

The group fell silent, in the presence of their stern taskmaster. The surgeon's mate spoke first.

"Hundreds of shoes ma'am. They came by wagon," he said.

"Who sent them?" she asked

"Don't know, ma'am, but they came from Québec I think."

"How do you know," she asked.

"There is this soldier, also from Québec. He offered to deliver the shoes to the men in Germantown."

"There is a soldier from Québec in the camp?"

"Oh yes, ma'am. He speaks English but he has the French

accent. A tall and handsome man. An officer I think," said the young medical worker.

Marguerite rushed from the temporary hospital and ran down the road to where the supply tent stood.

Benjamin, his clothes and boots splattered in blood, trotted and ran to the edge of the British encampment.

"Stop or I'll shoot."

Captain Stuart's aide easily recognized Benjamin as he ran from the camp.

"The captain has released me," said Benjamin. "I am free to go."

As the aide approached, Benjamin made a clumsy attempt to hide the evidence of his crime. He wiped his cheeks with both hands and squatted to remove his shoe. He shook an imaginary pebble from it. He crouched to hide his blood-stained trousers and held the shoe close to his chest, an effort to hide the large, red splotches.

"Why would the captain release his favorite prisoner," said the aide, a knowing grin plastered on his face.

The aide raised his musket.

"That's blood. Lots of it." he mumbled.

Benjamin replaced his shoe and rose to his feet.

"You will come with me and we will ask Captain Stuart if you are free to go," said the aide.

Benjamin walked at a snail's pace, calculating his next move.

"Get moving boy or I'll shoot you in the back," said the aide.

Benjamin stopped when he reached the tent, the canvas door still closed.

"Move," said the aide, shoving Benjamin to one side. Benjamin saw his chance and reached for the aide. They wrestled briefly, but

Benjamin prevailed, pushing the soldier into the tent. He pointed the weapon at the aide.

"Scream and you die," said Benjamin.

The aide noticed the body. The uniform belonged to Captain Stuart, but the officer's head and face, bludgeoned beyond recognition, gave no hint as to the dead man's identity. When the aide noticed one of the captain's eyeballs, resting by itself in the blood-soaked grass, he bent at the waist, and threw up.

Benjamin used the butt of his stolen musket to knock the aide to his knees. Another blow, this one to the head, sent the poor fellow crashing to the ground. Benjamin exited the tent and retraced his steps to the edge of the camp, forcing himself to walk in measured paces. In less than a minute, he reached the deep woods and began running as fast as he could through the trees, across a creek, and through a small swamp.

He didn't stop running, until exhaustion forced him to the ground.

Adolphe Lezard darted from building to tent to alleyway and to any other object large enough to hide a small man.

At every stop, he searched the horizon, the alleyways, and the occasional group of pedestrians, for the tall, dark-haired, Frenchman. Lezard checked his sidearm several times. He clutched his musket, in a useless effort to assure himself that Captain Dauphin walked in danger and not the other way around.

At the edge of the settlement, Lezard spotted a horse drawn wagon, covered in canvas. A single horse, tethered to the rear of the wagon, occasionally obscured Lezard's view, but did not prevent it. The tall, dark-haired man, driving the team of two horses, traveled in the direction of Germantown.

Lezard raced to his horse.

Marguerite arrived at the supply tent, breathless.

She required a nearby railing to remain standing and gasped her questions in between deep breaths. The guard could not understand the woman, still wheezing from lack of oxygen. He gave her a drink of water from his wooden canteen. Marguerite gulped, inhaled deeply, and tried to speak again.

"A tall dark-haired man. Heavy French accent. Acts like an officer. Did you see him?" she asked, her eyes filled with desperation.

"Yes, ma'am," said the soldier.

Marguerite stepped closer.

"Where'd he go? Where is he?" she demanded.

"He left, ma'am, with a wagon full of shoes. He intends to deliver them to Sullivan's men in Germantown. Left about an hour ago," said the guard.

Marguerite's eyes squeezed shut and she slid to the ground, leaning on the soldier as she fell.

"Antoine. My beloved Antoine."

Benjamin rested at the base of a large tree, surrounded by a dense patch of forest.

Although his knowledge of the area did not include the local roads, the boy knew enough to avoid roads altogether. He planned to follow the creek north at a safe distance, hoping the waterway led back to the rebel encampment. When the stream split in two, he took the smaller creek, assuming it unlikely that soldiers or travelers would do the same. After several hours of searching for the rebel line, he heard voices. But the distance between him and the voices, made it impossible to determine whether the voices belonged to rebels or Redcoats.

He chose to go no further, straining for the sound of British accents or New England mannerisms. He heard neither. The voices spoke German. Benjamin swallowed his panic and let his mind race. He stood yards from several Hessian companies. Recalling his original capture, the boy didn't move an inch, for fear of making a sound. Minutes passed. Afraid to go forward, unwilling to go back, and certain that the large creek would be dangerous, Benjamin tiptoed in an easterly direction. After a short while, he noticed a road and on the opposite side, a large stone residence. He stopped. Through the sunlit haze, he could make out a handsome lawn and a large white, three-story home with numerous windows.

He watched, as twenty or so Redcoats ran out of the woods. They scurried into the home, slammed the doors, and shuttered the windows. In seconds, he saw the business end of muskets protruding from second and third story windows. After a short period of silence, an ear-splitting volley, of musketry and field guns, pelted the house. A number of American rebels followed their own bullets and attempted to break open the doors and undo the shutters. But the English troops resisted. Given no choice, the rebels returned to the safety of the woods.

The position of the rebels now clear in his mind, Benjamin ran due north as quickly as he could, keeping the large stone house behind him and to the right. In minutes, he encountered rebel patrols.

"Stop or I shoot," said the voice, clearly a soldier from New England.

Benjamin's head jerked in the direction of a large tree. A rifle with a bayonet attached, wagged at the boy.

"On your knees and drop the musket," said a second rebel.

Benjamin did as ordered, placing both hands on his head, as a sign of abject surrender. Three Rebels emerged from the woods and surrounded their prisoner.

"Where you goin' boy?" asked one.

"I escaped from the British camp. I am a surgeon's mate," said Benjamin.

"You talk like they do," said another soldier, as he stood behind the kneeling prisoner.

Benjamin pleaded.

"I serve the rebels not the King."

"He's covered in blood," said one of the Rebels.

Benjamin pleaded some more.

"There are people back in Skippack that will confirm what I have told you. You must believe me," said Benjamin.

"And when you escaped the Redcoats, they gave you one of their muskets as a gift?" asked the oldest rebel, as he raised his own musket to eye level.

Another large and noisy volley of musket fire and field artillery interrupted their interrogation. The senior-level soldier shook his head.

"We don't have time for this shit," he grumbled.

He took aim and pulled the trigger.

"But I spoke the truth," said Benjamin, as the dark red stain on his white shirt slowly grew.

He fell face forward onto the forest floor.

CHAPTER TWENTY-FOUR

Bullets

Adolphe Lezard followed Antoine from a safe distance.

The winding road and the noise, of horses pulling a rickety wagon, effectively obscured the predator from his prey. The Skippack road led straight to the rebel troops, now forming into four separate armies. Sullivan's regiments lay in wait, west of the main road and south of Allen's lane.

Antoine found Sullivan's column and presented the gift from Hazen. Hazen's men cheered the loudest. Their anticipated battle, with the fiercest army on earth, would wait. The soles of hundreds of men were at stake. While Antoine renewed ties with his former French-Canadian Regiment, Lezard lurked on the edge of the enemy camp. The traitor, unwilling to risk an attack on Antoine, with such a large crowd in attendance, decided to wait for the perfect opportunity.

Dense fog hampered the rebels as they moved forward to engage the British. Antoine, still bothered by occasional pangs of his nearly mortal wound, watched in dismay, as his fellow 'Infernals' disappeared down the road and into the woods. He lingered with several companies of men, ordered to stay in reserve.

Lezard waited for the fog to lift and for Antoine to wander off by himself.

"I can't sit here," Antoine grumbled, to no one in particular.

After checking his musket, he tightened the girth on his saddle, untethered his horse from the wagon, and proceeded south at a gallop. Lezard did the same but at a safe distance. As Antoine approached, he could see a large, white home. Hazen's troops pounded the three-story structure, with musket fire and repeated volleys of their field artillery. Antoine joined the fray. When the Redcoats refused to budge, Antoine and his fellow rebels simply bypassed the white home. They travelled further south but slightly west.

Their arrival at the next clearing triggered a volley from a large number of British troops, hiding in the woods. Antoine thought this unusual for the Redcoats, as they preferred to fire in an open formation. He looked again and yelled at both sides to cease fire. The hidden troops did not wear Redcoats. They wore the uniforms and ragtag clothing of the rebels. Antoine pulled his mount up short. The unexpected attack caused both sides to break and flee. The surprise encounter triggered widespread panic.

When Antoine noticed a sea of Redcoats on his right, he circled back toward the camp, urging the remaining stragglers to follow suit. Lezard waited and steadied his musket against a small tree. He never pulled the trigger. A loud explosion spun him around and sent him to the forest floor in a crumpled heap. A musket ball shattered the bone in his upper arm and left a gaping hole in his flesh.

Dozens of Redcoats, from across the road, prepared their second volley. The contingent of rebels ran for their lives. A number of them scampered past Lezard and offered no assistance. Lezard yelled and two soldiers stopped. They dragged the traitor, moaning and groaning, into the woods. Lezard caught a brief glimpse of his prey. Antoine continued to fire his musket while most of the men ran to safety.

"I have three shots left," yelled a voice in the woods.

And nearer to Antoine, a second voice complained that he too would soon be out of ammunition. Antoine, down to one musket ball, groaned and shook his head. Telegraphing the fact that you could no longer defend yourself invited an immediate attack by the enemy.

He waited for the silence that comes when the other side reloads, and immediately sprang to his feet. He trotted his horse to the shoe wagon, tied it to the back end, and used the cart as a makeshift ambulance. Antoine retrieved fellow soldiers, wounded or too exhausted to walk, as he hurried to the rear of the battle. When he encountered a few more wounded, he ejected those soldiers that were ambulatory, and drove his team of horses back to Skippack for medical help.

Now, slowed by a wagon load of soldiers, Antoine spotted a body, in a small ditch, yards from the road. As he approached, Antoine could see a swathe of red leading from the deep woods to the motionless figure. The man had crawled a long distance on his belly to be nearer the road, Antoine thought. He rolled the soldier onto his back and stared into the wide-open eyes of a young boy. The dead man, his mouth frozen open, silently screamed for help.

Antoine recognized Benjamin as the surgeon's mate who worked with Marguerite.

Antoine's arrival at the temporary hospital in Skippack could not come soon enough.

During the several hour trip, three of his passengers succumbed to their wounds. Several healthy soldiers helped Antoine, as he variously dragged and carried wounded comrades, into the makeshift hospital. The dead stayed on the wagon for burial later in the day. One of Antoine's fellow soldiers, a young recruit from Montreal, suffered from horrendous wounds and lay close to death. Antoine, ignoring his own fatigue, carried the man to the far end of the temporary hospital, stopping feet from the operating theater.

"This man goes next," announced Antoine, out of breath and straining under the weight.

"I'll decide who goes next," said Marguerite, too busy to recognize the voice she yearned to hear. Antoine, also preoccupied, placed his friend on a nearby litter. Marguerite turned to her next patient, already lying on the operating table. She focused on the man's shirt, using her blade to cut and remove the blood-soaked garment. When she looked at the man's features, she jerked to a complete halt, unable to breath. The man's face, contorted in pain and covered with scars, temporarily paralyzed the woman. When she noticed the man's missing ear, her eyes bulged in disbelief.

"What are you waiting for?" asked the surgeon.

Still, Marguerite did not move. The surgeon shoved her to one side and yelled for a replacement nurse. Marguerite recovered and flew into a rage. She pushed the surgeon to the floor. With both hands on the knife, she raised her arms to shove the blade deep into Adolphe Lezard's unconscious body. Antoine flew to Lezard's rescue and grabbed for Marguerite. His muscular grip stopped the blade, inches from its target. He scrambled around the table and pulled Marguerite away, as she kicked and screamed. The surgeon suffered a slight cut on the arm, as he and Antoine wrested the blade from her unyielding grip.

When Marguerite realized Antoine foiled her murderous intentions, the pent-up anger of years gone by exploded in his face.

"You bastard. You miserable bastard. How dare you protect the man who attacked me? The man who murdered our son. The monster who did *this* to me," she cried, pulling her red hair back and exposing the scarred hole where her ear used to be.

Several onlookers gasped in shock when they saw her wound. The surgeon, although accustomed to the wounds of war, squeezed his eyes shut and looked away.

"Marguerite. Please," said Antoine, as he held the woman close and refused to let her go.

"He tried to kill me. Will you do nothing? Will you do nothing at all, you coward?" she yelled, repeatedly striking his chest with closed fists.

Antoine absorbed her angry blows and said nothing.

"You fight for France. You fight for the American rebels. But you refuse to fight for me."

"Marguerite. Listen to me," Antoine pleaded.

Marguerite slapped Antoine, leaving the clear red imprint of her hand on his face. Every eye in the tavern-turned-hospital focused on the couple. Antoine reached for Marguerite, holding both of her hands in his. He brought them to his chest. His unblinking eyes stared into hers as he pressed his lips against her hands and whispered.

"Marguerite. Please. I'm begging you. Let it go. It's over. Our son is gone and there is nothing we can do," he said.

Marguerite's breathing slowed, her eyes softened, and filled with tears. Antoine pulled her close. Her silent weeping became loud, uncontrollable sobs. For the first time since giving birth, she wept for their stillborn son.

Antoine held her close, his own tears hidden by the woman's brilliant red hair.

Lezard regained consciousness later that evening.

In moments, he discovered the loss of his left arm and began cursing at the orderlies.

"What did you do? I demand to see the butcher that did this to me," he screamed, thrashing and twisting in his bed. He attempted to sit but surrendered to the excruciating pain and fell back.

"Lie down and be still. Your stitches will not hold," ordered the surgeon.

"You butchering bastard," cried Lezard, throwing a pillow at the doctor and a shoe, for good measure.

The surgeon stormed off. A female orderly, scolded Lezard.

"Without the amputation, you would surely have died," she said.

"Get out of my sight," Lezard screamed. "Now! You bloodsucking whore," he said.

The nurse left and Lezard lay alone with his angry thoughts. A bedridden cripple did not stand a chance against Captain Dauphin and the redheaded whore. His tortured existence, now considerably worse, made the possibility of a normal life, impossible.

It would have been better if the bullet struck him in the head.

Marguerite and Antoine found limited privacy in a back room of the temporary hospital.

"Why did you save him?" Marguerite asked Antoine, through blood shot eyes.

"Killing Lezard changes nothing, said Antoine.

"He is a monster and deserves to die," Marguerite replied.

Antoine shot back.

"And the two of us? Are we any better?"

"You live to fight. I fight to live," she snapped.

Antoine's head drooped low and he slowly exhaled.

"You are correct," he whispered.

Marguerite, momentarily stunned by the man's admission, looked away. She focused on the dirty window.

"And you too are correct. Nothing I do will bring our dead son back to life, she said. "War has brought us nothing but death," she added.

Antoine reached for her hand.

"I am the one who brought you nothing but death," he said. "And for that I am sorry."

Marguerite sat in silence, wiping her moist eyes, with a bloodstained apron.

"Until today, I refused to cry for our son. I vowed that I would first have my revenge," she said.

"And, until today, I have always welcomed the next battle," he said. "No more."

Marguerite's eyes darted in his direction.

"But the war, the British. You will be a soldier no longer? I don't believe you." she said.

"I have been a soldier all my life," he said. "But I am tired, Marguerite. I am so tired."

Antoine looked away, unable to face her unbroken stare. For minutes, the only sound in the back room of the tavern-turned hospital, came from the noisy buzz of horse flies in the dirty windows. He reached for her hand.

"And in all those years, I have never been a husband, or a father, or even a friend. For this too, I am sorry. Truly sorry," he said.

Marguerite pulled away and rose to her feet. She turned her back, in a desperate attempt to hide the tears that streamed down her cheeks. When she heard the sound of his chair scraping the floor, she squeezed her eyes shut. Her chest heaved as she struggled for air. His long muscular arms encircled her shoulders. He buried his face into her flowing red hair and whispered.

"Please, Marguerite. I need you. And I love you," he whispered.

They embraced and his lips found hers.

Antoine refused to leave Marguerite's side while she performed her rounds at the hospital, both of them keeping a watchful eye.

As they shared a modest meal, at a nearby boarding house, a strange voice interrupted them.

"He's gone," said the orderly, whose duties included the care of Adolphe Lezard. "The man with no ear has disappeared," he said, wide-eyed and breathless.

"He need not run. I will chase him no more," said Marguerite.

Antoine reached for his musket.

"And he will not hurt you again, Marguerite, I promise."

CHAPTER TWENTY-FIVE

Candlelight

Adolphe Lezard staggered and stumbled, through the dirt roads and alley ways of Skippack.

Although the aftereffects of his surgery made him weak, Lezard wanted revenge–revenge against the surgeon who removed his arm and revenge against Marguerite for his monstrous appearance. And revenge against the perfect Captain Dauphin because he *was* perfect and because the captain protected Marguerite. And now, for the first time in his life, it didn't matter if the price of revenge included his own life. His fear of dying, extinguished by the pain of living, no longer prevented him from meting out the punishment his enemies deserved.

From the dark shadow of a large barn, he watched and waited as the sun set in the evening sky. Slowly, the supply tent grew quiet. When a lone sentry stood at the entrance, Lezard crossed the street. His remaining hand held a blade, covered by the sleeve of his coat. Lezard approached the guard.

"Good evening, my friend. A word with this old soldier if you will," said Lezard.

The sentry stepped forward, mesmerized by Lezard's appearance–the scars, the missing ear, and the jacket, its empty sleeve swinging like a pendulum as Lezard walked.

"Yes, sir," said the soldier, his eyes darting, searching every aspect of the man's grotesque features.

"My request is rather personal," said Lezard, as he motioned to the opening in the tent.

"Would you mind?" asked Lezard.

The sentry held the canvas door open, but the amputee insisted the young man enter first. When the canvas flap returned to its closed position, the sentry reached for a candle.

"We need light in here," he said.

Lezard approached from behind. He waited until the soldier's candle burned brightly in the dark. The French traitor stretched his only arm around the man's neck and pulled. Quickly. Smoothly. The soldier made a gurgling noise and fell to the ground with a thud.

Lezard moved as fast as his wounds and the dim light of a slivered moon would allow. He verified his motionless victim posed no danger and began the search. In minutes, he found not one, but several kegs of gun powder. Using his remaining hand, he emptied a burlap bag filled with hard tack biscuits. After several attempts, he clumsily poured much of the black powder into the sack. Enough gun powder to blow a hole in a wall. Or kill a half dozen occupants in the hospital.

Lezard placed the sack on the ground and cut an opening in the rear of the supply tent, enabling his discreet departure. The small slice of moon made his trip to the hospital, difficult but worry free, as he slithered through the dark shadows of tents and buildings.

Finally, he stood across the street from the tavern which housed his intended victims.

Marguerite lay sleeping on her cot. Antoine sat on the floor with his back to the woman, keeping watch.

Hours later, he too closed his eyes, and, except for the snoring of a few sick men, the hospital went silent. Lezard appeared at the entrance, searching for a means with which to detonate his weapon. A lone candle held by a copper holder, its tiny flame flickering wildly, forced him to cross the room. Despite Lezard's careful steps, the wooden planks in the old tavern creaked in protest. He heard the sound of someone rustling. Lezard stood motionless, trusting the near darkness to obscure his appearance. When the noise stopped, he resumed his cautious journey. After reaching the candle, Lezard abandoned any attempt at stealth, dropped his sack of gunpowder to the floor, and held the candle aloft.

The loud thud and the moving light caused Antoine, Marguerite, and several patients to stir. Lezard suspended the open flame over the sack.

"My apologies for the disruption, he shouted, standing several yards from his intended victims.

Antoine jumped to his feet. Marguerite bolted upright in her bed. Lezard grinned while Antoine retrieved his flintlock rifle and verified that the powder charge remained intact.

"Please don't shoot me, Captain. I am likely to drop this candle on my bag of black powder. People could get hurt," he grinned.

Marguerite climbed out of her cot and lit a second candle. Several ambulatory patients scampered to the exit. Lezard's smirk mutated into a snarl.

"And where is the good doctor, this evening?" asked Lezard, searching the room with his beady, black eyes.

"The surgeon was called away," said Marguerite, her gaze fixated on the deranged man.

"Madame Valtesse, or should I say, Sister Marguerite, or perhaps you prefer, Mrs. Dauphin. I care not what you are called. I prefer to address you by your most accurate title. Whore," he hissed, spitting in her direction for emphasis.

The monster's vitriol no longer triggered Marguerite's anger or even fear. She spoke in a calm, almost matter-of-fact tone of voice.

"It is me you wish to kill. Please allow the captain and our patients to leave," she begged.

"I will not leave," said Antoine.

The expert marksman sighted his weapon on the flame and pulled the hammer back. He waited for Lezard and the flame to line up. Lezard's head jerked when he heard the sound of Antoine's musket.

"The Captain hopes to kill me, before I kill myself and all of you," said Lezard. "Gallant but predictable," Lezard observed, an evil grin crossing his face.

He held the candle higher, poised to let it drop. Antoine exhaled and squeezed the trigger.

The musket ball missed the candlestick but struck Lezard in the left shoulder. The candle flew out of his hand. He spun backward into the wall and crumpled to the floor. The flame extinguished itself, but the wick continued to burn red. Lezard leaned forward, his remaining arm outstretched, desperate to rekindle the flame. Antoine tripped and struggled as he rushed to Lezard in the near darkness. Lezard retrieved the broken candle as Antoine approached. With his dying breath, Lezard coaxed the hot, red, line into a flame. Antoine threw himself onto the sack of black powder, sending a spray of explosive dust in Lezard's direction. Antoine and Lezard locked eyes. A shower of sparks bathed Lezard in a combination of light and darkness. For a brief moment, the monster's face appeared normal, its scarred features, hidden by the semi-darkness. The traitor's lit candle arced in the air. The captain swatted at the flame and missed. Lezard grinned through his mortal pain. As the flame approached the floor, Antoine rolled over the candle. He winced when the hot wax singed his skin A few grains of black powder burned through his shirt. Lezard sat motionless, his lips parted into a half smile, his eyes wide open. He neither saw nor heard an explosion.

Adolph Lezard was dead.

EPILOGUE

The sound of steel scraping on whetstone, floated into the night air.

A stiff, North Country breeze carried the noise across the Great Chazy River and into the deep woods.

Marguerite sat on a porch rocker, knitting her latest project, and stealing an occasional glance at the man with the blade. The American war for independence ended several years ago. For his extraordinary military service, Congress deeded a plot of land to Antoine Dauphin. It bordered on Corbeau Creek, near the boundary line, in Champlain, New York. While the American colonies feasted on their first taste of freedom, Mr. and Mrs. Dauphin basked in the peaceful aftermath of a long and horrible war.

"If it's a boy, his name shall be Noah," Marguerite announced.

"I like that name," said Antoine, as he focused on the sharp steel, completely missing the implications of her pronouncement.

After a few seconds, the news hit the captain like an artillery shell. He dropped the blade, dashed to her side, and fell to his knees.

"Are you sure?" he asked.

"Yes," she said, holding a child's mitten in his face.

"But, what if–?"

She gently pressed the fingers of one hand over the man's lips.

"We will manage."

"I love you Marguerite."
"And I love you, Captain Dauphin."

CPSIA information can be obtained
at www.ICGtesting.com
Printed in the USA
FSHW010048150920
73771FS